BLACK STORMS

LLLL institut
ramon llull

Corylus Books Ltd
corylusbooks.com

ISBN: 978-1-7392989-7-5

BLACK STORMS

TERESA SOLANA

Translated from Catalan by Peter Bush

Published by Corylus Books Ltd

For Clàudia, Ruth and Tom.

Give sorrow words. The grief that does not speak
Whispers the o'erfraught heart and bids it break.

William Shakespeare, *Macbeth*, Act 4 Scene 3.

Black storms shake the air
Dark clouds blind us

A las barricadas
Anarchist anthem from the Spanish Civil War,
based on the Polish *La Warszawianka*, the Varsovian.

1

The man who was about to commit murder left home at six-thirty, after telling his girlfriend Mary he'd business to see to and checking his car keys were in his pocket. He'd not driven his third-hand Seat Ibiza for days. Its shabby appearance was protection against petty thieves even in a street like theirs where he usually parked it. Nonetheless, when he saw the thick layer of dust and the obscenities a finger had scrawled on the bonnet, sides and windows, he decided a filthy car would attract attention and it might be worth his while to shell out on a wash. The queue he found at the garage started to wear his patience thin. However, he cooled down after taking a glance at his watch: the professor had given him an appointment for eight forty-five and there was no point being early. He had more than enough time. No need to worry.

He drove his gleaming Seat up the Gran Via towards the Plaça d'Espanya, and then turned down Entença on his way to Roma. As soon as he reached the Plaça dels Països Catalans, he left the car in a parking lot and went into Sants station, all set on melting into the crowd. He was sure nobody would notice him in that chaotic, crowded spot— that's why he'd chosen it—and hurried into the lavatories gripping his black backpack. It contained all he needed to carry out his plan of action: a disguise, latex gloves so he didn't leave fingerprints, and a length of plastic-covered clothesline. It was an old, light backpack, nothing too flashy to attract thieves on the lookout for easy pickings from commuters and tourists.

He found an empty stall in the gents, checked the catch was working and rather nervously shut himself inside. He took a wrap from his pocket, prepared a line of coke and racked his brain wondering how he'd eke out his meagre supplies until Mary brought a fresh consignment. The cocaine revitalised him, and with the drug still buzzing in his brain, he took off his shirt and jacket and donned the disguise he'd crammed into his backpack. All he needed from now on was inside a corduroy bag he slung over his shoulder that radically transformed his appearance when it was combined with the jeans, the shirt with the Mao collar that was a couple of sizes too big, and a Palestinian scarf he'd bought at the same hippy stall where he'd found the shirt. Just in case, a khaki cap and fake Ray-Bans hid his eyes, hair and part of his face. When he emerged from the lavatories and glanced at the queue at the ticket counter, he could only smile. Nobody would ever recognize him in that jazzy disguise.

He went to the left-luggage office and deposited the backpack in a locker before catching the Line 3 metro. Twenty minutes later the man who was about to commit murder was walking along La Rambla on his way to the history department. While he progressed steadily, trying to dodge the bustling pedestrians and bedazzled tourists in his way, he felt altogether pleased with himself and his brainwave pseudonym and doctoral-student status. Had the professor smelled a rat, he might have caught him out and told someone, even informed the police, but his ploy had worked a treat. The professor had swallowed the lot and agreed to see him in his office in the evening, after classes, when the corridors of the department would have shed their daytime throng of students and professors, and he could avoid dozens of potential witnesses eyeing his every move. If everything went to plan, terminating the professor's life would be simple enough. So far, the man about to commit murder had calculated right. But only so far.

When he had rung him mid-morning the previous day, he was surprised by how accommodating the professor proved to be. Something he hadn't anticipated. He'd expected to hear a self-satisfied, smug academic at the other end of the line, but quite against all odds the latter immediately agreed to see him at an untimely hour the following evening and asked for no further explanations. Before phoning he'd prepared a little spiel, convinced he'd have to produce good reasons to insist on that urgent, late appointment with the professor outside teaching hours. As a last resort, he'd invented a sad tale about a car accident or a mother in hospital, but finally he hadn't needed to invoke any such tearjerker. The professor had been very pleasant from the start and agreed straightaway; it never struck him that the time or urgency to meet was at all out of the ordinary. He'd kindly told him where his office was and apologised for only being able to offer him a half-hour slot at the very most.

'It's All Saints Eve and I must be home by nine-thirty because we have invited people over,' he'd said on the other end of the line.

The professor had returned to the department only three weeks ago and was feeling rather happy. He'd not crossed the university threshold for six months, and now sensed that his ability to re-engage with the tediously placid pace of academic life was a sign that everything was indeed returning to normal. His long convalescence had sorely tested his mental stamina, particularly at the beginning when he'd been forced to give up reading because the medication meant his eyes kept wandering and he lost his thread. The setbacks occasioned by cancer were compounded by the dismal threat of retirement that preyed on his every moment like an unjust life sentence he'd soon have to accept as inevitable. In a couple of years when he reached seventy, the university would organise an emotional homage, pat him on the back and declare him unfit to teach. It would dispatch him coldly back to his home and he, the dedicated professor, would be forced to bid farewell to his students, because that was the will of an administration that ignored intellectual ability, merit or personal factors. Although he'd grasped the nettle, trying to acquiesce benignly to the idea of the changes he'd face when the moment came to give up his chair to his successor, the ageing professor struggled to imagine a life far from the halls of knowledge, the routine of classes, the invigorating banter of students and never-ending disputes in departmental meetings. He'd surely have more time to write when he retired, his wife and children piously argued. Despite that welcome prospect, the professor was clear-sighted enough to realise that retirement amounted to concluding another chapter in his life at a time when there were few pages left to turn.

His illness had involved giving up sex, and incipient diabetes had long since banished fat, sugar and alcohol from his diet. Gone were the days when he could head all alone to the countryside at the weekend on the pretext that he was going to pick mushrooms because mobiles couldn't reach the places where he liked to go, even though it meant making his wife and children suffer. As he wasn't as strong or agile as he used to be, he could no longer swim out to the open sea in the summer or clamber over rocks with his grandchildren to collect mussels when they went to the beach. However, as he'd never been that excited by sex or desired to excel at sport, growing old and abandoning those activities had always been a secondary preoccupation: *that* wasn't what he found depressing. He'd become resigned to ageing. Conversely, the prospect of being forced to stay cooped up at home like a redundant item of furniture, as if the mere fact of hitting seventy meant one had to wind down like a clockwork toy, was intolerable. True enough his body was failing him, but his grey matter had matured like vintage wine and that was something to be proud of. He could still boast a prodigious memory that was the envy of his younger colleagues, and the very same years that had wasted his flesh had transformed the erudition he'd patiently accumulated into a solid store of wisdom. Cancer had made life difficult over the last year and a half, but his inopportune sickness had at least left the good health of his neurones intact. Stoic in outlook, the professor was happy to harbour a lucid mind in a shipwreck of a body.

His wife had started grumbling the second he informed her at lunchtime that he'd agreed to see a doctoral student at the end of the day. To avoid a row, he'd promised to take a taxi as soon as he left the department rather than meandering leisurely back, as he preferred. He'd be home by half past nine at the latest. In the give and take over dessert, she'd persuaded him to take his mackintosh and scarf, arguing that the television weatherman had predicted a cooler night. As he sat in his office and watched the black clouds now gathering and threatening to release a deluge, the professor was pleased he'd listened to her. Even though October had been extremely hot and the citizens of Barcelona were still in short sleeves, his wife was right. The weather was changing and, when he left the university in the evening, autumn would very likely make its presence felt with a display of gusting wind and rain. He was still convalescing, and it was better to err on the side of caution than risk catching a dangerous chill.

'Professor Parellada?'
The man who was about to commit murder knew the academic was in his office, and he opened and closed the door quietly behind him without waiting for his reply. He was relieved to find a frail little man who looked older than

he'd expected and thought this was going to make his task much easier. The professor's jacket and shirt hung on him as if he'd shrunk, and he glimpsed the highly respected scholar's atrophied muscles under his dark, conventional suit, the fruit of half a century of deskbound existence, peering at books and shuffling papers. At a glance, the man who was about to commit murder calculated that slight body could barely weigh in at sixty kilos, and, when he saw the professor's sluggish movements and emaciated, pallid face, he deduced he must have fallen foul of an illness that was implacably wasting his body. He grinned as he realised that would also facilitate his task. Luck seemed to be on his side.

The professor got up from his chair, and slowly walked towards him, smiling broadly and holding out a hand. It all happened very quickly. The stranger simply had to wait for the tiny man, sapped by his last round of chemotherapy, to trustingly turn his back and he would slip the cord around his neck and stifle any cry he might try to utter. He'd seen it done in a film and felt it was a simple, effective, and above all clean procedure. He couldn't risk blood splattering his clothes, as happened the previous time; nor could he take any chances on the professor screaming and being heard, even though the department was almost deserted on the eve of a holiday. The best option, he'd calculated, was to strangle him from behind, taking the professor by surprise before he realised what was happening. After all, he was experienced now and murder wasn't the big deal he'd initially thought it would be.

The old man barely offered any resistance and his frail body stopped convulsing after a few seconds, eight, maybe ten. As a precaution, he tightened the cord for longer than was necessary and counted silently and unhurriedly to sixty, determined to carry out his plan to the letter. He might as well do it properly. After that minute, one of the longest he'd ever lived, he gradually let go and the professor collapsed like a puppet, all limp in that old-fashioned, oversized suit. It *had* been a silent, quick and extremely clean operation. Not a speck of blood anywhere.

He immediately found the packet he'd come for on the desk. It was a brown business envelope he stuffed inside the corduroy bag along with the piece of cord he'd used to strangle the professor. After listening to make sure nobody was in the corridor, he switched out the light, put his cap back on and stood in the dark holding his breath. He had to be careful, because a few students were still lingering in the building with folders of notes tucked under their arms, and the cleaners had started work and were opening and shutting doors, emptying wastepaper baskets and vacuuming. If he didn't want to be caught, he shouldn't waste time. He should get out of the building fast.

He was about to open the office door when he noted an unpleasant smell in the air, one he didn't remember being there when he walked in. It was an acrid stench he immediately identified, one that transported him to the sordid nursing home where he'd parked his mother for the last ten years. The professor had pissed himself and his urine stank of old age and the medicines he had been taking to fight the disease that had been exacting such a toll. As he glanced at the body on the ground, a pathetic scrap of flesh, supine in its own secretions, the man who had just committed a murder thought he had perhaps done him a favour.

He nudged the door open, took the gloves off and left the office. He walked past some students in the lobby but, since he was sure nobody would recognize him with his fake Ray-Bans and young leftist garb, he strode by them unfazed by the curious looks coming his way. However messy this business became, he reflected, who would ever dream of connecting him with the murder of an old professor?

'Hey, 'scuse me! You got a light?'

He'd just stepped out into the street and lit a cigarette with hands that were still shaking when two twenty-year-olds, their cleavages hidden behind folders emblazoned with the university logo, suddenly stopped and blocked his path. His heart missed a beat, because the man who had just committed a murder hadn't anticipated that two brazen students might accost him with unlit cigarettes. As he swerved to avoid them, he unintentionally knocked into one. He continued walking as if nothing had happened, didn't even turn round to apologise, and the girl he'd accidentally shoved out of his way screamed a 'Fucking bastard' after him that echoed down the street. The man who had just committed murder hurried in the direction of La Rambla in his search for urban anonymity. When he'd finally disappeared into the stream of people bustling there, he took a deep breath and told himself it was a totally trivial incident. However messy things got, as soon as he got rid of his disguise and recovered his usual look, no one would ever recognise him, let alone identify him. His plan had worked to perfection. He shouldn't give it another thought.

The professor's wife had been right: it had cooled down and an icy, cutting wind was gusting down the streets making everyone rush along. He regretted he hadn't chosen thicker clothes. Luckily it hadn't started to rain, even though the clouds scudding over the tops of buildings were soot-black and the air smelled as if a storm might break any minute. The man who had just committed murder went into the Plaça de Catalunya metro and down to the platform. When the train came, he sat in the corner of a compartment and looked at the floor. At that time of night, apart from a few youths going out on the town, sporting their respective urban tribal uniforms or imported Halloween garb, disguised in wigs and scary masks on their way to a disco, the rest of the passengers were too exhausted to notice a dozing student gripping a bag in which he was no doubt carrying his lecture notes. But he wasn't asleep. A tiny voice was echoing around his head in a deathly cadence of litanies and spells: everything had worked out just fine.

2

Norma had been looking at her watch for some time while trying to join in the conversation and prove she wasn't nervous. She didn't want to make a drama out of something she knew was no such thing, and above all wanted to avoid her family spending supper consoling her or, worst of all, making her feel even more agitated with their pessimistic speculation and impractical advice. As they were familiar with Norma and her moods, they'd been keeping calm and biting their lips for over an hour, but she'd only have to give them the slightest excuse to start lamenting for that festive occasion to turn into a psychodrama where everyone would stick their oar in. Norma worried about her daughter, of course she did, but she preferred not to show it in front of her family. Her husband Octavi was in complete agreement.

Her colleagues had assured her that it was a matter of time, a few months, a couple of years at the most. 'These blasted young people and their idealism!' Chief Superintendent Nebot had commented sympathetically when he heard the news. He had even concurred that it wasn't such a big deal and tried to soft-pedal the subject. He'd had teenage children and knew from experience that this kind of rebelliousness was an adolescent thing. Naturally, his children had never gone so far, the chief inspector had added, with a smile of relief on his lips, but in any case, they'd be on the alert. They'd keep a watchful eye on the girl and keep Norma informed. Open confrontation, he'd declared in that half-authoritarian, half-affable tone he used towards his subordinates, would only make matters worse. Norma should be extremely patient and let time take its course.

Octavi had said almost as much. Octavi kept his anxieties to himself, and the calm way he approached those tensions helped ensure Norma didn't go overboard. Violeta's decision had taken everyone by surprise, although perhaps not that dramatically, because Violeta was a girl who was used to speaking her mind and everyone at home knew her strong opinions on certain subjects. But to do what she had done! Sure enough Guillem, Violeta's biological father, had handled his daughter's unexpected turn with equanimity, but, as he was Guillem, Norma reckoned, any consolation her ex might offer was of little use because he was always so accepting of his daughter's ways. Octavi was rational and even-handed, but Guillem, in Norma's view, was a dreamer and she could have no confidence in his judgements.

Norma had always thought, when it came to character, that her daughter and her biological father had little in common, but now she wasn't so sure. Up to that point, Norma had always relied on clichés and put Guillem's impulsive manner down to his homosexuality, making her ex's rather outlandish ways a feature of the whole gay community. Clearly, perhaps his being gay was irrelevant, Norma now reflected when she thought about the adventure Violeta had embarked upon, but Guillem's tendency to dream *was* a trait her daughter had inherited. After all, he was her father and they were bound to be similar in some respect, considering that physically she wasn't like him at all. Violeta resembled her mother, everyone said so, and the pair of them, as Great-grandmother Senta was continually reminding them, were cut from the same cloth as Great-grandfather Jack.

As they owed her leave from time immemorial and they

had no urgent cases on their hands, Norma had taken, most unusually, a whole day off. She'd got up early, cleaned and tidied the house, gone to the market, and done the cooking. You can't improvise supper for ten people in half an hour, particularly when it's a festive celebration. Norma hated cooking, but she defended the idea (an antiquated one, according to her girlfriends) that hospitality means making an effort to prepare a good meal when you have guests. Not that it happened very often, because with Octavi's and her professions it was difficult to plan ahead, but maybe that was why Norma thought it was in bad taste to invite someone to dinner and offer them a pitiful pre-cooked meal or the usual pa amb tomàquet, as if tasty food wasn't important. That All Saints Eve they were celebrating her birthday, and, before gorging on chestnuts, sweet potatoes, and the traditional panellets, Norma had decided her family would enjoy home-made mushroom soup and fresh sea bass cooked in the oven.

All Saints Eve is a peculiar time to come into the world. Deputy Inspector Norma Forester had done so thirty-eight years ago, around midnight, in a surprisingly short labour for a woman who was giving birth for the first time. Mimí, Norma's mother, would recount how the following day the room in the clinic where she'd had Norma saw a toing and froing of bunches of chrysanthemums and people dressed in black. As All Saints Day is a holiday, everybody decided to take the opportunity to drop by the clinic on their way to the traditional visit to the cemetery, so that the cheerful baskets of flowers they brought Mimí were accompanied by mourning dress and other sadder bouquets for the deceased. Norma's mother also recalled the blank expressions on the faces of relatives who couldn't decide whether to fuss over the baby or console her, as they were unable to accept that Mimí had decided to bring that child into the world all alone, without a husband by her side. It was the year 1971, and, according to Mimí, despite the

Bocaccio nightclub, the cosmopolitan veneer of the Gauche Divine and trips to Perpignan to see banned films, being a single mother was still considered shocking in a schizophrenic Barcelona suffering the final throes of Franco's dictatorship. When she told that story all smiles, but with the hint of sadness in her voice of someone who'd long left behind her the best years of her life, Senta looked at her and nodded silently.

'Maybe we should start. I don't think she's going to come...' said Norma, looking at her watch and getting up from the sofa. 'It's gone half past ten.'

'We're in no rush, love. We can wait a while longer.' In her way Mimí also felt anxious about her only granddaughter. 'You could ring her, perhaps she's on her way.'

'Norma's right.' Octavi cut short any possible family wrangle over whether they should or shouldn't wait for their daughter. 'Let's start on supper.'

He said it gently, but everyone stood up without arguing and took their places at table, while Norma and he headed off to the kitchen. Octavi never raised his voice, but, as is often the case with doctors, his voice possessed an imperious tone and natural authority that was difficult to challenge. Octavi wasn't angry with his daughter, but he was much more worried than he seemed. After all, Violeta was only eighteen and, even though he'd never said as much to Norma as a matter of prudence, he too was worried by the reckless genes of that English great-grandfather that ran through his daughter's DNA. Octavi was convinced that externalising his anxiety would change nothing, or would rather complicate matters, so he said nothing. He knew Violeta and trusted in her judgement, but most of all he trusted in the eighteen years of patient instruction during which he and Norma had made every effort to inculcate in that girl the only three things they considered vital in life: generosity of mind, a sense of justice and common sense. You had to expect at her age that she wouldn't always keep her feet on the ground, thought Octavi. Violeta was an only child. As were Mimí and Norma.

Every year, on All Saints Day Eve, Norma organised that small family dinner party to celebrate her birthday. Together with the big party they organised for Violeta, whose birthday fell in May, and Christmas Day (Octavi's birthday wasn't a good date, because it fell in the middle of August), these were the only occasions when she and Octavi gathered their respective families around a table for dinner. Norma's work didn't respect timetables or holidays as they were always eager to point out, and they were quite right, because, more than once, with a fridge full of delicious food, Norma had been forced to call everyone at the last minute and postpone a lunch or dinner that had been planned weeks before. However, that evening, Norma had everything under control, or at least so she thought. As she'd officially not seen her daughter for a couple of months (in fact, she'd gone more than once to spy on her in the streets of Gràcia and see for herself that she was all right), Norma had succeeded in forcing her boss to promise that, whatever happened, they would forget her phone number that night and let her eat supper in peace with her family. Inspector Bernat Roca was Norma's superior in the murder squad and Norma was convinced that something horrendous would have to happen for a man like the inspector to go back on his word.

For the first time since she'd been organising those suppers, Norma had decided to invite Guillem and his partner Robert to the party. This was the lure she'd thought of to ensure her daughter turned up at her traditional birthday supper, to which she'd also invited Octavi's parents and Aunt Margarida who, being a nun in an enclosed order, had to contrive an excuse every thirty-first of October to leave her convent.

Norma's mother and Great-grandmother Senta had lived with Norma and Octavi ever since Mimí had been widowed, and Norma was conscious that the absence of her stepfather had turned a birthday party into a rather melancholy celebration. That it fell on All Saints didn't help, and even less so that Great-grandmother Senta spent her time lighting candles and distributing small bunches of flowers throughout the house in front of the yellowing photos of deceased relatives. Senta, despite her tiny stature and absent looks, was still sharp-witted at ninety plus, and Mimí, ever loyal to the hippy aesthetics of her youth, still wore her hair long and dyed orange, although she was sixty-nine.

As well as being Norma's ex-boyfriend and Violeta's biological father, Guillem was Octavi's little brother, and that initially uncomfortable coincidence had in the end helped cement a closeness they had never enjoyed as boys because of the age gap. There were ten years between Octavi and Guillem and they weren't at all alike, or, as Mimí liked to say, they were as alike as an egg and a chestnut. It was as if in each of the pregnancies the features of the two progenitors had remained separate in the womb without ever mingling, the outcome being that physically Guillem resembled his mother, and Octavi, his father. Guillem had inherited Isabel's dark, curly hair and olive-toned, round-featured face, whereas Octavi had inherited his father's athletic complexion, prematurely grey hair and his lively, short-sighted eyes. Anyone observing his angular face would be unable to deduce that Guillem and he were brothers, and any interaction with them only confirmed that impression: where Octavi used cold reason and logic, Guillem applied enthusiasm and intuition. Octavi was a man of science, disciplined, sensible and methodical, whilst Guillem, who from childhood had revealed an artistic bent that never blossomed, was more bohemian in attitude and a dilettante who quickly got bored with everything.

Guillem's partners never lasted, though he'd been living with Robert for almost a year and Norma was sure it was working this time. Robert, who knew Violeta and Norma but not the rest of the family, couldn't stop feeling on edge. He'd had other partners in his life and several times had experienced the unpleasantness of reticent fathers- and brothers-in-law, but it was the first time he'd had to dine with a forensic doctor and a female officer, and he really didn't know how to approach it. He wasn't overjoyed by the idea that Norma was a cop, and, being a sensitive soul, felt sick at the thought of Octavi carrying out autopsies. When he discovered his future brother-in-law worked at the Hospital Clinic de Barcelona and that he was head of the forensic pathology department, he immediately assumed he would be dealing with a sinister character out of one of those Gothic novels he collected in bibliophile editions, and took fright. What kind of person decided to devote his life to slicing up corpses, and earning his living from the nasty realities of death? A psychopath? A doctor unable to cope with the suffering of the living? Robert was horrified by the dead and couldn't understand how someone would opt to spend their life dissecting corpses in a gloomy basement. Out of respect he'd said nothing to Guillem, but deep down he was certain there must be something sadistic or perverse in the character of individuals who, like Octavi, embraced such a grim profession. A susceptible fellow like him began having nightmares the moment he discovered he'd have to meet him and shake his icy hand. To make matters worse, they'd invited him round on a particularly lugubrious date like All Saints Eve, and, as he was polite and hadn't dared turn down the invitation, he'd now have to sit down for dinner with that outlandish family and all the souls in limbo of the unfortunate folk Octavi had opened down the middle.

Robert was at once highly impressionable and extremely superstitious, and he reckoned this was altogether a joke in bad taste.

However, the truth is that he felt rather annoyed when, after a few minutes of conversation, he was forced to admit that Dr Octavi Claramunt was not only not at all sinister but sensitive and attractive enough to arouse the interest of both sexes irrespective of his profession. Perhaps he did have the distant air of a learned professor, but Robert immediately realised that, as well as possessing a dangerously seductive myopic glance, his future brother-in-law was pleasantly extrovert with a wry sense of humour. Reluctantly, because all that macabre paraphernalia in his fantasies had come with a delicious thrill of Victorian decadence, Robert had to accept that his fear and loathing were completely unfounded.

Distant thunderclaps stirred the cat Hamlet from his nap, and he raised an ear and gave a huge yawn before dozing off again curled up on the sofa. Norma's father-in-law, Maurici, began to speculate on the imminence of the storm, and the conversation immediately focused on the weather and the power of Senta as an oracle, as she had forecast rain hours before. Of late, Senta had taken to predicting the weather, thinking that this was a skill she'd magically acquired with old age. Since she mostly got it wrong, nobody took any notice of her except for Mimí. Nevertheless, the icy wind blowing that evening seemed to confirm her prediction, and now and then Senta looked at her family, nodding and smirking like an inspired seer. The long summer had finally decided to beat a retreat, taking with it the heat of a sun that was beginning to fade, and the smell of autumn, rough seas and dry leaves was in the air. Octavi had to quickly stand up and close a window after the wind blew it wide open and scattered sheets of paper around.

'Are you alright?' Guillem whispered anxiously to

Robert. 'You don't look too good...'

'No, I'm fine. I slept badly last night,' Robert lied. 'It must be the weather.'

Everybody could see that Robert was looking pale, but no one said anything. That evening before setting out, without saying a word to Guillem, Robert had taken a tranquiliser to help him survive the grotesque dinner party he'd been expecting, and now, after that pill and a couple of glasses of excellent Ribera del Duero had hit his empty stomach, his head was beginning to spin. Norma started ladling out the soup and Octavi was opening another bottle while Robert nibbled on a piece of bread hoping to bring himself round. He wasn't feeling so on edge now, but his eyelids felt heavy and he was sleepy.

'This soup smells divine,' said Maurici, who had a soft spot for the young woman. 'Norma, when you make your mind up, you're a dab hand...'

'Octavi helped me clean the mushrooms. Today we must share the praise!' Norma replied, smiling and winking at her husband.

Robert tried the homemade soup with freshly picked penny buns, chanterelles and trumpets of death and was in awe, so he joined in Maurici's praise. Rather shamefacedly, he reflected that before setting foot in that house he'd imagined his dandyish sophistication would lead to titters, that they'd make him drink cheap wine that would provoke acidity in his stomach and that he'd have to listen to jokes about poofters from the lips of a foul-mouthed female officer and pretend he found them amusing. But he'd got it totally wrong, because that supper wasn't at all the surreal soirée he'd imagined. Norma and Octavi seemed quite civilised despite their professions, and even Isabel and Maurici, Guillem's parents were polite enough to just smile and exchange knowing looks.

'It can't be at all easy to get used to handling the dead. I suppose you must see all kinds of things...' Robert suddenly said, unable to restrain himself any longer.

Everybody sighed, and Norma, who in the fifteen years she'd been with Octavi had heard similar comments thousands of times, couldn't stop smiling. Like the rest of the family, she was used to it. In fact, Robert had promised he'd not be so banal as to ask his brother-in-law anything about his profession, but the tranquilliser, glasses of wine and convivial atmosphere had led him to relax and his troubled subconscious to voice his thoughts out loud. He immediately regretted having done so and turned bright red. He stammered an apology.

'I'm sorry. I shouldn't have brought the subject up. It's inexcusable. I mean...'

Octavi smiled and quietly rested his spoon on the rim of his soup dish. He drank a mouthful of water, straightened his glasses and adopted a professorial air. Everyone went quiet, very aware of what was coming next.

'Please, not at the dinner-table,' Mimí protested half-heartedly.

'The transformations undergone by the body from the time of death are part of a completely natural process, the stages of which are extremely well-defined ...' Octavi began solemnly, ready to respond to Robert's curiosity.

But the noise of keys opening the door interrupted the keynote lecture Dr Octavi Claramunt was about to impart for the benefit of his guest.

3

Antoni Falgueres was the man who had killed Professor Francesc Parellada; he was forty-nine and a lawyer. His was a third-rate legal mind, to the extent that the only clients he represented came from a prestigious practice that often had recourse to his services to ensure their name did not circulate in the courts in connection to certain subjects. For the last eight years Antoni Falgueres had only signed claims and statements written by others and acted as a frontman in complex operations designed to defraud the tax authorities via fake invoices, shell companies and tax havens. In exchange for lending his signature and administering a handful of companies created expressly to hide income and avoid taxes, the lawyers in the practice religiously paid him a wage on the side that was no great shakes but that allowed him to pay the rent on his tiny office on the Ronda de Sant Antoni, keep up appearances and make it to the end of the month. As there were thousands of failed lawyers like himself in Barcelona ready to sell their soul for a dish of lentils, he was in no position to negotiate. Antoni Falgueres had to accept the miserly crumbs they offered, paltry amounts given that he was such a key player. Now and then, depending on the degree of dodginess of the deals that required his signature, they'd give him a small bonus that he and Mary soon spent on paying off debts owed to local drug dealers and new ones they soon acquired.

However, the job that had led him to murder Professor Parellada had nothing to do with the swanky lawyers he worked for, and even Mary knew nothing about it. He wasn't a professional killer, not even one of those thugs he sometimes had to hire to intimidate a witness or beat up someone, and he couldn't stop feeling nervous. Up to that point, and apart from the unfortunate episode with the two students, he was sure everything had gone smoothly, but even so he was worried his inexperience might let him down and they'd end up catching him. He could get twenty years, he reflected, with a bit of luck that might be reduced to ten or fifteen, but that, at his age, with the damage inflicted by coke and alcohol, was the most he could expect before he kicked the bucket. He had wasted most of his life, and time was catching up on him. He couldn't allow himself to make a mistake.

As soon as he arrived at Sants station, he went to the left-luggage office and retrieved his backpack. He went to the station lavatories, removed his disguise and recovered his anodyne appearance as a respectable citizen that served him so well to pass unnoticed. After that, he sniffed the remains of the coke still left in its wrap and, his confidence restored by the drug, he took scissors from the bag and cut the gloves and cord he'd used to strangle the professor into small pieces which he patiently flushed down the pan. He had to pull the chain ten times to avoid blocking it, and, once he was sure those compromising items were definitively lost in the city's sewers, he left the station pretending not to be in a hurry and went to the parking lot to pick up his car.

He drove from Sants to Hospitalet to get rid of his disguise. When he reached La Florida market, he double-parked his car and took out of his backpack the three crumpled supermarket plastic bags he'd remembered to take when he left home. He put the scarf, cap and glasses inside, and, trying not to attract any attention, threw the bags into three different containers knowing that sooner or later they'd fall into the hands of the poor guys who spent their time looking for treasure among the rubbish. He still had to get rid of the shirt, but he'd had a rethink and decided to do that at home following the same procedure via which he'd dispatched the gloves and cord in the station lavatories. The corduroy bag, that now contained the envelope he'd taken from the professor's desk, wasn't a problem because he'd decided to wrap it in fancy paper and give it to his niece for her birthday, and, as far as his jeans and trainers went, they weren't a worry, because they were part of his normal wardrobe and there were thousands like them in Barcelona. The cheap brand of trainers were ones he wore when he went out for a ride with Mary at the weekends before she started work, and the black jeans he wore were on the tight side and hardly his favourites, a present from Mary, and they could return to oblivion at the back of the wardrobe. Everything was under control.

When he was going back to his car, he saw it was about to rain and decided to hurry. His old Ibiza didn't have a GPS, and the last thing he wanted was for the first storm of the season to catch him driving around a district and streets that were totally unfamiliar. Once inside the car, when the first drops started to fall, he switched on the radio and took some deep breaths. The days of poverty and making ends meet, of drinking the last drop in every bottle and suffering because local dealers wouldn't give them more wraps of coke, were now a thing of the past.

If everything went well, he and Mary would travel abroad and forget their debts and problems for a while. They'd fly to a place with tropical beaches on the other side of the ocean, where daiquiris and Mary's caresses would help him forget the two deaths he had on his conscience, that is, if he ever began to feel remorse. They'd go to the Caribbean, perhaps to Cancun, although he hadn't a clue how he'd manage to find there the coke they'd been hooked on for some time. However, with money in his pocket, he imagined it wouldn't be hard to track down suppliers, and he was sure the ever-resourceful Mary would soon hunt down where dealers and fun were to be had in Cancun.

At well after eleven it wasn't easy to find a space to leave the car and he was forced to drive round and round. When he did finally manage to park, it was some time after one of the cleaners had found the professor's body and the first patrol car had parked by the entrance to the department. It had also started raining—dense rain, large drops splashing noisily on the ground—and, as he didn't have an umbrella and didn't want to be drenched, he had to run back to their flat seeking shelter under balconies. There wasn't a soul in the street, and, as usual, the rain meant some street lights were no longer working.

Even though he knew Mary wouldn't be back from her club until seven or eight a.m., when he reached the flat, he took the precaution of locking the door and leaving the key in the keyhole. As his feet were soaked, he removed his trainers and left them in the lobby, not so much to avoid dirtying the floor as because he loathed feeling wet. Then he went to the dining room, put the backpack on the table and closed the curtains, an absurd precaution because the windowpane was so dirty the neighbours in the buildings on the other side of the road could have seen nothing. He took off his tie and jacket in the dining room, scoured out the coke still clinging to the wrap by rubbing his gums on the inside, and then poured himself a whisky. Curled up on the sofa, he whiled away some time pondering what he would say to Mary when he turned up in a few days with a huge wad of notes and told her they were rich. Mary was totally in the dark, and he tried to imagine the surprise on her face when she saw the notes and he told her to pack their cases because they were off to Cancun on holiday. Mary hadn't been lucky in life either, but all that was about to change for the pair of them.

The whisky soon relaxed his muscles and muddied his brain, and, when he realised his eyes were closing and he was beginning to feel drowsy, he went to the bathroom to wash his face and wake himself up. He came back to the dining room, grabbed the backpack and emptied its contents. He extracted from the corduroy bag the brown envelope he'd taken from the professor's desk, and, before putting it away, decided to take a peek at the manuscript it contained. *Too many words*, he thought as he returned the pile of papers to the envelope, he'd give them a read later. He put the envelope back in the backpack, took it into the bedroom and hid it in the wardrobe among other travel bags. Finally, he wrapped the corduroy bag in the same fancy paper they'd used in the shop where he bought it, and then patiently cut the shirt to ribbons that he flushed down the pan. He took the trainers into the kitchen, and gave them a thorough clean in the sink with a brush and washing-up soap. It would have been a better idea to do it in the washing machine, he reflected while turning them under the tap, but his mother's old machine hadn't worked for ages and Mary washed everything by hand.

After leaving the trainers on the washing machine to dry, he stripped off and took a shower. He couldn't make it a long one, because the heater didn't work and the water came out freezing. Shivering with cold, he put on his pyjamas and drank the last drop of whisky to give himself the energy to smoke a couple of cigarettes. There was nothing to eat in the kitchen, although, frankly, he didn't feel hungry. What he needed was a line, but as he'd run out of coke he tried to distract himself by fantasising about the way he and Mary would live it up in Cancun. He thought about the expensive clothes he'd buy in luxury fashion shops, the five-star hotels where they'd stay and the dinner-jacketed waiters who'd treat them like royalty. For the first time in his life, he had the world of the wealthy within his reach. He only had to stay calm, be patient, and play his cards right. The worst was over.

When he was in bed, he felt dizzy and his stomach was queasy, but drunkenness and withdrawal symptoms soon sent him to sleep. Under the influence of the cheap whisky Mary had stolen from a local supermarket the day before, Antoni Falgueres didn't dream of Cancun or a tropical beach surrounded by palm trees, but of a city's labyrinthine streets, at once familiar and strange, a place of nightmares and fantasies, where he walked, scared, lost and terribly alone.

4

'Violeta, my love!'
'How wonderful!'
'You must be frozen...!'
'Let her take her coat off...!'
'The soup's still hot.'
Violeta kissed everyone, cuddled Hamlet who'd jumped off the sofa to go and rub against the girl's legs, and apologised for arriving late. She'd had a class at the university and, after that, couldn't possibly miss a meeting that had gone on and on. She went around on an old bike so as not to add to the pollution, and had a puncture on the way and wasted time mending the tyre and reflating it. Before joining them at the dinner table she must wash her hands, she added with a smile, showing them her dirty, grease-covered hands as she went up the passage to the bathroom, humming all the way. When they saw she was in such high spirits, everyone in the dining room breathed a sigh of relief.

'She's so pretty!' whispered Mimí.

'But she's lost weight...' piped up the mother-in-law. 'And did you see her hair?'

'They're dreads, Isabel. It's all the fashion,' replied Mimí knowingly.

'I suppose she does look well...' Isabel conceded.

'And seems happy enough...'

Octavi, who, like the rest of the family, felt calmer now

he'd been able to check the state of his daughter with clinical scrutiny, raised an eyebrow and glanced reproachfully at his mother and mother-in-law.

'I said you were both making too much of it. If she'd heard you a few days ago...' he said, shaking his head.

Isabel and Mimí smiled and looked down rather sheepishly. As ever, Octavi was right. Their granddaughter hadn't turned into a cadaverous junkie or a hooligan, as they'd both predicted, and it was obvious that none of their apocalyptic predictions had been fulfilled. Violeta was the same loving, cheerful young woman she'd always been, or at least that was how she seemed at a glance, and, indeed, Norma's expression also changed the moment she saw her walk through the door. Yes, perhaps she did look thinner, but beneath the dreads, the piercings, the tattered t-shirt and the filthy jeans, anyone could see that Violeta was radiant. Nonetheless, despite the rich aroma of patchouli the girl gave off, Norma did detect the smell of the weed she or her flatmates must have been smoking. She hadn't spent three years in the narcotics squad in vain and, unlike Octavi, her sense of smell was too sharp to be fooled by a sickly perfume she'd always detested. Norma raised her eyebrows and looked askance at her husband, who got the message immediately, but neither said anything. That silence formed part of the strategy they'd agreed on to deal with such a situation.

'What were you talking about?' asked Violeta as she sat down at the table and ladled herself a generous helping of soup.

'Your father was about to tell Robert stuff about his work,' Guillem jumped in impishly.

'Dad!' Violeta opened her eyes wide, tipped her head back and smiled broadly. 'I know it's Halloween, but don't upset Robert with your grisly tales. The poor man isn't used to them!'

'How foolish!' Octavi took the hump. 'We are here to celebrate roasted chestnut day.' And added, professorially, 'In truth, Halloween is a celebration with Celtic origins that Irish immigrants took to the United States in the nineteenth century and...'

Violeta yawned comically and, realising he was the reason, Octavi interrupted his peroration. But went on, as if apologetically, ready to pick up his thread: 'In fact, I was only going to explain...'

Norma's mobile rang at that precise moment, and she gave a start. A spanner in the works. She and Octavi exchanged annoyed glances and she got up reluctantly to answer the call. When she saw the number on the screen, she shook her head and clicked her tongue. She'd not begun to speak when another mobile rang. It was Octavi's. He also had to jump up quickly to answer the call. As he did so Mimí sighed and Violeta gasped. Everyone, except for Robert, knew what those calls meant. They were party poopers.

'It's my birthday. All the family's here having dinner, I did warn you,' they heard Norma whisper. 'Are you sure Carrasco can't handle it?'

For a couple of minutes that seemed like an eternity to everyone, a tense Norma listened silently to the patter at the other end of the line. Now and then she looked up, nodded quietly and stroked her forehead anxiously. Apart from Great-Grandmother Senta, who was dozing in her chair, all eyes concentrated on gauging the seriousness of the situation from those monosyllabic responses and the gloomy expression on their hostess's face. Finally, they heard her agree resignedly: 'Alright. I'm on my way. I'll tell Gabriel.'

Octavi, who'd taken refuge in the kitchen to take his call, came back with his mobile, looking serious. He also seemed to be the bringer of bad tidings, and Isabel and Mimí, who were sitting next to each other, stared at him incredulously.

'Don't tell me you've got to go as well!' exclaimed Norma, gesturing dramatically, although she could guess his reply from the expression on his face. Octavi pursed his lips and nodded.

'It was Nebot. I don't know what the hell is happening, but they want me personally to investigate.' And he continued, addressing all the other guests, 'I'm sorry, but I think you'll have to continue the party without us.'

'Dad!' Violeta dropped her spoon in her soup and pushed her chair back.

'I'm sorry, darling. They're orders from the very top.'

It wasn't the first time Norma had received a call in the middle of lunch or dinner and had to abandon her family to deal with a case, but for Octavi to rush off too, as if he were the junior in the department, was something new. The Mossos, the independent Catalan police, didn't usually call Dr Octavi Claramunt late in the night when there was a murder or they'd found a corpse, that was why duty forensics existed. It was quite unusual for his mobile to ring at such an hour. They all looked at each other, worried and nervous.

'Something big must have happened, if you've both been summoned,' muttered Guillem nervously.

'Apparently there's been a murder at the university, in the School of History.' Norma didn't want to go into detail.

'Hey, dear, aren't you studying history?' Isabel blurted at her granddaughter.

'No worries, Grandma. I'm studying philosophy. Who have they done in, Mum? Is it a student?'

'We don't know,' Norma lied.

'Hell, Mum, can't you stop being fuzz for one second?'

'Don't you talk to your mother like that,' Mimí scolded her.

'Come on, Mum... tell us what's happened.'

'I said I don't know.'

'A load of shit!' Violeta erupted. 'It's always the same tune! You cops are all the same...'

Violeta shut up and, in a rage, pushed her chair back even further. Mimí, who'd been muttering and moving nervously in her chair for some time, couldn't stand it anymore and shouted, 'I can't believe it! Both of you going off on a day like today...! Don't those people have other police and doctors to call on, I mean...'

'They're orders from the very top,' Norma defended herself.

'Are you sure they can't send anyone else?'

'Or tell them you're ill?'

'You could say you got food poisoning from supper.'

'Or better still, that the oysters were off.'

'But, Aunty, we've not eaten any oysters...'

Norma was going to speak up to shut down that surreal dialogue, but had second thoughts. The least she and Octavi could do in those circumstances was to allow their family to let off steam and stoically suffer the string of laments and protests. While Mimí and Aunt Margarida competed in an impromptu brainstorm coming out with ever more ridiculous excuses to avoid Norma and Octavi having to go and do their duty, Violeta continued to scowl and simmer.

'Family,' Octavi finally declared in an authoritarian tone, 'I'm sorry but the orders have come from the very top.' A minute later he implored more quietly, 'Please, don't make it any harder for us...'

Chief Superintendent Josep Maria Nebot, with whom Octavi had just spoken, was the overall head of the criminal investigation division. Even though he was reputed to be a reasonable enough man, his rank meant you couldn't go against him, particularly in moments of crisis. Octavi could have refused his request because forensics didn't work to his orders but to the judges', but he reckoned that the chief wasn't in the mood to argue about matters of procedure that evening, given his harsh tone of voice. It had sounded much more authoritarian than usual, and everyone knew that when the chief adopted the curt tone that went with his position it was because something really dire had happened. He'd refused to go into detail, but the fact that he personally had bothered to call Octavi to ask him to go and examine a corpse in situ, bypassing the involvement of a judge or the forensic on duty, could only mean one thing: that the entire murder squad had been mobilised.

'In any case, Norma,' Mimí insisted, 'you could give us a clue! Nothing you say will leave these four walls.'

'Stop fishing, Mum.'

'Forget it, Grandma. It's not worth it.' Violeta grimaced and gave her a gesture of support. 'You know Mum never tells us anything about her work. It makes her feel important.'

Norma snarled and decided not to respond to her daughter. She hoped that sooner or later she'd get over her tantrum. From a very young age, Violeta had had to get used to calls that dragged her mother out of bed or, even worse, in the middle of Violeta's birthday party, with a house full of children in fancy dress, presents to open and candles yet to be blown out. Her daughter's reaction was always the same: she could never fathom why Norma couldn't have a normal job that would mean her little girl didn't have to be on tenterhooks whenever the telephone rang, suffering because of calls that woke her up and snatched her mother away in the pitch dark, when she was at her most defenceless, when she most needed her. Norma wasn't aware those midnight calls still gave Violeta nightmares.

'I imagine the police are obliged to maintain secrecy about their investigations,' noted Robert, who in fact was dead keen to know more. 'I mean, they probably don't even know who the dead person is.'

'You can be sure it's some big fish. If a homeless person or a sex worker had kicked the bucket, you can bet they wouldn't be ringing at this time of night,' retorted Violeta, po-faced. 'At least not Dad, who's the one who gives the orders. Right, Dad?'

'So you're still our clever daughter...' Octavi opted for irony. 'I'm pleased some things haven't changed!'

Violeta reacted with a scowl that turned into a smile, while rolling stray breadcrumbs into little balls. She knew it was futile to carry on because her mother and Guillem would either not answer or be evasive. Unlike Octavi, who used to regale his family with all the gory details of his labours as naturally as he would do if he worked in a grocery store or an insurance company, Norma went out of her way never to talk about the cases she was investigating. Now and then she'd deign to reveal an anecdotal detail, but when it came to her daily dealings with criminals and murderers, she sank into a hermetic silence that no pleading ever broke.

'So will you sleep here tonight?' Norma asked her daughter as she hugged her and kissed her hair. 'I'd like us to have a chat, maybe tomorrow morning...'

'Fuck, Mum, it's always the same...'

'Don't go overboard.'

'Sleep here tonight and I'll bring you ensaïmades for breakfast,' suggested Octavi, in a conciliatory move.

'Dad, I'm *veggie*...'

'What did she say she is?' cried Great-grandmother Senta, suddenly returning to the world of the living and upsetting Robert, who gave a start in his chair.

'Vegetarian, Mum,' explained Mimí, raising her voice because Great-grandmother Senta was going deaf. 'She says she's gone *vegetarian*. It means she doesn't eat *meat*.'

'I know what it means! I may be deaf, but I'm not an idiot!'

'But you can eat ensaïmades, can't you? Now I see why you're thinner...' said Norma, whose alarm bells rang when she heard that news.

'Mum, ensaïmades contain saïm, pig fat. And it's not true, I'm not any thinner.'

'But you've no bum on you! Your trousers are falling down!'

'Now who's overreacting!'

Before they started screaming at each other, Octavi said it was getting late and they should change. He gently steered his wife towards their bedroom while gesturing to Violeta to shut up, trying to avoid a shouting match. He suspected Violeta had been rehearsing one of her inflammatory little speeches to infuriate her mother, something she'd recently made a habit of doing, and it didn't seem the right moment to begin a debate on animal rights and the advantages and disadvantages of vegetarian diets. Above all, Octavi reckoned, because Mimí would end up siding with her granddaughter as usual, and the argument would get strung out and they'd end up bawling at each other. Octavi had deduced from the call that a reception committee of top brass would be waiting for them at the university, so they should hurry. Until he'd finished examining the body, the members of the detective squad would be waiting around and suffering the jibes and moods of Superintendent Mistral, which was torture, and knowing Mistral, Octavi wouldn't wish that on anyone. Norma said nothing and meekly allowed herself to be led to the bedroom by her husband.

'Violeta is right. It's always the same story!' she mumbled despondently as she took off her dress. 'And Bernat had promised me he wouldn't...'

'Don't worry. She'll be here tomorrow morning, you just see. And, by the way, Deputy Inspector, I'd also made plans for tonight...' said Octavi, hugging her around the waist and kissing her shoulder.

Norma slowly turned around, put her arms around his neck and whispered, 'In that case, doctor, we *had* better get a move on.'

5

While Norma and Octavi were changing, Isabel and Mimí swapped a few quiet words and announced they were going to the kitchen to get the second course.

'We should eat the sea bass before it goes cold,' said Mimí, springing to her feet, adding for Violeta's benefit, 'I bet you've not tasted sea bass for weeks. At the price it's selling for...'

'I don't eat fish either...' piped up Violeta.

Mimí stopped dead, half turned and faced up to her granddaughter.

'Stuff and nonsense. As long as my name is Mimí, you will eat the sea bass your mother has cooked! That would be the last straw...!'

Violeta scowled but didn't respond. She knew that when her grandmother adopted that assertive tone it was best not to go against her. Isabel didn't say anything either, but was secretly pleased that for once Mimí had taken the initiative and saved her from having to play the role of the baddy it always fell to her to perform with Violeta. Isabel and Mimí had little in common, apart from their worries about Violeta's well-being and a vehement desire that Norma should leave the force. Unlike Mimí, who came from a bourgeois neighbourhood and a prominent family, Isabel was of humble stock and was so disconcerted by her daughter-in-law's mother's brazen attitude and outlandish appearance she sometimes couldn't decide how to react.

Shy and conservative in her train of thought, way of behaving and dressing, Isabel remained loyal to an outmoded, austere elegance she enhanced on special occasions with her necklace of fine pearls and toned-down makeup. For that dinner party she'd chosen a sea-blue jacket and cream blouse that contrasted with the youthful designer dress her daughter-in-law's mother had put on, an ensemble she'd not hesitated to round off with garish red lipstick. Nevertheless, Isabel couldn't avoid glancing enviously down at the flat, black, soft velvet shoes Mimí was wearing, much more comfortable than the elegant high heels into which she had funnelled her own feet. With the exception of the rings, the other jewels Mimí wore were the costume kind, and all those adornments, with her wavy, yellow-dyed hair made her look like an old Hollywood actress who'd gone to seed or an eccentric fortune teller. Robert, who had transvestite friends who revered that aesthetic of sequins and dissonant colours, had been admiring her the whole evening. Quite discombobulated by the way the dinner was unfolding, he couldn't decide whether to get up and make a gentlemanly offer to help in the kitchen or stay seated at the table like Guillem.

'I suppose you know Mum is an anthropologist,' said Violeta, taking advantage of Norma's absence to address Robert. 'Everybody was shocked when she decided to join the force.'

'We've had our fair share of shocks in this family...' muttered Maurici, shaking his head and looking at his son out of the corner of his eye, particularly at the small earring he was wearing. Although he said that in a neutral tone, his comment inevitably sounded like a criticism.

'Hey, Father, don't you start...' Guillem said with a sigh.

'Did I perhaps say something out of order?' snapped Maurici, whose nose glowed red and who was starting to slur his words.

Guillem looked the other way, as it'd been directed at him, but Violeta, who was sitting next to Maurici, gently scolded her granddad and gave him a peck on the cheek. Maurici growled something inaudible, and finally lowered his eyes and shut up. Visibly ill at ease, Robert started fiddling with his cutlery.

'Don't worry, it's only the wine talking...' whispered Aunt Margarida as she took the bottle and poured herself a generous glass. In defence of Maurici, she added, 'Our generation was brought up differently. It's all changed now.'

'Not according to the pope,' retorted Guillem with a sly smile. 'In Rome little has changed...'

'Let the pope be,' retaliated the nun touchily. 'Ugh, if we had to take notice of him...' she added contemptuously.

'I mean, he *is* supposed to be your boss...' went on Guillem, wanting to make fun of the nun.

'You can laugh, but you just see how we'll soon have a popess in Rome, then things will really start to change,' she retorted.

She removed her toque to reveal silvery tresses that weren't as short as you'd have expected and declared, 'The days of celibacy are numbered too. And not before time...'

'Hell, Aunty, don't tell me there's a monk who fancies you...' Violeta interrupted, upping the ante.

'Shut up, you silly thing! I'm too old for such things! But if I were twenty, or, even, thirty years younger...' she replied, winking and guffawing.

Aunt Margarida was, in fact, Mimí's step-cousin, and both of them shared a peculiar sense of humour that made Isabel blush, and a liking for cava and firewater that the rest of the family found worrying. She belonged to the order of the Clarissas, the female wing of the Franciscans, and Norma was convinced the adolescent devotion her aunt felt for the Abbot of Montserrat verged on heresy. She'd become a nun in the convent in Pedralbes twelve years ago, and the closed nature of the order had led her to discover her ability with computers: as well as making pastries and gardening, she was also hard at work digitising the convent's historical archive. As hers had been a late vocation, more aesthetic than mystic in character, she was sensible enough never to discuss theology with her family, let alone religion.

Now raging claps of thunder enveloped the house in darkness. Terrified, Senta screamed and covered her ears. Recently Senta had been mistaking those thunderclaps for the bombs Italian aeroplanes dropped on Barcelona during the Civil War, and when it thundered, she always started to tremble. Mimí took her hand and soothed her.

'It's all right, Mother. It's only thunder.'

'I'll go to the kitchen to get a torch,' suggested Violeta, jumping up and finding her way with a small cigarette lighter.

Violeta was back in a couple of minutes, grumbling, and holding a candle. The torch, she said, was broken, or didn't have batteries. Luckily, the light came back straightaway and everyone breathed a sigh of relief. Aunt Margarida took advantage of the fact that Violeta had lowered her guard to intercede on behalf of Norma.

'You should show a bit more sympathy towards your mother, my love. I'm sure she's not overjoyed at the idea of leaving. If you'd seen how her expression changed when you walked through the door...!'

'But it's the same old story!' retorted Violeta, as she did a balancing act on the chair to land herself in the lotus position. And she added, by way of explanation, addressing Robert, 'It's what life is like when your parents are police: someone gets killed and they disappear!'

'Your father isn't police, my love. He's a doctor,' said Isabel, who'd just walked into the dining room with a tray fresh from the oven. She was very proud of her son's profession.

'Yes, but he works for them, like Mum.'

'*They*,' interjected Guillem in a tone she wasn't expecting, 'are also the people who put rapists, pederasts and murderers behind bars. Don't forget that.'

'And illegal immigrants, and squatters... And, not too long ago, they also put you in the nick,' Violeta counterattacked, rather taken aback by Guillem's emphatic tone.

'Not anymore. Now they defend our rights, because things have changed. Or do you think there aren't police who walk on the other side?' Guillem, who unlike Robert wasn't in the least flamboyant, emphasised his words with a very feminine whirl of the hand that Isabel and Maurici pretended not to see.

'That doesn't mean they've stopped beating people up.'

'Please don't be so stupid!' Guillem shifted on his chair and raised his voice slightly. 'Your grandmother is right. Your father is a doctor and your mother works in the murder squad, not the anti-riot brigade, as you know very well. They don't spend their time bashing people. In any case, don't be so disingenuous: the ones who take the decisions on beating up demonstrators are the politicians, not the police. The cops simply carry out orders.'

'They are instruments of repression,' mumbled Violeta, still rather shaken.

'They're a bit of everything, dear...' said a conciliatory Robert.

Guillem decided not to continue squabbling with his daughter, and a tense silence descended over the dining room. Fortunately, Mimí reappeared with a second steaming tray, and with Norma and Octavi who were ready to leave.

'Such elegance!' exclaimed a jocular Guillem. 'A tie and the whole caboodle!'

Octavi had merely put a woollen waistcoat over his shirt with a bland tie, while Norma, who'd chosen a low-necked purple dress for dinner that almost reached down to her ankles, had had to change everything. She was going to investigate a murder, not going to a party, and she'd be more comfortable visiting the crime scene in trousers, t-shirt and flat shoes. In her new, much more sober outfit, Norma realised that the makeup she was wearing was perhaps a little over the top but decided to stick with it. They'd already kept them waiting for too long, and, she reflected, everybody must be very nervous at the School of History.

In her bedroom Norma had caught some of the argument that had erupted in the dining room, but Violeta's radical opinions and anarchist harangues were not news to her. She went over to her daughter as if nothing was amiss, gently put her hands on her shoulders, and kissed her on the cheek.

'You're a silly!' she whispered with a smile.

'You're sillier!'

'No, you're the silliest!'

From when Violeta was a child, that affectionate exchange of insults had become a kind of ritual that cooled any ill-feeling. But they were late, and reluctantly Octavi decided to interrupt that tender scene of maternal-filial reconciliation that had reduced the emotional temperature.

'Take your helmet. And a jacket. We'll take the bike,' suggested Octavi.

'I'm not sure that's a good idea. It looks as if it's about to rain.'

'It'll only be a few drops. We'll be there in no time.'

'But the power went! And Grandmother said it would rain... Better take the car.'

'You won't find anywhere to park. The streets are narrow,' retorted Octavi, holding his helmet. 'And I don't remember your grandmother ever getting the weather right.'

'She does sometimes, you know, like everybody else. And don't forget I'm police. They won't give me a fine!'

'Yes, but you'll find someone to give you a lift home later, while the way this is looking, you can bet I'll have to go to the clinic. If I don't take a taxi, you tell me how I'll get there, at that time of day...! Come on, get your helmet,' Octavi insisted, staring at his watch.

Octavi went everywhere on his motorbike, but Norma didn't like motorbikes as a means of transport. She had seen too many accidents, too many cracked skulls, too many people in wheelchairs, but despite her arguments and all her ploys, including risqué lingerie, she'd never been able to persuade her husband to change his old Guzzi for something safer. In any case, she calculated she'd drunk some four glasses of wine that evening and would probably show positive in an alcohol test, and as Octavi had a bike but no car licence, if they opted for the Volkswagen, she would have to drive. She was sure Octavi, who was more moderate in everything, had only drunk a couple of glasses.

'All right...' Norma agreed half-heartedly. 'But don't go too fast.'

'When did I ever...?'

A fresh lightning strike shook the whole building and returned them to darkness. Robert was the one to scream now. Hamlet hid under the table, between their legs, and Violeta quickly lit the candle while complaining there were thousands of books and pieces of bric-a-brac in the flat but not a single torch that worked. In a timely move, before the issue of the torch started another row, Aunt Margarida declared it was the moment to crack open another bottle, and did so deftly, which Robert found astounding in a nun from an enclosed order. Guillem proposed a toast to good health and the thirty-eight years Norma was about to embark on and the forty-eight Octavi had reached in the summer, and immediately Isabel got to her feet and proposed a third toast, this time to Robert.

'Welcome to the family, lad!' she said shyly, raising her glass in the eerie candlelight.

It was the first time that Isabel had reacted in that way, and it wasn't any the less courageous for being feigned, and Guillem was really moved when he saw his father raise his glass to join in the toast. Robert sought out his boyfriend's hand under the napkins and squeezed it hard.

'Know what?' he whispered. 'Your family *is* peculiar. But I reckon I like them.'

6

The School of History is very close to the Museum of Contemporary Art, halfway between La Rambla de Canaletes and the still un-gentrified Ronda de Sant Antoni, in a neighbourhood of old side streets that until recently had been narrow and dark, which, after demolishing a few buildings and evicting a good number of locals, the Town Hall had incorporated into the monstrous theme park Barcelona had become in the wake of the Olympic Games. Norma and Octavi had visited that museum not long ago but the exhibition they saw was a big disappointment; both had sworn they'd never again give a chance to post-modern artists with glib tongues and doubtful talents. '*Ars longa vita brevis!*' Octavi had declared after he'd let off steam saying what he thought of contemporary art in general and the Barcelona variety in particular. The next exhibitions they'd go to see, he said, would have to be by someone who'd been dead at least fifty years. At his age he could ill afford to waste time on such nonsense.

By night and on a bike they barely took ten minutes to reach the School of History. It was close on midnight, but the streets weren't exactly deserted. From the moment Barcelona had been transformed into a city for tourists with cirrhotic livers looking for cheap alcohol, it was quite normal to see gangs of people ambling around in the centre, especially at night. The streets were full of cars, and the long weekend meant there were more nocturnal pedestrians and tourists than usual. At that time of night many were tottering or plastered out of their minds, and fraternised with the locals, jaywalking, and forcing the traffic to slow down. As soon as they reached La Rambla, Octavi had to stop his bike when he drove into a contingent of grinning skeletons flourishing plastic scythes and bottles of beer in a kind of macabre carnival.

'What a crowd!' grunted Octavi trying to open a way through. 'It's not midnight yet and they're already sozzled!'

They were both well aware that for some years All Saints Eve had become a problematic night. Inspector Roca had already phoned Norma to forewarn her that the other homicide squad detective, Deputy Inspector Agustí Carrasco, was already busy on a case of death by overdosing at the other end of the city. When he'd finished his preliminary investigation, Carrasco would have to take the lead in what looked like a settling of accounts in the Barceloneta which had ended in a couple of hoods being hacked to pieces, and the night was still young. The next few days, the inspector had ominously predicted, endorsing his reputation as a pessimist, Octavi and his team would have their hands full.

There must have been well over fifty people by the entrance and in the vicinity of the department, what with ambulance paramedics, municipal police, Mossos and milling bystanders. Octavi parked his bike by the main entrance, and some of those onlookers came to inspect it. Octavi was riding a Guzzi, an old 1985 model, the California 1000, and when he parked it in the street, somebody always stopped to have a closer look. Octavi's was all black and gleaming chrome, because he kept it spick and span, and its design, at once futuristic and old-fashioned, made it look like a museum piece. Octavi, who'd been a teenage fan of motorbikes, had bought it brand new over twenty years ago, and, despite Norma's grumbles, his old Guzzi was one of the few things he wasn't prepared to give up.

A nervous Inspector Roca was waiting for them at the entrance to the department, and the moment he spotted them, he gestured to them to come over. The inspector seemed quite anxious among so many curious bystanders and uniformed police, and Norma sighed when she saw his grimy jeans and tattered shirt. A once-white cotton shirt that now veered somewhere between dingy yellow to dirty grey. As usual, the inspector was unshaven and looked comatose.

'Good evening, ladies and gents,' he said, relieved to see them. 'I know I'm a party pooper, but they were orders from the chief superintendent. Nebot and Mistral are upstairs. And there are rumours that the minister will drop by at some stage...'

Norma and Octavi exchanged perplexed glances.

'Christ, Bernat, the top brass, minister included?' Norma yelped in surprise and Octavi raised his eyebrows quizzically, indicating how amazed he was. 'But who the hell's been done in? Wasn't it a professor?'

'A chair in contemporary history, to be precise, a certain Parellada. It appears he was strangled.'

'And couldn't Puig deal with it?' Octavi rasped. Before answering, the inspector looked around and lowered his voice.

'He happens to be Mònica Muntaner's father-in-law,' he said. But when he saw that name meant nothing to either of them, he added, 'I mean, *the* Muntaner family, the owners of the laboratories. You must have heard of them. They own some of the most important pharma business in the country.'

'Oh, so *that's* why we are here!' growled Octavi, annoyed to be vindicating the opinions of his daughter and her gang of punk friends.

This time Violeta had been spot on. There were class differences even among the dead: upper-class corpses that led to frantic investigations and second-class corpses that were processed routinely. This was an attitude that drove Octavi spare; he obliged his subordinates at the Hospital Clinic to show the same degree of professional attention to all the victims that passed through his department, independent of the size of their bank accounts. In the end, he couldn't hold back anymore:

'Hell, Bernat, is *this* why you insisted I came? Have things sunk so low?'

'Hey, it's not every day they do in a university professor. Besides, you know how upstairs behaves when the murder victim has got a name with clout...'

'And can you tell me what the fucking point of protocols is? Or do you think I can do something that Puig can't manage?'

Octavi had raised his voice more than was warranted, and Norma, who'd noticed a few Mossos in uniform listening in discreetly, waved to him to calm down.

'Don't take it so to heart, doctor,' retorted the inspector. 'Everybody here is feeling edgy. It was the chief's idea to call you, so don't look at me like that. Besides, Puig is still a bit wet behind the ears...'

'Puig is perfectly capable of dealing with this, as you know full well!' Octavi replied curtly. 'I mean, since when did Mossos give orders to forensics?'

The inspector kept his head down, sighed and shrugged his shoulders.

'Fine, shoot the messenger, if you want... But I told you it was all down to Nebot. I can tell you the chief is not having a good day.'

'As we're here, you might as well give us some info.' Norma decided to cut short the round of complaints and get on with the job. 'What do we know?'

'Apparently, he was strangled. In principle, it doesn't look like a robbery, but it's too early to draw any conclusions.'

'Have you informed the family?'

'We've spoken to the son, who was in Cerdanya with his wife, but we've not told the widow yet. Her son says she's got heart issues and he told the chief he first wants to prepare her for the news. When the chief spoke to him (he called him personally), he said he was going to drive here immediately. He'll be here any minute.'

'Provided he doesn't meet a patrol car and get stopped for speeding,' Norma interjected sarcastically.

'I doubt it. I think Nebot sent out an alert.'

'The chief is right on top of the case, I see.'

'That's why he's the chief,' tittered the inspector.

'Is this son an only child?'

'He's got a sister, who's with her mother right now. And, by the way, the victim was a sick man. He was being treated for cancer.'

'Do we know how old he was?' asked Octavi.

'Sixty-eight. They don't retire them at the university until they're seventy...'

'Where exactly did they find him?'

'In his office. The chief's waiting for you there.' The inspector hesitated for a few seconds: 'With the judge... and Mistral.'

'Fuck!' said Norma, put out.

'The superintendent asked for you several times.'

'I was celebrating my birthday. Remember?'

Superintendent Antònia Mistral was an authoritarian, unpleasant woman who had few fans among her subordinates. Everyone in the murder squad knew how much Norma and she loathed each other, and people gossiped that the superintendent pulled every string she could to ensure Norma wasn't promoted to inspector because she considered her to be too lenient and too left-wing even to be in the police. Norma, for her part, couldn't stand the superintendent's feminist façade and tired sloganising, always keen to turn on the discourse about oppressive males and atavistic injustice the moment she was criticised. Norma hated the superintendent's fondness for persecuting male chauvinist attitudes and converting all women in the world into victims. She felt it was a puerile, counter-productive attitude in a woman of her rank. The superintendent spent the whole day defending political correctness and threatening to instigate disciplinary actions, and, although she was sometimes right, Norma detested those witch hunts. In any case, she'd long concluded she preferred her colleagues' coarse banter when they went for a beer together to feminist harangues that, in her view, changed nothing. 'I'd better go up,' said Octavi, straightening his glasses. 'I'll expect you upstairs.'

While Octavi strode down the passage, Inspector Roca took Norma's arm and guided her into a quiet corner. The inspector was six years older and had been her mentor in the murder squad, and, although he was a good policeman, everybody knew he got flustered when the pressure was too great. Some people thought the post of head of homicide was too much for him, but the truth was that all the inspector's problems went back to a divorce that had taken him by surprise, and that he was still recovering from. The eight kilos he'd put on so quickly were down to the fact he now spent his free time slumped in front of the television drinking beer and eating pizza, and, at the station, his own colleagues laid bets on how long it would take the inspector to go from beer to whisky and from porn films to whores. When she saw the stains on his shirt and his stubbly face, Norma decided she should urgently put together a list of her available friends who could save the inspector from such a decline.

Before he became Norma's boss, they'd both worked under Superintendent Mistral, his predecessor in the post, and that traumatic experience had led to a good friendship that had survived his appointment as head of homicide at

Les Corts station. Everyone in the department had speculated that post would be Norma's, and, among the Mossos, the unexpected news of the deputy inspector's promotion was received with undisguised shock. It was in his favour that he was divorced and childless, but everybody was convinced the superintendent's hostility to Norma had done the rest. In truth, Norma might envy her busy colleague's salary, but not the meetings, the hysterical screaming and the red tape. Basically, Norma was pleased to have the freedom to operate as she wanted, and even more so, now that her immediate superior was her old colleague, and not the prissy Mistral.

'Nebot wants you to take charge of the investigation. Mistral wanted Carrasco, but the chief insisted we called you. He said you are the best.'

'Mistral must be climbing up the wall.'

'But don't get it wrong, because we'll be attacked from all sides. We should get used to the prospect,' said the inspector rather despondently.

After taking a first glance at the crime scene, drawing on his years of experience, Inspector Roca knew they were facing a complex case.

'It probably won't be so bad, you know...' Norma decided to adopt an optimistic front to counter the inspector's pessimism. 'If it's not a professional, with a bit of luck we'll catch him quick, you mark my words.'

'Unfortunately, luck is a factor that's beyond our control,' the inspector retorted sourly.

'Hell, you're just like Octavi, you... I'm sure Permanyer will find a hair, a fingerprint, a drop of sweat... Knowing him, he might take his time, but sooner or later he'll serve us the murderer's name on a silver platter.'

'It's that "sooner or later" that's worrying me. As you can imagine, I'm not overjoyed to have Mistral on my back the whole day.'

'I've heard she's dyed her hair and gone all blonde. And

she'll be dressed to the nines, now the top brass are paying us a visit,' joked Norma.

'Frankly, I'd not noticed,' the inspector lied.

'Well, you could try to land her. Though you'd have to shave and change that stained shirt first...'

'I like this shirt. And thank you very much, I'm not that desperate.'

Norma smiled at him sceptically, and patted him affectionately on the back.

'Don't you worry, I'll get weaving tomorrow. I've got a bunch of friends who are desperate and they're good-lookers to boot. But, to get back to the case, you said he'd been strangled.'

'So it seems.'

'At least there'll be no blood...'

'You're right. You've struck it lucky this time.'

Even though she'd been getting used to it over time, there were sights Norma preferred to be spared. If necessary, she could dirty her hands or witness an autopsy imperturbably before finding a quiet spot to throw up, but everyone in the department knew that, when there was a lot of blood around, Deputy Inspector Forester would pretend she had to make a call and vanish. Fortunately, her colleague Gabriel wasn't so susceptible, because he was like Octavi and could look at everything with professional eyes and maintain a prudent level of emotional distance. Norma justified herself by saying she could gather enough information from the photos and autopsy reports, and in part that was true. Her job was to look for motives, check alibis and question the living. It was her husband's job to extract information from the dead.

'At first glance, I don't think the murderer has left many clues,' said the inspector, shaking his head. 'But we'll have to wait for your guy to finish.'

'Octavi is on the warpath.'

'I'm really sorry to have messed up your dinner. I know

it was below the belt. How's Violeta?'

'In total teenage rebellion against her parents. Or, rather, against her mother...' Norma sighed, before adding, 'She looked fine, but smelled of weed. I imagine she smokes joints.'

'My love, she's eighteen, she calls herself an anarchist and lives in Gràcia with a bunch of squatters. What did you expect? Smoking joints is the least...'

'Well, thank you. That's so very reassuring...!'

'And I know it's a minor detail, but you were more or less her age when you had her...' the inspector reminded her.

'Shush. I'd rather not think about that now!'

Inspector Roca didn't have children or nephews or nieces, but he had known Violeta since she was a kid, and, in Norma's flat, he became Uncle Bernat. He and Octavi had known each other from childhood, and Norma knew the inspector loved to play the role of fake uncle he'd adopted towards Violeta and which included taking her cake on Easter Monday and the most spectacular presents on Twelfth Night.

'We'd better go up before Mistral starts breathing fire and...!' said Norma resignedly.

'After you, Deputy Inspector,' said the inspector, theatrically making way for her, 'the case is all yours.'

7

Norma and the inspector went along the corridor towards the Department of Contemporary History and the victim's office where one of the cleaners had found him dead only an hour and a half ago. This woman, a forty-five year-old Ecuadorian who looked easily ten years older, was in a state of severe shock because when she found him spread-eagled on the floor, she thought he'd fainted and tried to move him and bring him round. When she turned the body over, the professor had looked at her from the beyond, his blood-streaked eyes almost leaping from their sockets, and she'd nearly had a heart attack. The building's security guard, alerted by her screams and those of her colleagues, had immediately called an ambulance and informed the Mossos.

'Didn't I tell you,' whispered Norma. 'Mistral has put on her Sunday best. She's hoping to get into the photo.'

'Shush! She'll hear you!'

Superintendent Mistral and Chief Superintendent Nebot were in the corridor in tense conversation with the head of the forensic squad. Inspector Francesc Permanyer and his men, with their cases of equipment, were waiting for Octavi to finish examining the corpse and for the judge to order the body to be removed so they could examine the crime scene. The judge's presence was quite unusual too because, generally speaking, when there was a murder, judges simply spoke on the phone to the duty forensics and gave them instructions from their office. On this occasion, however, the judge had taken the trouble to show up in person and was inside talking to Octavi. Norma scowled when she set eyes on the magistrate in charge of the case. The judge, by the name of Óscar, a man in his fifties, was reputed to be as pernickety as he was ambitious and macho, renowned for his dislike of the Mossos. Everybody knew he was going to make their lives difficult.

'You took your time, Deputy Inspector,' said Superintendent Mistral, staring at her watch and raising a disapproving eyebrow.

'I'm so pleased to see you too, Superintendent.' Norma tried to make her voice sound icy, but, when she addressed Chief Superintendent Nebot, her tone changed immediately. 'Good evening, Chief Superintendent.'

'I heard it was your birthday today, Norma. Many happy returns.'

'Thank you, senyor. Octavi and I were indeed celebrating at home with the whole family,' she replied sarcastically.

'I know. And I am really sorry,' he apologised politely.

The chief ran his fingers through his hair, that had been cut back to almost zero to conceal his more-than-incipient baldness. Looking askance at Superintendent Mistral, he added, 'I mean, I promise we'll try to make it up later for spoiling your party, but I do need you to take charge of this murder. Deputy Inspector Carrasco is an excellent detective, as I hardly have to tell you, but you're more sensitive to certain issues. We can't afford any slip-ups on this case, as you can imagine. We must give the best impression possible.'

Norma knew perfectly well what the chief was referring to. Nobody could deny that Deputy Inspector Agustí Carrasco was a good cop, but everybody knew he was mostly characterised by his unsubtle methods, and foul-mouthed, politically incorrect outbursts. In the sordid streets of El Raval where he usually operated, his dinosaurian tactics gave excellent results, but the chief didn't want even to imagine him bluntly questioning one of the country's most powerful families in the presence of their sophisticated, sharp-as-nails lawyers. Norma behaved differently, she was more level-headed, and even though some in the department thought she wasn't police material, the chief was aware her refined air helped communicate the image of efficient modernity they were trying to fashion for the force.

'The inspector informed me the victim is a historian and the father-in-law of one of the country's wealthiest women. I suppose that explains why half the station is here,' she observed, quickly glancing around.

'He is Professor Francesc Parellada, who holds a chair in contemporary history,' the chief confirmed. 'The woman who found him identified him, and, moreover, he was carrying his ID.'

'The security guard has only been working three months at the university, and clearly didn't know him,' the inspector added timidly. 'Obviously he doesn't know all the students either. The cleaning lady told us the professor had been on a lengthy sick leave. He'd only just returned to work.'

'His son endorsed that,' the chief corroborated with a nod, 'he had lung cancer.'

Octavi and the judge emerged from the office, and a blast of expensive eau de cologne got up Norma's nose and made her sneeze. The judge was dressed smartly in an elegant dark suit which showed off a swanky silk tie he was surely wearing for the first time, and his greased hair was combed back. At his side, with his round glasses, messy hair and black corduroy jacket, Octavi looked exactly what he was: a disillusioned lefty who hadn't totally given up on his ideals.

'I'm done,' said Octavi, taking off his plastic gloves and shoe coverings and looking for somewhere to ditch them. 'I took his liver temperature and he must have been dead a couple of hours max.' And turning to the judge, he added, 'If you're in agreement, they can take him to the clinic now. We'll do the autopsy first thing tomorrow.'

'Tomorrow? Can't you do it tonight?' the chief begged him.

'Come on, Chief, do you expect me to drag everybody out of bed at this time of night? Off the record I can tell you I think he was strangled, probably with some kind of thick, rough cord. There are lacerations and bruising to the neck, but the skin hasn't been punctured. I couldn't see any traces, but I'd have to have a proper look. And, as I just said, he died at most three hours ago.'

'That would put the death at...'

'We'd be talking about somewhere between half past eight and half past nine this evening, give or take a minute. In any case, we'll have to wait to see what we find when we do the autopsy.' However, when he saw the look of despair on the chief's face, he added, 'All right, when he gets to the clinic, I'll do a preliminary examination.'

'It would be a good idea if I took a glance as well,' said Norma, rummaging in her bag.

Norma was looking for a band to tie back her hair and took some time to find one. After fixing it in a ponytail, she asked her forensic colleagues for plastic shoe covers and gloves and went into the office. The victim was an old man who looked fragile and sick, and the expression of pain on his face, caused by the strangling, gave him grotesque features that reminded her of the horror masks on sale in fancy dress shops during Halloween. Still reeling from the judge's strongly scented eau de cologne, Norma now sniffed the bitter smell impregnating the room and went over to the corpse to give it a closer inspection. Incontinence of the bladder is a secondary effect in some kinds of death, and with the lesions visible around the neck, it was a clue reinforcing the hypothesis that the victim had been strangled to death.

The professor's body didn't seem to show any other signs of violence, and, from the position of the corpse, Norma deduced the victim had his back turned to his executioner who'd surprised him from behind. The professor hadn't suspected his life was in danger, which meant he either knew his attacker or didn't see him as a threat. As far as the office went, it was an anodyne den of some ten square metres and its walls were lined by book-crammed shelves. The windows were shut: even though it was cold in the street, it was beginning to heat up inside. There was a desk, a coffee table with two small armchairs and a couple of smaller tables piled high with books and papers. Every item of furniture expressed that same urge to be ultra-modern you felt as soon as you entered the building, and the whole place was imbued with that impersonal air of synthetic materials and cold colours so highly esteemed by Barcelona's architects and designers. It was, however, a shoddy design, deliberately conceived not to resist the passage of time, Norma reflected after taking a closer look. In ten or fifteen years all that expensive furniture would have fallen apart and been thrown into the garbage containers. An association of ideas led her to think of the antiques she had at home and her sturdy furniture polished by the veneer of time. Bad business for antiquarians a hundred years on, she muttered to herself, shaking her head. Very little of what was being made now would survive.

Apart from the chaotic mounds of paper you would expect to find in the study of a man of letters, nothing caught Norma's attention. The office wasn't particularly messy and there were no signs of a struggle. Inspector Roca was right, the attacker had left few clues.

'You can take him, as far as I'm concerned. There's not much to look at,' and she added, for the benefit of the photographer, 'I suppose you've already taken the photos...'

The photographer yawned and nodded sleepily. Two men dressed in grey were in the corridor carrying a stretcher and a black plastic sack, and they too were yawning. The judge looked quizzically at Octavi and then gestured to the two men to go in and start the process of removing the body.

'We were fortunate the police patrol got here before the ambulance and didn't allow anyone in...!' sighed Inspector Francesc Permanyer. 'The people who found him said they didn't touch a thing, we'll see...'

'Well, let's hope your men don't mess up this time, Permanyer!' said Óscar Gallardo, who so far had only directed condescending glances his way, accompanying his sarcasm with a much-practised Mephistophelian smile.

'My men don't usually mess up. But they can make mistakes,' the inspector shrugged, 'it's only human nature. As a judge, you should know that.'

The magistrate leaned back and smiled, happy to have hit one of the inspector's sensitive spots.

'Come now, Permanyer, no need to go all philosophical on me...' he said smugly. 'I was only making an observation...'

Inspector Permanyer shrugged his shoulders again and adopted one of his stoical stances.

'I suppose we must discard the possibility it was an accident or suicide,' the chief interjected, changing the subject and introducing a hopeful note.

'Absolutely.' Octavi raised his eyebrows and straightened his glasses. 'I don't know how this gentleman could have strangled himself, deliberately or accidentally, and once dead, got rid of the cord or whatever he used. Obviously if you have some insight...'

'No need to be unpleasant, Dr Claramunt,' Superintendent Mistral interjected. 'You know that from the onset nothing can be off the table.'

'They should search the vicinity, and perhaps we'll strike it lucky,' said Octavi, ignoring the superintendent. 'If you find the cord and the guy who did it wasn't wearing gloves, there may be epithelial cells.'

'It might have been a woman. The victim was an old man, on the skinny side and, sick into the bargain. A woman could perfectly well have taken him by surprise and strangled him,' the superintendent suggested.

Octavi looked at her sceptically, but said nothing.

'What do you think?' The chief turned to Norma, who had only been listening without butting in.

'It's statistically unlikely,' she replied, shrugging her shoulders. 'But fortunately statistics change...'

'This isn't the attitude we expect from you in this investigation, Deputy Inspector Forester.' The superintendent raised an eyebrow and looked at her scornfully from her height of one metre eighty-five. 'Or could it be that now your daughter is living in a squat, with one of those anti-system groups, you have a different opinion about delinquents and are no longer interested in putting them behind bars?'

Norma wasn't expecting such a snide remark, and blushed a bright red. She'd have liked to forget her good upbringing and punch her in the face, but she simply clenched her fists and gave her a withering look. So as not to up the ante, and because squabbling with Superintendent Mistral wasn't a good idea, everybody stared into space and stayed silent, but Judge Gallardo whistled as if that revelation had come as a surprise. In fact, the news that Norma's daughter had joined one of the radical groups in Gràcia had spread like wildfire and he was perfectly in the loop.

'Do you really have a daughter who lives in a squat, Deputy Inspector Forester?' After a studied theatrical pause, he added, 'Well, I imagine it's in her blood. Because I did hear your grandfather also belonged to one of those anarchist...'

'One of which groups, senyor? You mean those the fascists murdered in the Camp de la Bota?' retorted Norma, giving him a look full of loathing.

The judge stared back for a few seconds, but finally decided to avert his gaze. Octavi, who was on the point of letting fly a caustic response, felt the chief gently tugging his sleeve and gesturing to him to shut up.

'Perhaps it's a student with a grudge,' Inspector Roca suggested on cue to avoid Norma and Octavi getting into a row with the judge. And addressing Norma directly, he said, 'We should look at the academic files and see whether any student has a record of mental issues or violence. And let's see what the family has to say as well as the other professors and administrators...'

'Let's hope the son knows something. He's on his way now.' The chief consulted his watch and looked down. 'At any rate, don't start questioning people until tomorrow, OK? He may be the father-in-law of a Muntaner, but it's no time to be dragging people from their beds for no particular reason. The last thing we want are more headlines about the bully-boy tactics of the Mossos. I don't want to be on the receiving end of a call from Roure. Got that, Norma?'

'Yes, senyor.'

The chief was referring to the Director General of the Police, the man who, after the minister, ruled the roost. The director general's name always made everyone nervous, especially after the reprimands they'd suffered after the outrages committed by some Mossos.

'Where's the woman who found him? And the security guard? I'd like to ask them some questions,' said Norma.

Inspector Roca cleared his throat.

'We've let them go home. They were only in the way here. I spoke to them myself and they maintained they saw nothing or nobody suspicious. In any case, I told them to come to the station tomorrow to sign a statement. Maybe they'll remember something when they've recovered from the shock.'

'I want to talk to them. Don't let them leave until I've questioned them, right?' Norma insisted.

They saw a Mosso in uniform marching towards them along the corridor, who couldn't have been more than twenty-two. He was looking for the chief.

'Senyor,' he said, addressing him, 'The dean of the School of History and the rector have arrived. And they've just informed us that Minister Roig is about to arrive.'

'Thanks, Laura. We'll be down straightaway.'

The chief looked at his watch again, rubbed his eyes and sighed. He'd got up this morning at four-thirty in order to be at one of those boring meetings on international cooperation that were held in Brussels from time to time and, what with one thing and another, he'd not had a minute's respite. Generally, when he was travelling by plane he managed a nap, but that day a colleague from Zaragoza had sat next to him and the chief had thought it bad manners to start snoring, so he'd chatted away. As his blood pressure was sky-high and his doctor had prohibited coffee, he was dead sleepy.

'We'd better go to welcome them,' the chief said wearily. 'I'm leaving everything in your hands, Norma, right? And, Octavi, do try to get a move on. And get hold of Gabriel. Where the hell is he? Shouldn't he be here by now?'

'He's on his way. He'll be here any minute,' Norma lied.

And, discreetly, while Chief Superintendent Nebot, Superintendent Mistral and Inspector Roca as per protocol headed towards the lobby to welcome the academic hierarchy, Norma took out her mobile and redialled Sergeant Gabriel Alonso's number while wondering what excuses she'd give her superiors if she failed to locate her colleague.

8

Norma had repeatedly tried to speak to Gabriel, but her colleague never answered her call. He was no doubt in some bar trying to get off with a Mossa, an activity to which he devoted much of his free time when he wasn't doing lengths in the swimming pool. Sergeant Gabriel Alonso was thirty-two and honest-looking, as well as one metre ninety tall with a muscular, chiselled body, which meant young women were invariably keen to get a closer look and accept an invitation to a nightcap at his place with high hopes of staying for breakfast. Warned off by his friends' divorces and incapable of remaining faithful to one woman, he'd pledged to take no relationship seriously until he hit forty, so he hadn't had one but multiple girlfriends. He was impulsive and a touch forward at work, but he was also imaginative, loyal and competent and Norma appreciated him as a colleague. Their age difference led Norma to tend to treat him maternally, and Gabriel played along with that and allowed himself to be scolded and advised by his superior as if he were a kid brother fond of playing practical jokes.

'About time you answered! Where the hell have you been? Even Nebot was asking after you...!' Norma lambasted Gabriel when he finally answered her call.

'Fuck! You mean the chief super?' shouted Gabriel. 'I'm sorry but it's on the wild side here!'

Very loud music was blaring in the background and

Norma had to hold her phone away from her ear.

'Well, start saying your goodbyes and head straight for the School of History on Carrer Montalegre,' whispered Norma, who didn't want anyone to know she was talking to Gabriel. 'Do you know where that is?' She thought Gabriel said he did. 'A professor's been murdered. There's a lot of hoo-ha because the victim belongs to an important family.'

'A what? Hell, Norma, I can hardly hear you and my hands are tied right now. Can't we leave it till tomorrow? I'll be there early, promise.'

'Sergeant Alonso, get a move on and come here this minute!'

'Blast! I clearly picked the wrong line of work!'

'No, you just need to change your nocturnal habits. You'll end up deaf!'

Gabriel was living it up in Castelldefels at a well-known club with a few Barça players and a bunch of skinny girls who aspired to be TV reality show regulars; even if he hurried, he wouldn't reach the department any time soon. Norma decided to kill time by mulling over first impressions with the head of the forensic team, a methodical, phlegmatic guy who drove everybody mad. She and Inspector Francesc Permanyer got on well, and over the years had learned to trust each other. Norma knew that if he was supervising the investigation personally, no clue would be missed, though it would be a long night and things would move slowly. The inspector had a reputation among the Mossos for being fussy, which sparked lots of jokes and wry comments, but he'd just shrug his shoulders when he heard snide remarks and ignore them. Hypotheses made by investigators must always be supported by material evidence, he'd always say when they tried to pressurise him, and it was his job to ensure every lead was thoroughly analysed, however long it took.

As Norma had imagined, the professor's office was awash with fingerprints, footprints and hair that would probably be of no use. 'His lads,' said the inspector, not seeming at all perturbed, 'are in it for the long haul.'

'It doesn't look like a robbery. The victim's wallet was still in his pocket with his credit cards and all his documentation. He was also carrying around a hundred euros in coins and notes. And they didn't take his ring or watch.'

'Maybe the thief heard the cleaning lady on her way and took fright. Or maybe there was a really valuable item in the office...' Norma didn't seem too convinced.

'A contemporary history professor's office doesn't seem like a place where anyone would keep valuable items. Besides, the cleaning ladies have keys to the offices and go in and out when they want, I mean it's not exactly a secure place.' The inspector paused and scratched his chin. 'Unless, that is, there were ancient documents or a rare book that might be of interest to a bibliophile...'

'We're in the Department of Contemporary History, as you yourself just said. In theory, there aren't any ancient objects here,' Norma retorted, surveying the office.

'On this occasion I agree with Bernat. This case doesn't give me good vibes.'

'Any special reason?' Norma knew the inspector was a wily old hand and that his hunches were usually helpful.

'I don't know what to say. It's all very turbid.'

'Premeditated, right?'

'Yes, nobody strangles on the spur of the moment, as you well know. If they'd shoved him and he'd collapsed on the floor... Or even if they'd stabbed him or cracked his skull open with some object, it would be different. But someone who walks around with thick cord in his pocket probably took the precaution of wearing gloves.'

'Who knows? We might be lucky with fingerprints...'

'I doubt it. Besides, if the guy isn't on file...'

'Or the gal. Didn't you hear Mistral?'

The inspector looked over the top of his glasses and smiled wryly.

'You can laugh,' noted Norma sceptically. 'You can be sure that Mistral will have a ball the day there are female psychopaths who disembowel guys. We'll have taken one more step towards equality!'

'You women don't disembowel guys,' responded the inspector in a would-be pedagogical tone. 'Your crimes are more refined, you don't usually splash blood everywhere. If the perfect crime exists, I'm sure you'll find a woman, not a man, behind it.'

'And you've seen the judge they assigned. Another stroke of bad luck...'

'That's the other side to it...' said the inspector, glancing around to make sure there were no eavesdroppers nearby. 'You know how Gallardo always likes to make our lives difficult. The nicest thing I heard him say was that my men and I are a load of incompetents who don't have a clue how cows piss,' he added, not hiding his irritation.

'You and I know that's not true. And so do the people upstairs.'

The inspector looked down and muttered, 'We cocked up the case of that girl...'

'Everyone cocks up now and then.' Norma turned her head and put her hand affectionately on his shoulder. 'I was lucky.'

On one occasion, Norma had lost her rag with a man under arrest in the interview room and, in a rabid fury, punched him a couple of times, broke his nose and knocked out a couple of teeth. For a time, the station was in turmoil, and the incident nearly led to her being suspended from the force for a good long spell.

'Water under the bridge,' muttered the inspector, aware that it was a delicate subject. 'Much worse was what the other prisoners did to him later in the Model.'

'I'd be lying if I said I regretted it... But the fact is I should be capable of a little self-control. We're supposed to be civilized, not barbarians.'

'The barbarians couldn't care less about guys who rape and murder young girls. That's why Nebot covered it up.'

Norma nodded and was on the verge of confessing she still felt remorse about that episode and that it prostrated her on a psychoanalyst's couch on a weekly basis. She wasn't a cop of the old school, she wasn't the daughter of cops or military, and, unlike some of her colleagues, she didn't feel a special fondness for uniforms and pistols. Her adoptive father was a linguist and chair of classical languages at the University of Barcelona, her mother was an old hippy pacifist who couldn't fathom why Norma had decided to join the force, and she herself had a doctorate in anthropology, read ancient Greek and Latin and had inherited her maternal family's passion for opera and theatre. Even so, none of that had stopped her from losing her marbles and behaving like a barbarian.

'Don't keep harping on... I'll go and see what the lads have got to say,' said the inspector, as he noticed one of his men leaving the office looking quite demoralised.

'The cleaning ladies here don't overwork themselves...' the cop complained. 'Boss, there's enough hair and fibre in there to start a sale. It will take us weeks to sort them!'

As usual, Inspector Permanyer shrugged his shoulders and assumed that stoic stance his forensic team knew and feared. 'That's what they pay you for,' he said. But then he immediately added, 'I'll come and give you a hand now.'

'I'll go and see if Gabriel has arrived,' said Norma with more faith than conviction. 'If that young man doesn't turn up soon, we'll both be in a fine pickle!'

9

Norma left Inspector Permanyer and his men collecting samples, and yawned her way to the lobby. The faculty entrance was thronged with police coming and going, but the person arriving wasn't Sergeant Gabriel Alonso but the brand-new minister of the interior in her official limousine, surrounded by an eye-catching retinue. When she received Chief Superintendent Nebot's call, the minister had decided to break off her holidays and rush back to Barcelona, well aware of the resonance a case like this would have in the press. It wasn't an option to stay put in the Empordà and turn a blind eye, she had concluded after weighing up the alternatives, even though her presence would only get in the way of the police investigation.

Minister Roig was welcomed personally by the chief superintendent, who opened the car door for her and held a huge black umbrella to keep off the rain. She was more or less his age, around fifty-five, and, as well being reputed to be intelligent and astute, she was also known for being super touchy. Thirty years of activism and political involvement meant she trusted nobody and, depending on the day, she could be rather paranoid. That morning she looked bleary-eyed with bags under her eyes. The two-piece she had chosen to visit the crime scene was made from a dubiously pink-salmon fabric that creased easily and was at least a couple of sizes too small, which, contrary to what she thought, wasn't stylish and made her seem fatter. What with a skirt that was too tight, the downpour and the stilettoes she tottered on, the operation of exiting her car was a risky business and ended in a very visible ladder to her tights on her left leg.

'Well, it just had to start bucketing down today!' the chief observed warmly as he offered her the umbrella and his arm.

'Thanks for the call. I know I can't do very much, but I consider it to be my duty. Has the family arrived?'

'We're waiting for the son who's on his way from Cerdanya.'

'I imagine you have everything under control, Chief Superintendent?'

'Absolutely, you have *no* need to worry. This way, Minister. Careful with the step.'

When she saw the chief and the minister scurrying inside, Norma decided to turn round and make herself scarce. She quite liked Minister Roig (or at least felt she was an improvement on her incompetent predecessor), but she was too weary to be soft-soaping. Besides, she didn't want the chief asking after Gabriel again, who was still on the motorway driving his finely tuned car at top speed.

While the minister and the chief made their way to the professor's office, Norma looked at the time and decided to get a breath of fresh air. But the rain wasn't exactly light, and she had to rush back inside to escape a drenching. She noticed rivulets of water were starting to stream down the street bringing a pile of rubbish with them, and immediately thought of Octavi and his old Guzzi defenceless amid the storm. But she reckoned her husband must be in the hospital clinic by now, and in any case she was confident Octavi would be too sensible to start driving on two wheels as long as it continued to rain cats and dogs. For a few seconds she wondered whether to call his mobile, but decided not to, and her thoughts drifted to Violeta and the leaky dampness in the squat where she was camped with her alternative friends. When she saw the quantity of water falling, she hoped her daughter had accepted the invitation to stay with them that night and let her bicycle be. Knowing her family, the cava and spirits would have started flowing freely with the desserts, making the most of her and Octavi's absence, and, with a little luck, Norma calculated, Mimí and Aunt Margarida's alcoholic excesses would leave Violeta plastered on her bed. Tomorrow morning she might have a hangover, but a headache was always preferable to a night sleeping in a dirty, damp house and catching pneumonia. With winter on its way, Norma pondered, that was a topic they both needed to address.

While waiting for Gabriel, she found a coffee machine and served herself a tallat. When she swallowed the first mouthful her stomach started rumbling, as she'd barely eaten a thing. It was almost one-thirty, too late to be thinking about a second supper and far too soon to be contemplating breakfast, since it would be several hours before any bar thereabouts opened its doors. As today was a national holiday, not everyone would open or they would do so much later than usual. Faced with the dilemma of having to cope with a hungry, rebellious stomach or gobbling down one of those tasteless, industrial chocolate bars the machine next to the coffee maker dispensed, she chose the second option. Although she didn't like that chocolate, she thought it would silence her stomach and the injection of sugar would help keep her awake.

Norma started chewing on the chocolate bar and her thoughts returned to Violeta. What if her mother and grandmother were right? What if Violeta had left home and joined a squat because her mother was a cop? It was true that Norma's line of work was incompatible with normal life, and, as soon as Violeta fled the coop, Mimí kept sticking the knife in, and she couldn't help feeling guilty. *That's all very well*, Norma pondered, *but what do women in the Abat family know about leading a normal life?*

For starters, they all had the eccentric names of opera heroines that, over time, had become a family tradition that was hard to change. She herself had yielded to it by naming her daughter after the protagonist of *La Traviata*, a name that nevertheless had seemed quite normal compared to others in the family. She'd been named after a Druidic priestess with matricidal instincts, and Violeta could be thankful, because being a Norma or a Violeta wasn't like walking the streets as a Mimí, Senta, or Antigone, like her poor great-grandmother. They even had an Electra in the family! Nevertheless, Norma had always suspected that all those outlandish names were only a symptom, and that, if there was one thing that didn't fit the Abat family, it was precisely the adjective 'normal' to which her mother seemed to have taken a liking of late.

The scatter-brained look on Sergeant Gabriel Alonso's face interrupted her train of thought and brought her back to the prosaic reality of the murder she was investigating. Gabriel arrived at the same time as Jordi Parellada, the murdered professor's son, and that coincidence meant Norma had to defer the dressing-down she'd prepared. Someone must have informed the chief superintendent and the minister, because he was still in his car when they both arrived in the lobby preparing their welcome. From the out-of-the-way corner where Norma and Gabriel had taken refuge, they heard the chief superintendent and the minister expressing their condolences, telling him they'd moved his father's body to the hospital clinic and that the head of the forensic pathology department personally would carry out the autopsy. While the chief superintendent and the minister were singing the praises of the high professional standards of the police who worked in the forensic department, a dazed Jordi Parellada listened in silence and merely nodded. Norma, who as a female officer had often had to witness such scenes, thought the man seemed genuinely overwhelmed by the situation.

The chief superintendent, who'd spotted Norma and Gabriel keeping a prudent distance out of the corner of his eye, signalled to them to come over.

'I'd like to introduce Deputy Inspector Forester and her colleague. They are the best detectives we have in the force and will be in charge of this investigation.'

And he added, in a would-be diplomatic tone, 'They'll need to ask you a few questions.'

'I can manage that.'

'I'm so sorry for your loss,' said Norma, shaking his hand.

'Thank you,' murmured a numbed Jordi Parellada. 'I've still not come to terms...'

Jordi Parellada was a courteous, serious and shy individual who, despite the flashy silver Mercedes his chauffeur had parked by the door, didn't seem particularly enamoured of glitter and ostentation. His way of dressing was discreet and conservative, and Norma reckoned he must be more or less Octavi's age, around the fifty mark. A doctor of Economic Sciences, with a law degree, his father-in-law had appointed him years ago as head of the Muntaner Laboratories, a profitable family business that was often cited as an example of a well-run company, whose production lines were on an industrial estate on the outskirts of Barcelona. Jordi Parellada was recognised as the man who'd been able to modernise the firm in time and, since he'd become director general, profits had increased fivefold.

'I hate to bother you at a moment like this,' Norma began tactfully, 'but I do need to ask you a few questions. Do you know if anyone had ever threatened your father?'

'Not that I know.' Jordi Parellada shook his head. 'My father didn't have any enemies.'

'I gather he was a professor of contemporary history. Perhaps he'd fallen out with a colleague, or a student who felt hard done by...'

'I don't recollect him ever mentioning anything of the sort.'

'I understand.'

'Of course,' Jordi Parellada added, 'there will always be students who think they've been marked down, or refused a scholarship... But that's nothing new at the university, and it's the best students, not the failures, who are the angriest, the ones who are expecting a first-class honours degree or to see their fees waived, en route to an excellent career.'

'What happens then?'

'Normally it doesn't go beyond a complaint to the dean, and often not even that. I mean I find it hard to imagine my father's death is down to a squabble with colleagues or the revenge of a student who didn't get a grant, if that's what you're thinking. But I thought something had been stolen...'

'Maybe,' said Norma cautiously. 'We've not discounted that possibility. Do you know whether your father had an appointment with someone last night?'

'No. In fact we'd not spoken for a couple of days. He's hardly been home since he went back to work. And as there was no way he'd get used to carrying his mobile... It's different with my mother. I speak to her daily.'

'Did you speak to her yesterday?'

Jordi Parellada looked as if he was trying to remember, as if 'yesterday' belonged to a very remote past.

'Yes, I spoke to her yesterday morning. She told me my father was feeling much better and they were going to have dinner with old friends as they did every All Saints Eve. A kind of tradition they inaugurated after their children left home.'

'And are you sure you can't think of anybody who harboured resentment towards your father?' Norma persisted. 'Someone who had a motive to...?'

'Deputy Inspector Forester,' interjected Minister Roig, wanting to make her presence felt, 'you may think I'm interfering in something that's not my business'—in effect, that *was* what Norma was thinking—'but I think you should leave your questions for tomorrow. Senyor Parellada must be exhausted and I hardly think this is the moment to be grilling him.'

'The minister is right, Norma,' the chief superintendent added quietly.

'My father was very ill. His cancer wasn't looking good, but the doctors were still giving him two or three years...' murmured Jordi Parellada with a lump in his throat.

'I am so sorry,' Norma apologised. 'Forgive me if I've upset you.'

'On the contrary, I'm grateful for all you are doing.'

'We can talk more calmly tomorrow. We understand these are difficult moments for you, but we will have to ask you a few questions.'

'Naturally, should I come to the station?' he asked without a hint of irony. 'I'm at your disposal.'

'No, of course not!' the chief superintendent replied before Norma could say a word. 'The deputy inspector and the sergeant will go wherever you say. But you know we have to respect procedures, and, in these cases, the family knows things they don't think are important but which will probably help our investigation.'

'I'd also like to speak to your wife,' said Norma, putting out feelers.

'My wife?' repeated Jordi Parellada, surprised.

'Women are more intuitive and attentive to detail than men,' said Norma with a half-smile, to avoid having to tell him that a victim's relatives are always the first suspects the police investigate. 'They sometimes notice things, focus on small things...'

'Mònica is still in Cerdanya. She'll drive back early tomorrow,' and, as if he needed to justify himself, he added, 'Our two children went clubbing with friends and it was hard tracking them down... Mònica and I thought it would be best if I took the car and returned first. I imagine she'll be here by midday.'

'What if we meet at around one?' Norma suggested.

'Yes, I think that's a good time. And if you don't mind coming to our place...'

'Of course not.'

'I'll stay with my mother tonight, but I'll have to be home first thing to start preparing the funeral,' he explained.

'We won't keep you any longer,' said Norma, holding her hand out to shake his. 'Please accept once more my condolences, senyor, and I assure you that we *will* catch the guilty person.'

'You'll need my address...' said Jordi Parellada, as he rummaged anxiously in his pocket for something.

'Don't worry,' Chief Superintendent Nebot replied gently. 'We know where you live. That's our job.'

10

Norma offered Gabriel a coffee from the machine and told him what they'd found out so far, namely, very little. Inspector Permanyer and his men were still collecting samples in the professor's office, and Gabriel decided to take a look. As there was nobody to question, and the forensic team were combing the area for the murder weapon, Norma suggested they leave it until the following day and go home to catch up on their sleep.

When they were leaving the department, she remembered she hadn't brought the car and asked Gabriel to give her a lift home. It was almost 4 a.m. and the streets were deserted, so it took Gabriel less than ten minutes to reach Norma's flat.

'Now you go straight to bed, Sergeant. I want you fully fit tomorrow,' she said, as she alighted from his car.

'Yes, Mum.'

In the lift Norma looked at her watch and realised that at most she could sleep for four hours. She gingerly opened the door to their flat so as not to wake anyone, but immediately understood there was no need to tiptoe because a concert was playing full blast: her husband was snoring, her mother was snoring and Great-grandmother Senta was snoring. The house was all but shaking. The only one not snoring was Violeta, who had slept over and was back in her old bedroom. For a moment, Norma was tempted to go into her daughter's bedroom and give her a kiss, as she always used to when she got back in the early hours when Violeta was little, but she had second thoughts. The concert of snores meant that if her daughter woke up, she'd struggle to get back to sleep and would be in an even worse mood in the morning.

As she left Violeta's room, Norma's heart missed a beat and she instinctively touched her holster to check her pistol was there: some strange noises were coming from the dining room. In the dark, she listened hard and realised there were four, not three, individuals snoring in that house. She relaxed, patted the pistol in its holster and smiled. She should have guessed. Taking care not to bump into the furniture, she went over to the sofa and saw it was Aunt Margarida sleeping peacefully, still in her nun's habit under the blanket someone had draped over her. However, Norma gave a start when she smelled her aunt's alcoholic breath, and instinctively stared at the array of bottles of spirits, more empty than full, and the cans of beer littering the table. *You can bet Violeta had polished off the beers*, Norma deduced, and her mother, grandmother and aunt had made inroads into the spirits. Reluctantly she had to concede that Octavi was right: you could never leave her family to their own devices.

Norma was so tired she fell asleep despite the thunderous concert of snores shaking the house and, within five minutes of slipping into bed, the quartet of snorers became a quintet. She slept deeply until half past eight, when her alarm rang. The light of a cold, grey day filtered through the window and Norma opened just one eye, not wanting to wake up entirely. As she'd barely slept four hours, she was dead tired and stretched her arm out looking for Octavi. Nobody was on the other side of the bed, which meant her husband was already up and she could linger in bed a while. If she went back to sleep, she could rely on Octavi waking her up. As he'd promised his daughter, Octavi had gone out to buy ensaïmades and was in the kitchen boiling up coffee.

Mimí, who for some years had been waking early after drinking alcohol, had also got up and was having breakfast in the kitchen with Octavi, but Margarida, Senta and Violeta were still fast asleep. Octavi, who heard Norma switch off the alarm, waited a few minutes before going in and reminding her it was late.

'Will madam rise or does she want me to bring her breakfast in bed?' he asked, giving her a kiss.

Norma grunted and turned over. She was currently trapped in the cobwebs of a nightmare of being in a third-year maths class at secondary school and was resisting waking up. Octavi had to shake her gently to get her to open her eyes.

'Hey, up you get, sleepy head!'

'Yes, I'd better. What time is it?'

'Don't worry, it's not nine yet. I expect you got back late last night. I'm sorry, I didn't hear you.'

'It was almost four. Don't remind me...' she said, jumping out of bed.

'At least you were able to get a bit of shuteye,' said Octavi, wanting to sound upbeat. 'It could have been worse.'

Norma scowled at him and started rubbing her eyes. She'd forgotten to remove her makeup, and her face wasn't a pretty sight what with the smudged eyeliner and eyes that were bloodshot from so much rubbing. After hesitating for a few seconds, still half asleep, she decided to wash her face with soap and water and leave her shower till after breakfast. She was starving and needed desperately to put something in her stomach, because apart from the three or four spoonfuls of soup she'd managed to swallow and that gooey chocolate, she'd been fasting for nigh on twenty hours.

Mimí and Octavi had just finished breakfast, but Octavi poured himself another cup of coffee while Norma ate an ensaïmada and gulped down a huge mug of coffee. Octavi had to be in the hospital clinic by nine-thirty, but there was plenty of time as it was a national holiday and he'd go on his motorbike. Norma had arranged with Gabriel that he would pick her up at ten on the dot to go to the station, but she still had to shower and dress, and she'd barely time. The rain had messed up her hair, and she'd have to wash it, and since, against all advice from her girlfriends and hairdresser, she refused to cut it, drying and combing her hair would take a good twenty minutes.

'I imagine our baby is still asleep,' said Norma drowsily when her mother left the kitchen and she and Octavi were alone. And she whispered, 'We must discuss her marijuana habit. I expect you noticed yesterday.'

'I guessed as much from the expression on your face. You know my sense of smell isn't my forte.'

'But you could smell it a mile off!'

'I only picked up that hippy scent she likes to use,' Octavi said, shrugging his shoulders. 'But you're the expert. If you say it was weed, then weed it was.'

Norma took another ensaïmada and a deep breath.

'So what do we do now?'

'For the moment, we mustn't make a drama out of it.' Octavi looked at his watch and got up. 'I must go, I've got the autopsy at ten.' But when he saw the worried look on his wife's face, he added, 'We can talk about that later. Better not to rush things.'

'And what if there is something else besides marijuana?'

'I thought she looked fine yesterday. Maybe she was a bit edgy to start with, after acting hard and not dropping by for two months, but her pupils didn't seem dilated and her cheeks had a good colour. Frankly, it's not her smoking the odd joint that worries me. If that's all it is...'

Norma shuddered and Octavi hugged her and kissed her on the cheek. From the moment her daughter had left home, Norma kept obsessing about how Violeta could get hooked on pot living with squatters in Gràcia as easily as from visiting exclusive clubs on the Avinguda del Tibidabo and the city's upper north side. She was absolutely convinced. Yet, hadn't she smoked a few joints when she was at university? When he saw her looking so preoccupied, Octavi took a see-through plastic sachet from his pocket and showed it to Norma. Inside was a handful of brown hair where you could see the henna highlights Violeta added now and then.

'What the fuck...?' asked Norma, shocked.

'I'll get them analysed on the quiet, in case there are traces of other drugs.'

'You clipped hair off our daughter?'

'Calm down, she didn't wake up. I did it very carefully. She only growled a bit.'

'Hell, Octavi, you've gone too far this time!'

Octavi, who'd anticipated that Norma would initially be horrified, had decided not to mention his initiative to his wife, but changed his mind when he saw her looking so anxious. For her part she knew that Octavi, as a good scientist, was a practical man keener on a hands-on approach than Byzantine arguments, but even so she reckoned that on this occasion he'd taken his positivist pragmatism too far.

'I really do think we should have a little more confidence in her,' replied Norma with a sigh. 'This can't be right. Imagine if all parents decided to spy on their daughters like this... Apart from the fact that Violeta isn't a minor anymore. I mean, if she finds out...'

'Love, not all parents have a laboratory to hand and a daughter with her head in the clouds living in Gràcia with a bunch of individuals without papers... You know, it's not that I don't have any confidence in her. What I don't trust are her raging teenage hormones and the bastard dealers.'

'I know. But can you imagine how I'd have reacted, if my mother had done something like this?'

'Your mother smoked joints. Let's not rake that up.'

And, shaking the sachet, he added, 'Should I forget it, or let Trias take a look?'

'Let him take a look,' said Norma wearily. 'But don't tell him it's our daughter's hair.'

'There'll be no need. He's got children Violeta's age. He'll put two and two together.'

Norma looked down and said nothing. It was clear she must give it some thought before continuing that conversation. It was one thing to ask the chief to send a patrol out now and then to keep an eye on Violeta and her friends' activities to avoid her getting into deeper water, but, whatever Octavi said, analysing a handful of her hair was a step too far. She didn't want to think of the consequences if Violeta found out.

'Hey, love...' said Octavi, downplaying the issue as he put on his jacket. 'If she's clean, we can stop all the worrying. And if Trias finds something, we can decide on our best course of action.'

Resigned, Norma sighed and nodded reluctantly. After getting a whiff of weed from her daughter's hair and clothes, she didn't like the idea of living in doubt about what substances Violeta was into. The tactic Octavi had taken was basically reassuring and she could always cop out by saying it hadn't been her idea, so she decided to drop it and change the subject.

'Did you find anything out at the clinic?' Being the wife of the head of forensic pathology had its advantages, she'd be the first to find out the results from the autopsy.

'I'm almost sure he was strangled to death, but I'll confirm that later, when we open him up. I reckon we'll be through by one.'

'Give me a ring. Or, better still, send me a message. I've arranged to see Gabriel at the station to question the security guard and the cleaning lady who found the body. Then we'll go to interview the victim's son.'

'I'll ring you the moment I know anything. And now I

really must be going. I'll be late.'

Octavi kissed her and left her eating breakfast in the kitchen. It was quite cold, because it was early November and they hadn't yet switched the central heating on, but Norma was pleased to enjoy those peaceful minutes before she got under the shower. She poured herself a drop more coffee, and after checking Mimí was in the bathroom and the rest of the family was still asleep, she shut the door quietly, opened the window on to the yard, jumped on a chair and extracted a box of green tea she had hidden behind some tins of biscuits in one of the cupboards. Nobody drank tea in that house and she stealthily took a packet of cigarettes and a lighter out of the box. Officially Norma was an ex-smoker, but she had the occasional smoke on the sly and right then she needed one. She'd been trying to give up the habit for years, but she found the idea of renouncing tobacco forever intolerable and had sought a compromise in that adolescent habit of clandestine smoking. Norma kept packets of cigarettes in different places for when she experienced that urgent need, and Octavi, who'd long suspected his wife had a smoke out of sight, acted as if he hadn't noticed. After giving it some thought, he'd concluded it was better to turn a blind eye to avoid an argument and the possibility of a total relapse. Luckily, Gabriel had never smoked. Nor had he.

Norma savoured that secret cigarette as she finished her coffee and went to the bathroom. She spent ten minutes under the shower, twenty drying herself and combing her hair, and ten more in front of the wardrobe wondering what to wear. She wanted something elegant and low-key, but that morning nothing there fitted the bill. As she found it hard to throw out old or unfashionable clothes, her wardrobe was full of items that didn't match and only stayed there gathering mites and dust, as she tried to tell Octavi whenever she complained her wardrobe was too small. First she selected black trousers, a lilac blouse and a blouson jacket that was also black, but, after looking at herself in the mirror, she realised those colours made her look as if she was in mourning, so she decided to change the blouse for one with more cheerful colours. Because of the rain the shoes she'd worn the previous night were splattered with mud and she had to wear boots. By a quarter to ten, hair tidy, lightly made-up and perfumed, she walked to her daughter's bedroom and opened the door.

Violeta was sleeping peacefully and looked as if she wouldn't say boo to a goose. Norma stood and observed her for a while, holding her breath, before sitting down on the end of the bed. She gently began to wake her up, caressing her hair.

'Darling, I'm sorry, but it's late and I have to go. How about meeting for lunch today?'

'I can't today,' said Violeta, rubbing her eyes.

'Let's do tomorrow then. If you like, I can come to Gràcia. There must be a load of vegetarian restaurants in your neighbourhood. It's on me.'

'We'll see...'

Violeta sat up, bleary-eyed, kissed her mother and mumbled that she had a headache before turning over. Norma gave her another kiss and offered to get her an aspirin, but, before she could finish her sentence, she realised Violeta was snoring again and let it go. As she left, she slowly pulled the door to and asked Mimí not to wake her up.

'Let her lie in. And, when she does wake up, don't get her into a state. I can't imagine what she was like by the time you got her to bed yesterday!'

'Come off it! Your grandmother and I never get that child into any kind of state,' Mimí protested, acting as if she'd been insulted. 'Besides, we didn't drink that much...'

'Alright, but don't give her lots of money.' Norma begged.

'Look, if your grandmother and I want to give her a little

present, that's our business. You can be sure she needs some clothes. Didn't you see her outfit? That faded t-shirt full of holes she was wearing last night...'

'It's the fashion, Mother. It's what youngsters wear in Gràcia.'

'Nonsense! It's one thing to dress like a hippy and another as a beggar. And I know all about that...!'

Norma didn't have time to start an argument, besides, she knew very well it was futile trying to make her mother see sense when it came to spoiling her granddaughter. She gave her a resigned smile and a kiss, looked at herself in the mirror in the lobby and went downstairs to wait for her colleague.

There wasn't a soul in the street. As it was a holiday, all the shops were shut and there was hardly any traffic. The impact of the storm was still visible, with the pavements hidden under brown leaves and litter, and although the sun was shining a cold breeze was blowing. Norma shivered and regretted not putting on a t-shirt under her blouse. One less summer, she thought as she zipped up her jacket and rubbed her arms trying to warm them up. How many summers did she have left? Thirty? Forty? It would soon be Christmas, all of a sudden Norma felt they'd celebrated Christmas two days ago, that the year had passed so quickly she'd not noticed. She sometimes wondered what her mother and grandmother felt about the passage of time. Would they think it was slipping by more quickly? Or more slowly? Did they ever think about death? Mimí was still in good shape at nearly sixty-nine, but Great-grandmother Senta was starting to lose herself in the foggy memories of her youth and was gradually ebbing away. Norma was aware that she too was growing old, because recently she'd had to make an effort not to voice nostalgic thoughts that were quite embarrassing, and her stepfather Roger's sudden death had been a blow she was still recovering from. Norma had always been very close to

Roger, as Violeta was to Octavi, although she knew he wasn't her biological father. Fortunately, the arrival of Gabriel, who was disobeying all municipal regulations and hooting because he reckoned his colleague was lost in the clouds, interrupted Norma's cliché-ridden reflections on the passage of time and a lost youth that her therapist, in contravention of all the teachings of maestro Freud and the specific school of psychoanalysis she belonged to, had told her to block out in no uncertain terms.

11

Despite the bad dreams, that morning Antoni Falgueres would have slept a lot longer if the shrill ring of the doorbell hadn't hurtled him back into the land of the living. The persistent ringing reminded him he had left the key in the keyhole, so he got up feeling resigned after concluding it must be Mary who couldn't open the door. Mary returned with a black eye and puffy lip, but happy and in a chatty mood. The beating she'd received a few hours earlier had produced a good tip, she said, her smile revealing gaps in her teeth, because the latest psychopath to cross her path had taken fright when he'd heard her scream and threaten to call the police. Her client had been forced to cough up, and Mary had quickly invested part of the proceeds in a bottle of gin and a couple of wraps of high quality coke. She'd go to the market, she added, and spend the rest on steak and cook that stew he liked so much. He knew it wasn't the first time she'd been battered by a client, but the tips they left when they smashed her face up or broke a rib, if they left one, weren't usually that good. This time, she said proudly, as she undressed and stood under the shower, she could be thankful she'd been so lucky.

Mary's chattering completely woke him up, and after a quick romp, because Mary was tired and her face was sore, he went into the kitchen to boil up some coffee and prepare a good line to boost his energy levels. It wasn't nine yet, and while Mary tried to get to sleep with the help of a few painkillers, he drank coffee, ate stale muffins, then went into the dining room and switched on the telly. He was curious to find out what they were saying about the murder he'd committed and what leads the police were following, and he soon found a channel where a po-faced newscaster was reporting on the murder. He turned up the volume slightly and leaned forward so as not to miss a detail, but suddenly went pale when he saw a very familiar face on the screen. His heart missed a beat, the cup of coffee slipped out of his fingers and the black liquid spread over the filthy dining-room carpet without him even noticing.

He changed channel several times secretly hoping the face he'd just seen was a bad trick played on him by the coke. When he was sure he wasn't seeing things and understood what the consequences were, he went into a state of shock and slumped on the sofa.

'It's not possible...' he muttered.

His body was drenched in cold sweat and his heartbeat raced out of control. Realising he must calm down before his raging heart exploded, he decided against snorting another line and went to look for Mary's bag. He found the anti-stress pills she took against withdrawal symptoms and his shaking hands placed a couple under his tongue, then stretched out on the sofa.

While he waited for the pills to take effect, he took several deep breaths and shut his eyes. That unexpected revelation turned everything upside down. No doubt killing the professor had been his idea, but his client had given him carte blanche and asked him to sort everything without going into any detail. He'd promised him a handsome reward if he resolved that issue, and now he knew who the individual was who'd contracted him and what he could hope for, he'd ask for more money and threaten to go public with their agreement if he refused. As soon as he had the dosh in his pocket, he'd go to a travel agency, and book a couple of plane tickets to put a reasonable amount of ocean between himself and the investigation that no magistrate could cross. He and Mary would be off at once, in just the time it took to be paid, buy their tickets, pack their bags, but, just in case, he'd invent an alibi and ask Mary to agree to endorse his version. Obviously, he'd end up telling her the whole truth, because Mary was no fool, and, if the cops questioned her, she'd put two and two together and draw her own conclusions. Mary would have him by the short and curlies, that was the risk, but she loved him, heaven knows why, and he reckoned she could handle the situation. In fact, everything was still under control, he repeated to himself to keep his spirits up, and considering he wasn't on any police file and knew neither of the victims, the cops wouldn't have it easy connecting him to the case. If he kept calm and avoided panicking, he and Mary would soon be starting out on a new life far from that sordid world around them, and everything would be different. Except that now, however much he tried, he couldn't hear that soothing little voice in his head that told him every once in a while that all was well.

12

Norma and Gabriel reached Les Corts station just before half past ten. Inspector Roca had summoned the security guard and cleaning lady for eleven, and Norma suggested to Gabriel they should pop into the bar on the corner before going in. That night Gabriel hadn't slept well either, and what with his drowsiness and the lambasting he'd received from Norma because he'd not answered his mobile in the disco, he was feeling rather down.

'I think we both need an extra dose of caffeine,' said Norma, as they walked into the bar.

There were a few Mossos in uniform eating breakfast and watching a car race on the telly. Norma said hello, sat at the bar, and ordered a couple of coffees. After swallowing the first mouthful, Norma was tempted to light up again, but she'd already smoked once that morning, and thought better of it. Coffee didn't taste the same if you didn't have a cigarette between your lips, but she didn't want to relapse and, above all, start smoking in front of Gabriel and have to tell him she occasionally smoked on the side, behind Octavi's back, as if she was a teenager. She was a murder squad deputy inspector, a woman able to make her own decisions in life, but she had to admit that clandestine smoking wasn't the best way to win the respect of her subordinate.

Just before eleven, she and Gabriel left the bar and went into the station. The two witnesses had been waiting for some time, and Norma and Gabriel thanked them for their patience, then questioned them separately. The security guard was first. He'd not been working long at the university and barely knew the professor by sight. He said he'd seen nobody suspicious on the day of the murder, or at least nobody looking more suspicious than was usual among the students. Accompanied by one of her daughters, because she was still very shaken up, the cleaning lady was no help either, because apart from finding the corpse, she had seen or heard nothing. The woman was a bag of nerves and kept rubbing her hands together, and Norma tried to calm her down because she was a foreigner and afraid of losing her job.

'Here's my card, with my number,' Norma told her, 'Ring me if you have any problems.'

Norma made them sign their statements, sighed, let them leave, and hoped they'd have more luck with the samples collected by Inspector Permanyer's team. For the moment, the Mossos had checked out the department building and the neighbouring streets looking for the murder weapon or some clue, but had found nothing, and given the lack of leads, Norma said they should concentrate on the motive.

'If the professor had an enemy with motives enough to kill him in cold blood,' she thought aloud, 'somebody near to him must know something.'

'Unless it's a lunatic,' Gabriel objected timidly.

'Don't be such a pessimist.'

They still had half an hour to kill, and Gabriel winked at Norma and said he'd go and catch up on his paperwork. Translated, that meant Gabriel was planning to answer personal emails and visit his Facebook page. Norma scowled at him but said nothing. She also went to her desk, switched on the computer and keyed in her email password – she had a stack of unopened messages. None seemed urgent, but, just in case, she reviewed the long list in bold before deciding not to open any. Suddenly she gave a start, looking around to check no one had noticed her surprised reaction. She'd just noticed a message she'd not seen before, and for a few seconds, finger on mouse, she was tempted to open it. Finally, she had second thoughts and decided to read it later when things were less hectic. In any case, she knew exactly what that message said: David Subirana was in Barcelona and wanted to see her.

She'd not had news of David for over six months, and had imagined he was hard at work excavating in Cairo. The idea she might see him soon was a shock to the system. How long would he be in Barcelona this time? She didn't want to call him from the station and risk someone overhearing the conversation; besides, she had to do her homework before going out to question the Parellada couple. She should Google the professor and Muntaner family to know exactly whom she was meeting and to see whether information online gave her any clue as to a possible motive. Inspector Permanyer had already dismissed robbery as a motive and she agreed.

Norma chased David from her head and dived into Google. Professor Francesc Parellada came up in thousands of entries due to his status as a teacher at Barcelona University and expert on the Spanish Civil War. He was the author of a dozen books and hundreds of specialised articles, and Norma thought she remembered seeing a few of those books in her stepfather's library. Most articles could be consulted online, and, as she had plenty of time, she decided to note down a few links to examine at leisure. As for the Muntaner family, whose name had brought the top brass out the previous night, its members had a rather unimpressive online presence. Even so, Norma discovered that Rafael Muntaner, the patriarch of the family, had died eight years ago, that half of Barcelona from the Diagonal and the upper north side had come to the funeral, and that Mònica and Gerard, his two offspring, had inherited an estate that was worth a billion euros all told. While she was taking notes, her mobile rang and Norma gave a start for a second time.

Octavi had rung to confirm that the professor had been strangled to death. They still hadn't finished, he said, but he'd been able to speak by phone with the oncologist who was treating him, and he'd confirmed the professor was a sick man and that they'd treated his lung cancer.

'They certainly strangled him with some kind of rope or plastic-covered cord. Or maybe a length of wire...' Octavi added, rather annoyed at being so imprecise. 'There was no trace of fibres on his skin, and I found nothing under his nails. Sorry!'

'In any case, send the professor's suit to Permanyer's team for analysis.'

'Hey, I'm not a greenhorn!' he protested, pretending to be offended. 'Don't you worry, I've done that.' He added, 'But don't get your hopes up... I don't think the guy even had the option of resisting, because he'd been really debilitated by the chemo. He barely weighed sixty kilos.'

'They strangled him from behind, right?'

'Yes, that's not in doubt. And I'd say whoever did it was taller than the victim.'

'How tall? Much taller?'

'How do I know? Do you think this is *CSI* or something?'

'OK, don't get annoyed. Will you be home for lunch?'

'As soon as we're done with him, I'll grab my bike and head home. Should I ring your mother?'

'No, don't worry, I will.'

After hanging up, Norma rang Inspector Roca to tell him unofficially what Octavi had discovered, which unfortunately was very little. At the time the inspector was in the School of History, meeting an anxious dean, while a couple of his men were scrutinising academic files and making lists of students and teachers in the department.

Norma and he agreed to meet later at the station to review the list, and then Norma rang her mother and told her she and Octavi would be home for lunch though she couldn't say when. Mimí, who saw to the cooking on holidays (or, rather, she heated up what her housekeeper left all prepared in the fridge), asked her if they'd fancy cannelloni or chicken stew.

'The chicken with some salad,' she replied after pondering for a few seconds.

Before leaving, she opened her inbox and clicked on the message David had sent. Her friend was indeed in Barcelona and wanted to see her.

'Let's be off,' she said to Gabriel, jumping up from her chair. 'I'd rather not be late.'

'Are you completely ruling out robbery as a motive?' Gabriel asked despondently as they walked to his car.

'We never completely rule out anything at the start,' joked Norma, parodying what Superintendent Mistral had said.

Gabriel couldn't decide how to interpret Norma's sarcasm, so he opted to say nothing. That morning Norma had given him a hard time. She reckoned that at least for now she should treat Gabriel sternly so he learned his lesson, and didn't mistake being on friendly terms with a lack of professionalism. Gabriel would make a good detective, Norma had told Inspector Roca, but he still had a lot to learn about discipline.

'You can drive,' she said, as the lift took them down to the car park.

Norma's head was aching so the idea of driving didn't appeal. Besides, she was used to her Volkswagen Beetle and hated Gabriel's finely-tuned Hyundai, particularly in the city. For his part, Gabriel detested being the backup driver and couldn't stand Norma's far too cautious style of driving, so he gave a relieved smile.

TERESA SOLANA

As there wasn't much traffic, Gabriel decided to put his foot down and make headway, assuming she would grumble and start lecturing him. Quite unexpectedly, Norma simply looked out of the window and said nothing. After his telling-off Gabriel wasn't sure what his colleague's thoughtful silence implied. Naturally, he knew nothing about David and his emails, so he reduced speed and started stopping even at the amber lights.

'It must be somewhere near here,' Gabriel said when they reached the convent in Pedralbes.

Absorbed in thought, Norma didn't hear him.

The luxurious villa where the Parelladas lived in the district of Sarrià was close to the Pedralbes convent. From inside the car, Norma gazed at the building and wondered whether Aunt Margarida would be back in the convent or whether, as happened the previous year, she'd take a few days holiday and hide away at their place. From a very young age, Aunt Margarida had dreamed of living in that old convent, not so much because she was deeply religious as because she felt a romantic longing to walk between its Gothic walls disguised in the sober habits of the Clarissas like a heroine from yesteryear.

Since she didn't have children and hated living alone, when her husband died she decided to realise that old dream after weighing up the advantages of growing old among affable nuns in a venerable convent rather than doing so alone in her flat, or, what most terrified her, surrounded by decrepit crocks in a shabby residential home watching that sinister procession of black bags on their way to the crematorium. The dearth of vocations and the generous gift she'd made to the bishopric after selling her flat helped ensure they welcomed her with open arms, and, from the day she professed her vocation, Sister Margarida diligently fulfilled her duties as a nun, fascinated by the monotonous, soothing discipline she discovered came with the habit. She'd been living comfortably isolated from the world and its problems for eight years, reciting ancient prayers behind those impenetrable stone walls. However, occasionally, she did miss the freedom of her secular life and, now and then, invented an excuse to go out and took advantage of her escape to go to bingo sessions, drink cocktails in Boades and hit the town with Mimí.

'It's too early,' said Norma, scowling. 'Let's wait a bit. Don't park in front.'

Gabriel restarted the car and parked it in a side street some two hundred metres from their mansion. Norma took out a packet of cigarettes and lit up. She hadn't smoked for three days, but this was her second that morning. David's message had jolted her badly.

'Christ, Norma,' Gabriel exclaimed, 'I thought you'd given up!'

'I only have a smoke now and then,' she said, trying to justify herself. 'Don't you dare say anything at the station... Least of all to Octavi. That's an order, got it?'

'You're the one dishing them out. But I don't think it's a good idea.'

'I'll bear that in mind. By the way, let me do the talking today.'

'Should we see them as suspects? The family, that is.'

'I don't know. I'll decide on that later.'

Norma extinguished her cigarette and, before ringing the bell, she checked the address to make sure she'd got the right one. In that spot there were only luxury flats and mansions, and the Parellada establishment was almost invisible from the road. The mansion, like the convent, was also isolated from the world by a crowded garden and a wall almost three metres high, painted a dark grey. They'd installed a security camera to check on the identities of visitors on the steel door that kept the unwanted ones out. Norma rang the bell and an unseen hand opened that heavy door inviting them to enter the property. Without hiding their curiosity, she and Gabriel stepped inside ready to meekly follow the dainty pebble path to the house. Before they got there, a second camera detected them and forewarned their hosts.

The house was a building of cubic dimensions, painted in that dismal, modern grey. No balconies or friezes enlivened the walls, and, of course, Norma reflected, as she looked it over, the architectural philosophy behind that mansion had nothing in common with the colourful aesthetic of mosaics and stained-glass windows the Barcelona bourgeoisie had adopted a hundred years before as symbols of their wealth and good taste. In fact, that overly sober, humourless house, with no neighbours to bid good morning or exchange a few polite remarks or gossip with, reminded her of a prison. Like most wealthy families, the Parelladas lived as if marooned on their small individual slice of paradise, but Norma's idea of paradise didn't encompass security cameras and concrete walls. That desolate form of existence didn't appeal to her at all.

Jordi Parellada and his wife were waiting for them in front of the main entrance holding hands. Both seemed genuinely shocked and had bags under their eyes, as if they hadn't slept much. Once the officers had introduced themselves, reiterated their condolences and been thanked for doing so, the married couple invited them into the house and ushered them into the drawing room. Norma made the most of that exchange of polite pleasantries to analyse the appearance of the heir to the Muntaner fortune, a straightforward-looking woman who, she deduced, didn't go around boasting about the string of zeros in her current account. Like her husband, she dressed comfortably and simply, and her grief-stricken yet calm demeanour was quite the reverse of the cheque-book arrogance she'd been met with in other wealthy women in her position. Mònica Muntaner was a fully modern woman, and, as Norma had discovered on Google, had a doctorate in chemistry and was head of the research and innovation section at the Muntaner Laboratories, a position of responsibility that was in no way honorary or decorative. On the other hand, it was a good sign they hadn't called any lawyer to be present at what was going to be a kind of interrogation, Norma reflected, even though they must imagine the police had no reason to consider them to be suspects. From the outset, they didn't appear to have any motive, and neither was in Barcelona when the crime took place.

The Parelladas walked them through a spectacular drawing room dominated by a modern steel fireplace that rose up in the very centre of the room opposite a disturbing Francis Bacon that Norma imagined was an original. There were three white leather sofas around the unlit fireplace. The couple sat on one, and Norma and Gabriel, following their indications, sat on the sofa nearest to them.

Acting like a good hostess, Mònica Muntaner offered them coffee or a cold drink, that the well-mannered Norma and Gabriel declined. Norma took her glasses and a notebook from her bag and began to ask routine questions. Gabriel, as Norma had ordered, sat there in silence.

The couple answered all her questions politely and patiently, and Norma felt they were really trying hard to cooperate. They repeated that they knew of no one who had any reason to feel resentful towards the professor, let alone to murder him, and also that, however much they'd thought back, they were sure he had never fallen out with any student or professor. The beneficiary of the will was his mother, Jordi Parellada explained before Norma even broached the subject, and he had bequeathed to her the flat on the Gran Via where his parents had always lived, the flat in Calella de Palafrugell where they spent the summer and savings that amounted to seventy thousand euros, give or take a few euros. Very little compared to the wealth of the

Muntaners, Norma reflected. That inheritance didn't seem like a motive.

'I understand your father was a specialist in the Civil War,' Norma said, testing the terrain.

'Yes, he was a real authority. He published many articles and quite a few books, and he was finishing another.' Forcing a smile, he added, 'He was particularly keen on the anarchists.'

'But he wasn't an anarchist, was he?' interjected his wife.

'No, he wasn't. But he admired the culture of the Athenaeums, the energy and bustle of working-class Barcelona, the idealism of the revolutionaries... As you must know, Barcelona was full of anarchists in the thirties. Father said they were dreamers, and that, except for a minority, they were mostly good people. According to him, it was the war that turned everything upside down, because it put the workers between a rock and a hard place.'

'Winning the war or starting the revolution,' muttered Norma.

'Exactly.'

'My grandfather thought the war couldn't be won without making the revolution,' said Norma, repeating what she'd heard said at home so often.

Norma's comment surprised everyone, and for a few seconds an uneasy silence reigned in that designer drawing room. When she realised she'd voiced her thoughts out loud, she blushed a deep red and looked down as if she was concentrating on her notes.

'As far as that went,' said Jordi Parellada with a smile, 'my father and I didn't agree. He said that, from the start, it was a war that was impossible to win. But I think if the Republicans had been able to bury their differences and act like a professional army...'

Norma was going to respond, but finally decided to grit her teeth and not open up a debate on why the Republicans had lost the war. Mònica Muntaner, clearly afraid the conversation might become awkward, looked at her watch and said softly, 'Jordi, remember your mother is waiting for us. And this lady and gentleman must have work to do...'

'As you see, my father passed his passion for the Civil War on to me,' Jordi Parellada justified himself, a sad smile on his lips.

Norma nodded and, taking advantage of the way the conversation had turned, she decided to ask whether Francesc Parellada had ever had problems with any extremists because of his opinions or writing.

'No, not that I am aware of. My father was a shy man and had very little public exposure. I mean he wasn't one of those who are always on the radio or telly, his publications were quite scholarly. None of his books became best-sellers, that's not what he wanted.' And he added proudly, 'My father was a true academic.'

'He loved teaching,' his wife continued in a tone that revealed the genuine admiration she felt for her late father-in-law. 'One of the things that most saddened him about being ill was not being able to see his students.'

'I will need to speak to your mother,' Norma said, trying not to sound threatening. 'Perhaps he told her something you don't know.'

For the first time Jordi Parellada reacted defensively and his tone of voice sounded much less friendly.

'Frankly, I would rather you left my mother out of this business. It's been a very hard blow for her, and it's already unpleasant enough.'

'I totally understand,' Norma replied diplomatically. 'But I need to ask her whether your father was particularly worried or anxious, or if anyone had threatened him. I promise not to upset her.'

'It's quite normal that they should want to speak to her, Jordi,' his wife interceded gently. 'Your mother will understand.'

'Perhaps tomorrow,' he sighed. 'I don't think she'd be up for it today.'

Norma nodded, put her glasses and notebook away and stood up, signalling to Gabriel to follow suit.

'It's most peculiar...' whispered Jordi Parellada, also getting up off the sofa. 'It's not two weeks since my father went to the funeral of a friend who also died in violent circumstances.'

'That's true, Víctor... I'd forgotten about him,' his wife chipped in. And seeing how Norma had looked up and was staring at her questioningly, she added, 'Thieves entered his house and stabbed him to death.'

Norma froze for a few seconds, then walked back and sat down again. Gabriel and the Parellada couple, surprised by her reaction, did the same.

'So who was this friend?' she asked, looking for a blank page in her notebook and putting her glasses back on.

'He was Víctor Porta,' said Jordi Parellada, rather disconcerted. 'He and my father were friends from childhood. In fact, they were both born in the same neighbourhood and went to the same school.'

'What happened to him?'

'I told you, thieves broke into his house, ran into him and stabbed him.'

'Apparently, he bled to death,' noted his wife.

'Is he the man who was murdered not long ago in Poble Sec?' Norma asked, trying to remember. She knew Deputy Inspector Carrasco was in charge of that case.

'Yes, Víctor lived near the Paral·lel, even though he lived most of his life in Mexico. He returned to Barcelona after his wife died.' He hesitated. 'But that was a robbery, wasn't it? According to the papers, it was one of those gangs from the east,' he added, realising it was a strange coincidence.

'You don't think they are connected, do you?' asked Mònica Muntaner, lowering her voice.

'I don't know,' responded Norma, shaking her head.

'It's a possibility. Do you have any idea when they last met?'

'I think it was shortly before...' said Jordi Parellada without finishing his sentence. 'But I couldn't tell you exactly. My father may have jotted it down in his diary.'

'Do you know if he lived alone?'

'Yes, Víctor liked to keep himself to himself. But his daughter and his grandson often paid him a visit.' He persisted, not sounding very convinced, 'But what happened to Víctor was only a coincidence, wasn't it?'

'Maybe,' Norma replied quietly. 'But coincidences are always suspicious. We'll have to look into it.'

Norma didn't recall that that particular case had been closed and, as she stood up for a second time, assuming their meeting was over, she added, 'Do you think we could drop by your mother's house tomorrow afternoon? I promise we won't upset her.'

'My mother lives on the Gran Via, near the Plaça de la Universitat. I'll jot down her address.'

'Of course, you can be there when we talk to her.'

'Do promise it will be a short conversation,' Jordi asked her. 'She's got a pacemaker.'

'You have my word.'

'I'll try to arrange it for tomorrow,' and, in a pleading voice, he added, '*You* will talk to her, I hope?'

'If you prefer, I can come alone. Your mother, you and me. Fifteen minutes, max,' replied Norma, recalling the chief superintendent's warning about taking it slow and easy.

'My wife and I are grateful for all that you are doing, we really are,' he said, holding his hand out to shake hers.

'And, of course,' his wife added, with no great subtlety, 'we will be happy to collaborate however and with whoever. I mean if the team looking into the case needs more resources or overtime...'

'Don't you worry about that,' Norma cut her dead. 'We have everything under control.'

TERESA SOLANA

13

As they walked across the leafy garden, still soaked after the previous night's downpour, a perplexed Norma looked around, then checked the time. Her watch confirmed it was just before two, but soot-black clouds had so darkened the sky that night-time seemed about to fall and engulf them in dense, damp gloom. A blast of icy wind gave her the shivers, and all of a sudden she sensed something wasn't right because her head was still aching and the coffees she'd drunk that morning hadn't energised her. She felt strangely exhausted, even feverish.

'Would you mind driving me home?' she asked, as they got into the car. 'I need to catch up on my sleep before going back to the station. I expect you do as well.'

'I'd love a nap.'

'Go home but make sure you're contactable,' said Norma, raising an eyebrow. 'I'll expect you at six.'

'Don't worry, boss. Message received.' Gabriel smiled and imitated a military salute.

Inside the car Norma started looking out of the window. Gabriel understood his colleague wasn't in the mood for chit-chat and drove in strict silence. When they reached Via Augusta, Norma noticed Gabriel was looking at her out of the corner of his eye and shifting anxiously in his seat.

'What's wrong?' Norma asked.

'Nothing.'

'Come on. Something's buzzing round that brainbox of

yours,' she insisted.

'I was wondering if what you told the judge yesterday was true, that your grandfather was an anarchist,' muttered Gabriel, keeping his eyes on the road.

In fact, ever since Officer Mata had phoned to tell him about the squabble between Deputy Inspector Forester and Judge Gallardo, Gabriel had been waiting all morning for the right moment to have that conversation.

'But what the hell...?' erupted Norma, who couldn't work out why her colleague knew about that.

'A little bird told me,' Gabriel confessed, with a shy smile.

'Right. I imagine it's that little bird who starts licking her lips whenever you're around.'

'Well, is it true he was an anarchist?' Gabriel asked again.

'Yes, he was an anarchist.'

'The kind that threw bombs and burnt churches?'

'Of course not, not all anarchists went around lighting fires... My grandfather came to Barcelona to fight the fascists.'

'And did he die in the war?'

'Why are you so fascinated by my grandfather?' Norma retaliated, rather upset by this intrusion into her private life.

'Nothing in particular. I was just curious.'

Norma turned her head and started looking out of the window again, hoping Gabriel would realise she preferred to end a conversation she considered too personal, but immediately regretted being so elusive and changed her mind. After all, Gabriel was her colleague, and considering her English surname, the gossip that went the rounds at the station, and the judge's perverse comments, it wasn't strange he felt curious.

'My grandfather was executed in the Camp de la Bota in 1939. He was twenty-five,' she eventually explained.

Still looking straight ahead, Gabriel shook his head.

'At the time, both sides did outrageous things. It's better we turn the page.'

'Better? Better for who?' Norma replied curtly, dismayed by her colleague's remark.

'Better for everyone. The Republicans weren't exactly angels...'

Norma opened her mouth to fire back a response, but finally opted to keep quiet. She'd just realised that she knew very little about Sergeant Gabriel Alonso, who was currently pretending to focus on his driving and avoiding eye contact. What lay beneath his butter-wouldn't-melt expression, that innocent air she suspected was rather an act? What were Gabriel's political ideas? Who did he vote for? Norma had deduced from his sarcastic comments and irreverent asides that her colleague was on the left, but in reality, if she thought about it, she had to accept they'd never openly discussed politics. After a while, and still looking straight ahead, it was Gabriel who broke the silence.

'The FAI anarchists killed my grandfather. I never got to know him either,' he whispered.

'I didn't know...' she replied, rather taken aback. 'I'm very sorry.'

Norma had always imagined that Gabriel belonged to the generation without a memory for the Civil War, which to them was a distant event they'd barely registered. Gabriel was two years old when the dictator died, and the democratic transition during which he'd grown up had developed at the price of giving a tacit amnesty to the Francoists, silencing the suffering of the Republicans and wiping from the map the atrocities of the winners. The predominant discourse was that both camps were equally good and bad, had committed a similar number of heroic and barbaric acts, and as such, according to that convenient premise, Nationalists and Republicans both had reason enough to be ashamed of what they'd done. It was better, so they said, not to open those old wounds and simply turn the page. By dint of insisting, the architects of the transition, many of them would-be reformed Francoists or Stalinists, had engineered a situation where many victims felt guilty and many of the guilty felt like victims. Since conversations about the war had been reduced to a mere exchange of flashbacks without a historical perspective—Guernica versus Paracuellos, so many women and children executed versus so many murdered priests and burnt churches—in schools it was decided to tiptoe around the subject of the war so as not to offend anyone's sensibilities or ideologies. The Historical Memory Law, passed thirty years too late, had been simply reduced to a rhetorical exercise, to a handful of bureaucratic permissions to dig up land in search of remains, as if that was all restoring the dignity of victims amounted to. Meanwhile, time moved on and the last generations of Francoists who had sworn loyalty to the regime quietly departed the world of the living without anyone bringing them to account or holding them responsible. The circus orchestrated in the corridors of power had succeeded in drowning the transition in a mist of amnesia, but, at the same time, the hint of bitterness Norma detected in Gabriel's voice made her realise that the phantom of a grandfather he'd never known had surely hovered over his childhood with the same epic intensity as the tragic figure of her grandfather Jack had over hers.

'In any case, my grandfather didn't belong to the FAI, nor was he a murderer,' said Norma, after a while.

'No, I wasn't suggesting...'

'Besides, a murder and an execution aren't the same thing. Wild animals murdered your grandfather, mine was executed on the orders of a court. I know the result is the same, but it's a crucial shade of difference.' She realised she might have come across as over-categorical, so she added, 'If you like, we can talk about this some other day, right now I'm too tired. My head's been aching ever since I left home this morning.'

Gabriel didn't know if that was an excuse because Norma was uncomfortable with the conversation or if it was true she was really ill. He'd noticed that Norma had been looking unwell for some time, but they'd only been working together for a few months and that had been the first time Gabriel had dared bring up the subject of the Civil War. Even though he was happy to work under her orders he found Norma intimidating, and, though they worked well together, they weren't what you'd call friends, certainly not in the way Norma and Inspector Roca were. On the other hand, Gabriel found his colleague's green eyes and casual way of behaving perilously sensual, and he was aware that, if he'd met her in a different context, he'd have tried to seduce her. Basically, he was happy with the big sister stance Norma had adopted towards him from the start, which made a fling impossible.

'Well, I was of the opinion,' said Gabriel, changing his tone and trying to take the angst out of the subject, 'that your grandfather was an aristocrat. A lord, or something similar.'

'A lord?' Norma turned and looked at him in astonishment. 'How'd you work that out?'

'You know what they call you behind your back at the station...'

'Well no, I didn't know I even had a nickname!'

'It wasn't me. Don't you really know?'

'Not a clue!' And when she saw Gabriel was hesitating and looked alarmed, she added with a smile, 'Come on, tell me. I won't be angry, I promise. What do you call me?'

'They sometimes call you Lady Norma,' he said quietly. 'Not that I ever have...'

Norma raised an eyebrow and gave a sigh of relief. Knowing the unsubtle sense of humour of some of her colleagues, it could have been a lot worse.

'Sorry to disappoint you, but my grandfather was no aristocrat. He was a worker, and as poor as a church mouse. I've not inherited any haunted castle, in case you had high hopes.'

'What a pity.' Gabriel clicked his tongue and smiled, feeling much more relaxed. 'A castle with ghosts would suit you.'

Norma knew that ever since Deputy Inspector Carrasco had set foot in her house, all kinds of rumours had gone round the station. The fact that Norma and Octavi lived in a modernist building in the Eixample, in a flat that was worth a small fortune, had fired the imagination of a deputy inspector prone to wild gossip-mongering, and he'd immediately registered that that huge flat, crammed with books and antiques, didn't fit the stereotype of murder squad detectives and wasn't within reach of the wages earned by Mossos.

'This afternoon we must take a look at the file on the Poble Sec case,' Norma said, while Gabriel stopped the car on the corner of Carrer Roger de Llúria. 'Carrasco's in charge. I'll give him a ring now.'

'Do you really think there might be a connection?'

'At the moment, we've got no leads.' Norma shrugged her shoulders. 'We might as well give it a go.'

As she got out of the car and took her mobile from her pocket to ring Deputy Inspector's Carrasco's number, Gabriel headed towards El Carmel, already savouring the hearty steak and chips he was intending to eat before stretching out for what he considered to be a well-deserved siesta. Norma saw Octavi's old Guzzi parked on the pavement, touched it and felt it was still warm. *Today*, she reflected with a smile, *is my lucky day*. It was more than likely she and Octavi would eat lunch together.

14

Norma opened the door just as her family sat down for lunch. Violeta had left, but Aunt Margarida, wearing trousers and a blouse Mimí had lent her, was still there energetically chewing salad and telling everyone about the petty gossip that reverberated down the cloisters of her small Clarissa community. She had put on eyeliner, powdered her cheeks and painted her nails red, but her rejuvenated appearance wasn't only sparked by the miracle improvised from the pots on Mimí's dressing table, as she thought: it was clear that convent life suited her. As usual, they were chattering nineteen to the dozen, and Mimí, who knew that at mealtimes the sisters had to stay silent, intuited the sacrifice that bygone rule inflicted on her cousin. Octavi sarcastically asked her what she'd done with her habit and she winked at him.

'You know, it didn't seem right to go to the movies and to bingo dressed as a nun...'

And she immediately justified herself by saying it had all been Mimí's idea, who'd persuaded her to think up an excuse and delay her return to the convent for a few more hours. If it was no bother, she said in a would-be humble tone she still needed to work on, she'd stay with them another night and make the most of it to relax.

'Make yourself at home, as always,' said Norma, giving Octavi a bad turn. He hoped Norma didn't really mean that and that the nun wouldn't take her seriously. And in complete good faith, she added, 'But, Aunty, wouldn't you prefer to leave the convent and strike out on your own? You could do whatever you wanted without needing to play truant like a fifteen-year-old schoolgirl...'

'Come off it!' the nun retorted. 'I feel great in the convent! Besides, now I have a laptop in my cell, with one of those wireless connections, I can chat away and download films for free. I don't even need to go to the cinema.'

'You nuns have computers in your cells?' asked Octavi, flabbergasted.

'Not exactly... In fact, I reckon I'm the only one...' And, as Octavi was still looking at her in amazement, she added, 'The truth is that we've left the Middle Ages behind, and they don't search our rooms nowadays. Indeed,' she leaned forward to lead them to understand she was speaking confidentially, 'I know the password for the Thyssen Museum next door, and, in the evening, when we retire, I log on. I do so on the sly, obviously.' And, as if it was the most normal thing in the world, she said, 'By the way, before I leave, remind me to give you my email address.'

'You know, love, I can't make head or tail of the Internet,' Mimí confessed. 'Computers aren't my thing.'

'Well, you must give it another try, Mimí.' The nun shook her head and attempted to imitate the mother superior's tone of voice when she caught her skiving off some unpleasant task or gossiping with the other nuns. 'If you only knew the things it is possible to do...! I won't elaborate,' she explained, lowering her voice and looking askance at Norma, 'but ever since the Internet came into existence, the ways of the Lord are inexhaustible.'

'You mean "inscrutable",' Octavi corrected her.

'I know what I mean,' said the nun, smiling sardonically, half closing her eyes. 'From now on, if you like, from eight in the evening you can call me on my mobile,' she added.

'You have a mobile too?' blurted Octavi. 'Darling, you've got the lot!'

'That's all very well, however much you've got the Internet and a mobile, you can't leave whenever you feel like it,' insisted Norma, who was trying to imagine the shock on the mother superior's face the day she caught Sister Margarida with a clandestine phone perched by her ear or surfing the Web on the sly.

'Well, you know I like a little bit of this and a little bit of that...' she said mischievously. And she winked at them again.

Octavi sighed and shook his head, and Norma, who knew her husband would never understand her aunt's idiosyncratic logic or her crazy love of convent life, glanced at him, signalling he should let it drop. She'd no idea what punishment they might inflict on her if the bishopric ever discovered the double life she led, and didn't dare ask her in case the question sounded like a criticism. In any case, Norma didn't think they'd ever expel her, and imagined that, at the very worst, they'd force her to pray a few more Our Fathers and scrub the convent floor on her knees. Besides, it was more than likely the bishopric was aware that Sister Margarida took a few days of holiday now and then and made whoopee with her cousin, and they surely turned a blind eye because they were short of people with religious vocations and couldn't allow themselves the luxury of expelling anyone. Obviously, Norma reflected, it might also be the case that they were fooled by her excuses and never imagined Sister Margarida might find a secret, almost adolescent pleasure in getting up to mischief. The Vatican had enough headaches covering up for paedophiles and recruiting adepts in the Third World, and Aunt Margarida's urban antics were purely innocent fun. Mere venal sins, Norma reckoned. A few weeks in Purgatory, and all sorted.

'Hey, love, why don't you want any more? Don't you like it?' Mimí asked anxiously, when she saw the chicken leg languishing intact on Norma's plate.

'I'm sorry, I can't eat any more.'

'You don't look at all well. You should put something into your stomach,' Mimí insisted.

'I really can't.'

Unlike Octavi, who was starving, Norma had barely touched her salad, but because Mimí insisted and she didn't want to argue, she agreed to nibble a few grapes. She'd been thinking for some time that the sickly feeling in her whole body wasn't simply about the four hours she'd slept, but, stubborn as ever, she refused to admit some virus had taken up residence to stymie her. Octavi observed Norma out of the corner of his eye and saw his mother-in-law was right. Apart from being lacklustre, Norma was pale and her eyes were shining bright. Quite out of character, she said she didn't want coffee and was going to lie down for a while.

'I think you've got a temperature,' said Octavi, putting his hand on her forehead. 'Use the thermometer.'

'It's nothing really. I just need an aspirin and a few hours' sleep.'

'Let me feel your pulse,' Octavi insisted, trying to catch her wrist.

'Just leave me alone!' Norma jumped to her feet. 'I told you I'm fine!'

Octavi raised his eyebrows and shook his head, but he let it drop. He knew his wife would refuse to admit she was ill until she reached 39° and was completely floored. Norma, who wanted to find out what Octavi could remember of the Porta case, beckoned to her husband from the passage to accompany her into the kitchen.

'I may be wrong, but it's too much of a coincidence that two men the same age who were lifelong friends have been murdered only a couple of weeks apart. There just has to be a connection,' she said rather hoarsely, as she opened a cupboard and rummaged in the medicine chest.

'Sentís did the autopsy.' Octavi vaguely remembered the

case. 'The guy was stabbed four or five times. I think we've sent our report to Carrasco.'

'I've arranged to see him this afternoon to review the file,' said Norma, chewing an aspirin.

'You should stay in bed. You're quite poorly.'

'I only need to sleep a bit. I'll be fine.'

Octavi glanced at her sceptically and went back to the dining room while Norma headed to their bedroom hoping the aspirin would work wonders. Before getting into bed, she took off her blouse and trousers, and, as she had the shivers, she put on thick socks and pulled the feather eiderdown over her. Even though she felt exhausted, her temperature kept her half-awake, but, when the alarm went off at a quarter past five, she'd finally managed to fall into a deep sleep and lose all notion of time. She didn't know if it was the morning or afternoon, but, when she realised she wasn't wearing pyjamas and that bright light was filtering through the window, she deduced she'd just enjoyed a long afternoon nap. Nevertheless, she was still sleepy, and for a few minutes she lingered between the sheets, tempted to turn over and carry on sleeping. She could always ring Gabriel and ask him to go and talk to Carrasco, but the latter would no doubt insist on giving her a call and they'd end up having a three-way meeting on the phone. She struggled to get up and put her clothes on, then went straight to the kitchen to make herself a cocktail of painkillers, trying to make sure Octavi didn't hear.

Fortunately, Octavi was in his study at the other end of the flat, absorbed in an article on the sudden deaths of adults from cerebrovascular haemorrhages associated with the consumption of cocaine, and he didn't notice Norma's excursion to the medicine chest. Mimí and Aunt Margarida had gone out some time ago, and Great-grandmother Senta, who was engrossed in a light entertainment programme on a German television channel, didn't hear her either. Over recent years Norma's great-grandmother had developed a few manias, like walking around the flat barefoot and refusing to take her medication, and, for some months, she only watched foreign television channels in languages which were a total mystery to her. Norma walked past, but Senta was so engrossed she didn't notice her great-granddaughter. Only Hamlet, who was lying placidly on her lap, lifted his head and half opened his eyes when he heard his mistress's footsteps before nodding off again.

Norma washed her face and dabbed a little colour on her cheeks to try to hide the pallor. However, when she saw the bags under her eyes and her sickly face, she wrinkled her nose and decided to gather her hair into a ponytail. Those tresses that had turned grey when she was a young woman usually conferred an exotic aura that Octavi found particularly sensual, but right then they only made her look sicklier and older.

'I'm off to the station,' she muttered from the door to Octavi's study.

'You're sick. You won't last long.'

'I'm feeling better,' she lied. 'And I won't be long.' But when she saw the worried look on Octavi's face, she added, 'When I get back, I'll check my temperature. Promise.'

Norma pretended not to see the thunderous glance Octavi directed her way and turned round. She took a thick parka from the wardrobe that she only donned on the coldest of days and left, trying to close the door quietly. She knew it was rash to go out in that state, but she was confident the mixture of pills she'd swallowed behind Octavi's back would make a difference. While she was walking to the parking lot to get her car, she dialled Violeta's number.

'Hello, darling,' she replied to her voicemail. 'Remember we agreed to have lunch soon. Will you give me a ring? I just want a chat. I promise I won't come down hard on you and start sermonising.'

That was a promise Norma knew she couldn't keep, and, after hanging up she immediately felt rather ridiculous that she'd spontaneously adopted the imploring tone of a desperate mother. After all, Violeta was a grown woman and lived her own life, and if she wanted them to be friends she should first abandon this emotional blackmail and stop acting like a nagging mother. Before reaching the station, she phoned Violeta and left a second message.

'Violeta, it's me again. Listen, if you don't have time to meet, don't worry. I'm rushed off my feet too...' And after hesitating for a few seconds, she added, 'In any case, if you need anything, call me, OK? Whatever...'

15

Even though it was a national holiday, it was all go that afternoon at Les Corts station. The Mossos had just arrested one of the mafia leaders most sought after by the Italian police in a spectacular operation, and journalists were parked outside the door trying to get a photo or statement. When Norma arrived it was exactly six o'clock, but Gabriel, still sore from his telling-off that morning, had been there for some time and was chatting amicably to Inspector Roca, who'd been deprived of the holiday by a mountain of paperwork. Norma used the presence of the inspector to tell him about her conversation with the Parelladas and her hunches about the Poble Sec murder.

'Just in case, I've decided to take a look at the Porta file. I know the two men died in very different circumstances and that maybe it's only a coincidence, but if you don't mind I'd just like to take a look,' she said.

'All yours. You know you have carte blanche. By the way,' the inspector suddenly remembered, opening a folder and handing her a sheaf of papers, 'I have the list of lecturers and students in the department. Apart from a couple of lecturers on the point of retiring who belonged to the Unified Socialist Party of Catalunya in the sixties and spent time in the Model prison, nobody has a record. And if there are students or teachers with psychiatric problems or a liking for violence, it's not on file.'

'What about the professor's students?' Gabriel asked.

'The list isn't very long. He only gave doctoral classes and directed doctoral theses. Seven students in total.'

'You talk to them,' said Norma, passing the list on to Gabriel. 'See if you can find anything.'

'Right. Do you want me to question the lecturers in the department as well?'

'Yes, of course.'

'See if you can find the last person to see him alive,' asked Inspector Roca. 'It must be a student or a teacher.' And noticing that Norma seemed a bit withdrawn and that her cheeks were pallid despite all the rouge, he asked her, 'You not feeling well, Norma?'

'No, I'm fine.'

'Well, you don't look a hundred percent,' the inspector came back at her, immediately regretting he'd opened his mouth because he recalled that his ex's face used to look off when she had her period.

'I think I'm coming down with the flu. My temperature is up,' she confessed.

'If you're ill, you shouldn't have come in.'

'Don't you start as well. I'm up to here with Octavi's lectures.'

'If you're sick, go home and stay in bed. That's an order,' the inspector rasped, trying to endow his voice with a ring of authority.

'I've got a meeting with Carrasco. After I've spoken to him, I'll go home and rest, I promise. The truth is I can't stand...'

'Carrasco? You've got Carrasco coming into the station today?' exclaimed the inspector, whistling in admiration. 'Fuck, Norma! That's a coup! How the hell did you manage that?'

I threatened to round up a few uniformed Mossos and go for a drink in his favourite clip joint,' she said, forcing a smile.

'Hey, boss, that was below the belt!' Gabriel whistled in admiration too. 'Carrasco will never forgive you.'

Norma shrugged her shoulders and looked at her watch: it was almost twenty to seven. As she'd agreed to meet the deputy inspector at six, she started to think the old dinosaur had had second thoughts and was going to stand her up. In fact, Norma had no authority over Carrasco who, if he was clear about one thing, it was that good relations between colleagues didn't include depriving him of his tot of whisky and his stool at the bar when he wasn't on duty. Norma was getting ready to pick up the phone and remind him they were waiting for him when she saw the inspector's vast paunch and one-metre-ninety bulk tottering down the corridor. The deputy inspector was sweating and panting, and, from the expression on his face, everyone could see he was breathing fire.

'Fucking hell, Norma!' he roared, banging the door open. 'Couldn't it wait until tomorrow? Or better still, Monday? Who the hell do you think you are?' When he saw Inspector Roca, he added, in a more conciliatory tone, 'I'm sorry, boss. But I'm fed up with being the dogsbody of the department!' And he spat in Norma's direction, 'Well, senyoreta, what the fuck is so urgent?'

'I told you on the phone,' replied Norma, trying to keep her composure. 'There may be a connection between the Poble Sec case and the case of the professor who was killed at the university.'

'You just wanted to screw with me!' the cop muttered, as he took off his jacket.

The moment the deputy inspector was in shirt sleeves, Norma started to retch and felt like throwing up. Carrasco wasn't over-fond of soap and water, and at the station it was common knowledge he rarely took a shower more than once a week. His clothes and thick, dandruffy hair usually stank of bar fry-ups and cheap eau de cologne, and his breath of cheap wine, black tobacco and vile bile. The deputy inspector never used deodorant because in his words he thought it was a 'poofter' thing, and his liking for raw onion didn't help matters; his sweat exuded a sour stench that turned Norma's stomach. In the murder squad rumour had it that most criminals preferred to confess rather than spend half an hour shut up in the small interview room with the deputy inspector, and Norma, who didn't usually believe the urban myths that were rife in the station, didn't have the slightest doubt that the rumour was true in this case.

Deputy Inspector Carrasco was fifty-eight and as ugly as sin. He'd been divorced for twenty years, and ever since had lived alone in a modest boarding-house near the Boqueria market. His scruffy appearance and penchant for whores in the Raval, whisky and clip joints, habits he proudly boasted of, made him an anachronistic figure that conflicted with the image of modernity and slick efficiency the Ministry of the Interior was trying to convey. The deputy inspector was uncouth and foul-mouthed, but knew the Raval inside out like no other cop, and, for him, the sordid nature of the dives where he hung out were an added attraction that led to excellent results in his work. Unlike Inspector Roca, whose face was still lined by the depression brought on by his unexpected divorce, the deputy inspector had been infinitely happier after his wife left him, and for ages couldn't imagine how he'd been able to exist for so many years without whisky, tarts and smoke-filled bars. He had no family and few friends, and he himself had predicted he would end his days in a hospital connected to an oxygen cylinder or vegetating in a dingy care home. He declared he couldn't care less, and frankly seemed to have accepted that less-than-glorious finale with the same resignation with which he embraced his excess weight or hangover headaches. Norma couldn't stand his stink, stained shirts and long, filthy nails, and she inwardly sympathised with the whores who were forced to inhale his putrid breath and feel his grungy one hundred and thirty kilos bouncing on top of them.

'Fuck it, Carrasco!' Norma shouted, throwing her head backwards and getting up to open a window, 'You need a shower!'

'My lovely, please don't rub me up the wrong way.'

'Norma's right,' interjected Inspector Roca. 'A splash of soap and water would do the trick... Come on, tell us what we know about the Poble Sec case.'

The deputy inspector was used to criticism of his personal hygiene and didn't bother answering back. He walked over to his desk grumbling and swaying his huge body, took a file from one of the drawers and started rummaging among the bunch of crumpled papers. Some sheets were stained with oil and a yellowy-red substance none of those present had any difficulty in identifying as choriço because it was still giving off a smell, but before Norma or Gabriel could jump in, Inspector Roca gestured to them to keep quiet. *The deputy inspector may not be very wholesome*, his glance said, *but he knows how to do his job*.

'The dead man is a Víctor Porta. Sixty-eight. A widower. He returned to Barcelona five years ago and lived in Poble Sec. One of the neighbours on his floor informed the city police because the guy's lights and telly were switched on but he never answered when they knocked on his door. The fire brigade got in through the balcony and found him in the dining room where he was starting to pong.' The deputy inspector paused to shuffle the papers. 'Let's see now... Right, he was stabbed five times, twice fatally. His flat was a total mess, and we concluded,' he said, shrugging his shoulders, 'that he'd been robbed.'

'I gather he'd lived in Mexico,' Norma said, remembering what the Parelladas had said.

The deputy inspector rummaged among the papers and extracted a handwritten sheet that only he could read, partly because the writing was illegible and partly because it was full of spelling mistakes.

'The guy left for Mexico when he was twenty-two and

married a Mexican,' he explained. 'When his wife died, his daughter persuaded him to come back to Barcelona.'

'Does his daughter live here?'

'She's married to a Catalan,' said the deputy inspector. And he added sarcastically, 'He ended up in shit creek... If he'd stayed in Mexico, he'd be sunbathing, laying young lasses and drinking margaritas.'

'Absolutely. I gather that's what everybody does in Mexico. I can't think why you're still with us...' responded Norma sarcastically.

'Have you got any leads? Did you find anything at the crime scene?' Inspector Roca asked.

'No, I haven't received Inspector Permanyer's report.'

'And when will you?'

The deputy inspector smiled and shrugged his shoulders.

'You know what Permanyer's like, boss. What the hell can I say?'

The inspector didn't respond, but turned round and quietly went to his office to make a call. A few minutes later he emerged and told them they'd have something Monday morning. Norma and Carrasco exchanged sceptical glances, but neither said a word.

'If the Poble Sec fellow is connected to the murder you're investigating,' said the deputy inspector as he stuffed the oil-stained sheets back into the file which he brusquely threw into Norma's hands, 'you can look into it, darling. I've already got too much on my plate.'

'It's not definite there is a connection,' retorted Norma. 'I only wanted to check it out.' And she added, remembering what Jordi Parellada had said, 'Are you sure it was one of those gangs from the east?'

The deputy inspector smiled once again, scratched his head and cleaned out the dandruff that had caught under his nails, using a yellowish thumbnail. Norma was too late to look away and heaved again.

'We've got to tell the journos something, right, boss?'

he grinned. 'The fact is right now we've not got a fucking clue.'

'What about witnesses?' asked Gabriel.

'Nobody saw or heard anything,' the deputy inspector replied with another shrug of the shoulders.

'Not even the neighbour who informed the city police?' Gabriel insisted.

'I couldn't say. She's dead.'

'What do you mean, she's dead?' asked Norma, bemused.

'It was the idiot firemen,' said the deputy inspector. 'They took them both away in the same ambulance. Two for the price of one. It's almost all in the report.' But as he noticed Inspector Roca giving one of those stares, he added, 'Hey, this time it had nothing to do with me, don't you look at me like that... By the time I got there, the old girl had already kicked it.'

'Could you be a little more explicit?' asked Norma.

The inspector, who'd put on his jacket and was about to make an exit, assuming that the meeting was over, sighed and reluctantly turned round.

'It seems that one of the rookies asked the old girl to go into the flat and identify the body, and naturally, the old girl took one look and had a heart attack.'

'What bad luck!' said Gabriel.

'The truth is blood was splattered all over the flat. And flies galore... You know, a right shit show, the kind you like,' the deputy inspector let fly, giving Norma a half-mocking, half-lecherous smile. 'In short, the slut curled her toes up.'

'Fucking hell, Agustí, "the slut" was a grandma...' Norma flared up wearily.

'Bah...'

'I don't know why you find it so hard to show a little respect,' she insisted.

'Hey, chick, you're far too touchy,' said the deputy inspector using that troglodyte tone he liked to adopt towards Norma.

'Don't call me chick. I'm not one of your tarts.'

In the doorway, the deputy inspector's bleary eyes looked scornfully at her and, in defiance of all the 'No Smoking' posters hanging throughout the building, slowly lit a cigarette.

'Hey, chick,' he repeated, 'you've got what you wanted. Now get off my back!'

And he slouched off.

16

Norma had driven her Volkswagen to the station, but what with the flu she was incubating and the painkillers she'd taken before leaving home, she was on her last legs. Inspector Roca, who'd anxiously watched Norma zigzagging down the corridor, her eyelids flickering, insisted on accompanying her home, seeing she was in no fit state to drive herself. Initially Norma refused his offer, but the inspector took the keys to the Volkswagen and forced her to get in, threatening to call Octavi if she didn't relent. As she was completely run down, Norma reluctantly gave way and the second she was in the car she fell asleep next to her chauffeur for the day. Noticing how she was shivering, the inspector quickly switched on the heating.

At home, Octavi helped her strip off and get into bed. He took her temperature, listened to her chest and examined her throat, and then gave his verdict: Norma had a high of 39° and showed all the symptoms of flu.

'Give me antibiotics,' she said faintly.

'You've got the flu. Antibiotics are no use,' Octavi retorted, as he got her to swallow a pill to lower her temperature.

'Just to help fight it off. They can't do me any harm...'

'Forget it. Antipyretics, analgesics and bed, that's what you need.'

'But...'

'Don't be so stubborn.' Octavi's tone turned authoritarian. 'Flu is a virus, not a bacterium. Antibiotics won't cure it.' And he added for good measure, looking angry, 'Don't be so obsessed...!'

Ignoring Norma's protests, Octavi walked out of the bedroom and, just in case, went to the small medicine chest in the pantry and hid the antibiotics in a drawer in his study. Just like Mimí, Norma would always have recourse to antibiotics the moment her temperature shot up, and Octavi decided it was better to take precautions before his wife paid a visit to the pantry and began to self-medicate. Whatever Octavi might pontificate, none of his explanations, based on scientific reasoning, made a difference. Norma and her mother worshipped antibiotics with the same faith as believers did the waters of Lourdes, and, at the slightest symptom, they swallowed them like sweets.

Octavi was about to offer to prepare something to eat when he realised Norma was already asleep. He decided not to wake her and, as quietly as possible, switched off the light, picked up the cat that had jumped on the bed and tried to get between the sheets, gave it some food and took two cans of beer from the fridge and a packet of crisps. Roca was waiting in the dining room, happily zapping the telly. Mimí and Aunt Margarida weren't back from bingo, and Great-grandmother Senta had long since retired to her room to watch a Japanese film without subtitles.

'Why don't you stay and watch the game?' Octavi asked, offering him one of the cans. 'Barça's playing.'

'You sure I won't be in the way?'

'Norma needs to sleep. The flu has to follow its course. Or have you got other plans?'

'No, I don't,' said the inspector, rather despondently.

'Pizza, or bread with tomato and ham?'

'I've got pizza coming out of my ears...' the inspector confessed with a smile.

'Let's go to the kitchen and see what we can find.'

Under the influence of the painkillers, Norma slept like

a log all night. In the morning she still had a temperature and a headache, and Octavi had to convince her to eat something before she swallowed the pills he'd prescribed. Mimí, who'd taken on the role of bedside nurse and spent her time going in and out of the bedroom, made sure her daughter ate a couple of breakfast tea biscuits and drank a glass of orange juice before going back to sleep.

Norma spent the whole day sweating, sleeping, swallowing pills and drinking the juices her mother prepared. Aunt Margarida, who offered to lend a helping hand, and had called the convent to say she wouldn't be back till Sunday because she had to look after sick relatives, went into the bedroom now and then and took her temperature to see if she was still feverish. Senta followed suit, assuring her she had the gift of precisely divining temperatures by touching foreheads with the palm of her hand. Norma was irritated by the constant attention from the three women, but as the flu had floored her and she had no strength to protest, she let them get on with it.

When Octavi returned from the clinic in the evening, Mimí and Aunt Margarida mobbed him, fearfully telling him her temperature hadn't gone down.

'It's because you won't give her antibiotics!' they reproached him.

Without flinching, Octavi went for his case and examined his wife again. After checking the illness was following its course and that there were no complications, he kissed her on the forehead and declared, 'She'll be better tomorrow, you just see.'

On Saturday Norma still had a slight temperature and spent the day in bed, but by Sunday Mimí finally let her get up and eat lunch sitting at the table. Norma took the opportunity to speak to Gabriel who'd phoned every day to enquire how she was faring.

'I know it's Sunday,' Norma probed, 'but... would you

mind coming by this afternoon? I'd like you to bring me up to speed on any developments.'

Gabriel was delighted to comply; he'd never set foot in that house, but had heard all the exaggerated gossip at the station about the so-called mansion where his colleague lived.

'I've got a basketball game today. I won't be able to make it before half seven.'

'No worries, come by when you can,' she replied, trying not to let Gabriel notice the hint of impatience in her voice.

After lunch Norma went to have a nap, as she'd promised Mimí, and when she got up two hours later, she called a couple of girlfriends she'd not spoken to for weeks. Octavi was busy preparing a paper for a congress, and Norma decided to shut herself in her study and read more of the novel about Trotsky's assassination she'd begun, while she waited for Gabriel.

It was past half seven when Gabriel, his hair still wet, rang the bell. The moment he saw Mimí, who'd hurried to open the door, he thought he must have got the wrong flat. He didn't know Norma's mother and was alarmed to see he was being welcomed in by a woman sheathed in a flimsy, cobalt-blue tunic set off by a bunch of necklaces and flowing yellowy-brown tresses. Mimí, who'd been making a fuss for months about meeting Norma's new colleague, asked him to come in, and a bewildered Gabriel crossed the doorstep and entered a lobby as big as his dining room.

He was gobsmacked to see his reflection in a huge mirror with a gold leaf frame that, as Mimí explained while he admired himself, dated from the First French Empire. Gabriel had no idea what that first empire might be or when the Ming dynasty had ruled over China, which was, also according to Mimí, the era of a porcelain vase covered in drawings of sea plants and golden carp that had been inherited from Great-great-grandmother Antigone. The vase had survived raids by German bombers during the war and was worth a small fortune, but in fact what really caught Gabriel's eye was the Manolete chair where Mimí had just deposited his jacket. With a beaming smile, Mimí gestured to him to follow her, and an intimidated Gabriel walked along a long passageway that led into a drawing room of Versailles proportions. Great-grandmother Senta and Aunt Margarida were intrigued and stared at him as Mimí did the introductions.

'Norma's coming, my love. Make yourself at home,' she said.

Aunt Margarida, who was wearing her nun's habit because she was about to go back to the convent, was still sporting red nails, and, when he saw them, Gabriel didn't know how to react. Great-Grandmother Senta gawped at him and nodded, and Gabriel wasn't sure if that was a sign of approval or to tell him he wasn't seeing things. Octavi, who'd heard the ring at the door, came opportunely out of his study to say hello just when Gabriel felt panic-stricken, thinking he must be hallucinating.

'So, she forced you to come on a Sunday...' Octavi said as they shook hands.

'I didn't want to disturb you, but she insisted...' Gabriel apologised rather sheepishly.

'Don't worry,' Octavi sighed. 'I know my wife. She's a law unto herself.'

'Badmouthing me behind my back, are you?' asked Norma with a smile from the doorway.

Gabriel got up and saw how Norma's appearance had improved spectacularly since the last time they'd seen each other.

'You look really well,' he said.

'We'd better go to my study. It will be quieter there. Like a glass of beer?'

'Yes, please! I'm not on duty today.'

'Follow me.'

Norma led him to the kitchen and offered a choice of three different beers, one imported and two local, while she opted for mineral water. Norma's study was at the other end of the house, and, as he walked along that long passage for the second time, Gabriel was forced to recognise that not only had Deputy Inspector Carrasco not exaggerated anything, he'd even under-reported. The flat where Norma and Octavi lived was a four-hundred-square-metre labyrinth of passageways and rooms, and Gabriel felt quite lost.

'Hell, Norma!' he whistled, 'this is quite a palace!'

'My great-grandparents lived here. It's a family inheritance.'

Mimí had grown up in that flat, and it now housed a mixture of inherited antiques and the modern designer furniture that Norma liked. Ever since her mother and grandmother had moved in, it also provided a home for Mimí's hippy bits and pieces and the black-and-white photos Senta had spread around the whole house. Gabriel imagined the fair-haired young man dressed as a militiaman, who appeared in some of the photos was Norma's grandfather, but he didn't ask. Despite the very warm welcome Norma had given him, he was under the impression the deputy inspector was rather dismayed by his intrusion in her family space, and that, if it hadn't been for the untimely flu, she'd never have invited him to set foot there.

Norma gently eased Hamlet out of the chair where he was dozing and asked Gabriel to sit down. She took off her shoes, settled down on the chaise longue where she liked to stretch out to read, and put a blanket over her legs. The cat jumped up and burrowed between Norma's legs and she started stroking his head.

'You're not short of a book or two...' Gabriel commented, surveying the shelves that lined the study walls.

'This was my great-grandfather's study,' Norma explained with a sigh. 'He was a pharmacist, but he was fond of history...'

'So your family has always lived in this flat...'

'No, my mother was born in Casa Batlló,' Norma replied with a smile.

'Hell, you mean that tourist place? On the Passeig de Gràcia?'

'The very same.'

'So what happened?'

'When the war was over, they had to sell the flat,' she sighed again. She then added, as she saw Gabriel was intrigued, 'It's a complicated story, but the truth is my grandmother Senta inherited this flat and decided to give it to me when I married Octavi.'

'And have you read all these books?' asked Gabriel who'd left the armchair, unable to resist the temptation to nose around.

'Basically, they are history and anthropology books,' she smiled. 'Novels are in the library. I can show you that later, if you're interested.'

Gabriel knew Norma had studied anthropology, but his idea of anthropologists was limited to English explorers wearing pith helmets in the jungle and boiling in a cooking pot.

'Have you spent any time with a tribe of savages?' he asked, while he tried to fathom why Norma had four different editions of Lévi-Strauss's *Tristes Tropiques*—two in French, one in English and one in Catalan.

'Anthropology isn't only about "tribes of savages", as you put it,' Norma smiled. 'And, by the way we don't say "tribes of savages" anymore but "primitive societies".'

'Sure, but have you ever been in such a place?'

'When I was studying for my doctorate, I spent four weeks in Brazil, with a Yanomami community.'

'Hell! Aren't they cannibals?'

'Endocannibals, to be precise,' Norma corrected him.

'And weren't you afraid they'd eat you?'

'The Yanomani only eat their dead. As a matter of fact, it's a funeral rite.'

'Yuck!'

'Yes, it's not for the squeamish.'

'You mean that instead of burying them, they put them in a pot and eat them?'

'No, they don't put them in a pot. They burn the bones, mix the ashes with the fruit of a palm tree and make a paste, a kind of purée.'

'And do they eat this purée?'

'They do.'

'That's what savages would do.'

'Depending on how you look at it. Cannibalism is basically a ritual practice, and the majority of peoples who have historically practised or practise anthropophagy do so because it is a way of appropriating the strength of their enemies, honouring their relatives or making sure their dead are gone forever so their spirits can't harm them. They don't sacrifice people in order to feed themselves, as we do with animals, but eat them once they are dead. That's very different.'

'Whatever you like, you can keep it,' replied Gabriel, entirely unconvinced. And a few seconds later, as if the possibility had just occurred to him, he asked, 'I suppose you personally never tasted human flesh, did you?'

'I thought you'd come to talk about the case?' Norma asked, smiling again, amused by the look on Gabriel's face caused by the idea of such a possibility.

'But...'

'Come on, let's stick to the case. What have you found out?'

Rather annoyed, Gabriel extracted his notebook from his pocket and started consulting his notes.

'The family's clean. We've checked their alibis. In effect,

the professor's son and his wife were in Cerdanya. The daughter Eulàlia and her husband dined with friends in a restaurant. They arrived at nine on the dot and the waiter remembered because that's when they open and they were their first customers.'

'Have you found the last person to see the victim or speak to him?'

'It seems to have been another teacher in the department, Dr Serrano. He popped into the professor's study at eight–thirty, and, as it was about to start raining, he offered to drive him home.'

'How considerate of him!'

'But the professor said he had to stay on because he had a meeting with another student.'

'And did he say who that student was?'

'No, but he did say it wasn't one of theirs. He told him it was someone from the Autònoma.'

'Well, at least that's something. Are you sure he spoke of him as male?'

'Completely sure.'

'So we should speak to his students.'

'No probs,' Gabriel smirked. 'I've traced them all and told them to show up at the department on Monday morning.'

'You're a fast learner,' replied Norma with a hint of irony. 'And what do we know about this Serrano?'

'He was a former student of his. And, according to him, Francesc Parellada had no enemies, at least none who had declared themselves. He was evidently someone who minded his own business and took no part in the squabbles in the department or the struggles for power in the uni. Besides, he was about to retire.'

'And what about the Poble Sec victim? Did you track down his daughter?'

'She's called Montserrat, and is a nurse who works in the Hospital de Sant Pau,' he responded, full of himself.

'So, you really have done your homework... I'll have to give you ten out of ten today!'

'Thank you so much.'

'Call her and arrange an appointment. I've a few questions I'd like to ask her.'

'But Carrasco has already questioned her,' Gabriel replied.

'I know he has, but call her all the same,' Norma insisted. And even though she suspected she knew what the answer would be, she asked, 'Do we have any news from Permanyer by any chance?'

Gabriel put his notebook in his pocket, leaned back in the armchair and smiled.

'He says we shouldn't worry. He's getting on with the job.'

'That Permanyer...' sighed Norma. 'I'm not surprised he has Mistral pulling her hair out. Come to think of it, how is the superintendent? Has she been on your backs these last few days?'

'Hell, I'd forgotten...' Gabriel's face lit up. 'I've got some good news!'

'Good news?'

'The superintendent came a cropper skiing and broke a leg. She'll be off sick for some time,' he said with a grin. And he threw his head back and added, 'They're still celebrating in Les Corts. Quite a few got bladdered.'

'You're real animals!' Norma shook her head but couldn't suppress a smile.

Gabriel returned her smile and raised his bottle of beer.

'Long live ski slopes!' he exclaimed.

Norma hesitated for a moment, but finally raised her small bottle of mineral water and, as if she was offering a reluctant toast, she shouted, 'Long live ski slopes!'

17

On Monday morning, completely recovered from the flu, Norma got up earlier than usual. It was still dark, but Mimí had set the breakfast table, made coffee and gone back to her bedroom to look at the news. Great-grandmother Senta would sleep on till past ten. Insomniac Mimí was an early riser but she was aware that if she and Senta prowled around the house the whole day, Norma and Octavi had little time by themselves, so she'd melted away so that her daughter and son-in-law could breakfast in peace. Octavi was also up and, like every morning, he was in the kitchen eating an orange, a yoghurt and a bowl of muesli. Starving as she was, Norma had yielded to the temptation of slices of toast generously spread with butter and plum jam.

'Soon you'll be complaining you've packed it on your bum,' Octavi said, shaking his head as he poured himself a coffee.

'Nah, this is a special treat... I'll be back on the muesli tomorrow.'

'I don't mind. I like big bums.'

'Silly!' Norma laughed, throwing a napkin at his face he wasn't quick enough to dodge.

Octavi smiled, sent it back to his wife using the same method and winked. That morning, now Norma had recovered and Aunt Margarida was back in the convent, Octavi was in high spirits. As it was Monday, in principle he didn't have to go to court and he had no tedious meetings in his diary, so if there weren't any complications, he could spend the day in the autopsy room on routine examinations and get home early.

'I'm more and more convinced the two murders are linked,' Norma murmured, buttering a third slice of toast.

'You mean the professor and the Poble Sec pensioner?'

'Yes, I'll be interviewing the professor's widow today. And I want to talk to the pensioner's daughter again. I'm pretty sure Carrasco missed something, though I don't have a clue what it might be.'

'Take it easy, you only got out of bed a day ago.'

'I feel fine and I'm raring to go. Which you may have noticed last night...' she replied mischievously.

'And you didn't need antibiotics!'

'Don't start on that...'

Suddenly Norma looked at the kitchen clock and jumped up.

'Hey, it's late. I must get going to the station.'

'But it's not eight yet!' Octavi grumbled.

'I've got a lot on today. And I need to make up for lost time!' she sighed.

And while she hugged him from behind and gave him a kiss, she added with a smile, 'You're not exactly in a rush to get to work, doctor.'

'I'm hoping they'll leave us in peace,' replied Octavi, looking sceptical. 'Recently I've been spending the whole day shut up in the office,' and added, with a shake of the head, 'I'm up to here with all the meetings and form-filling.'

'Don't complain,' Norma ribbed him, giving him another kiss. 'It's what you always wanted!'

After brushing her teeth and applying a quick touch of lipstick, Norma put on her jacket and left the house, happy to be back on the street. It seemed to be a cold morning, and as she walked towards the parking lot, under the light from a tepid sun that was just beginning to emerge between the buildings, she thought of the message David had sent her before she fell ill, to which she'd not yet replied. She'd thought about it several times while she was getting better, and although she couldn't help feeling guilty, she was delighted he'd contacted her. She knew that one day David would fall in love with another woman or simply decide to end the absurd relationship, and, after two months without any news of him, she was often afraid they'd never see each other again.

Following an incident with Violeta, Norma had instructed him never to phone her; if David wanted to communicate with her, he had to send her an email and patiently wait for her to reply. Until now David had scrupulously respected their agreement, and Norma decided the first thing she would do when she reached the station would be to call him and apologise for taking so long. She'd tell him the truth, that she'd been languishing in bed for several days, and as always happened when David was in Barcelona, they'd organise a time and a place and spend an afternoon together. She too was dying to see him. She couldn't help herself.

He and Norma had met three years ago, just before her stepfather Roger had died from a heart attack. Chief Superintendent Nebot had decided to send her to Madrid to participate in a series of seminars to encourage collaboration between the different police bodies within the Ministry of the Interior, convinced that the deputy inspector's refined manner would make a good impression on the sceptics in the capital. Rather than staying in a hotel with the rest of her colleagues, Norma preferred to sleep at the house of a lifelong friend who worked as a curator at the Reina Sofia, whom she'd not seen for a long time. One evening, when the sessions were finished at the ministry, her friend picked her up and persuaded her to go to an exhibition of Egyptian art that was being launched that day. While they were visiting it, her friend introduced her to Professor David Subirana, the Egyptologist who'd been commissioned to curate the exhibition. David was a couple of years younger than Norma and they immediately hit it off.

Norma couldn't claim in her defence that when she met David she was going through a bad time with Octavi, or that she didn't love her husband anymore. They'd just returned from a romantic trip to Scotland to celebrate their wedding anniversary, and, after eleven years of married life and thirteen of blissful coexistence, Norma's emotional life seemed firmly on track beside Octavi. In other respects, Violeta was still a docile adolescent who got top marks and gave them few headaches, and Norma was pleased to have returned to the murder squad after a disastrous period in the narcotics department. Indeed, when she met David Subirana she was a happy woman, that was beyond any doubt. Or at least, happy enough not to be able to account for David's intermittent presence in her life over the last three years.

That night after leaving the exhibition, Norma had drunk enough G&Ts and exchanged enough amorous chit-chat to fall in love with David. Feeling a brief infatuation with another man six hundred kilometres away from Octavi under the influence of gin was no big deal, she told herself, it was only an innocent one-night stand, so she allowed herself to be seduced by his warm lilt and tales of tombs and mummies. When they went to bed, Norma thought that little extramarital adventure, the first she'd ever had, would be over the second she returned to Barcelona and David to his classes in Oxford and excavations in Cairo. But ever since, they'd continued seeing each other, making the most of David's trips to Barcelona to see his parents. At best, they saw each other two or three times a year, and, apart from that, at Norma's express wish, they had no other contact. For his part, Octavi had never suspected a thing.

Even though she treated it as an affair that was going nowhere, Norma soon realised that an overemotional liaison with David could end up endangering her relationship with Octavi. Despite the adolescent passion the Egyptologist aroused in her, Norma loved Octavi and had no intention of breaking up her marriage, so she refused to have a long-distance affair with him and forbade him to write or call her. She still felt ashamed when she remembered the day he rang her mobile and Violeta took the call because she was in the shower. Her daughter, who was just sixteen, forgot to pass on the message, and it wasn't until they were all around the dinner table and Mimí was ladling out the soup, that she let slip that a fellow called David had rung her and wanted her to return his call. Her mother often received calls from people she didn't know so Violeta didn't suspect anything, but that evening Norma turned as red as a tomato and was speechless; she froze like an idiot, gripping her spoon tight. Fortunately, neither Violeta nor Octavi noticed anything, because at that precise moment Mimí screamed and all eyes were on her: Mimí complained she'd twisted her neck and couldn't move it. Octavi immediately got up and went to fetch some ointment, and while he was on his way to their medicine chest, Norma asked Violeta to go her bedroom and bring her the bag where she kept her pills. As soon as Octavi and Violeta disappeared, Mimí's neck underwent a miraculous recovery to the amazement of Norma and Senta, and, before Norma had time to react, Mimí stared her in the eye and rasped, 'Make that the last time you blush in front of your husband when you hear another man's name!' And she added, looking at Senta out of the corner of her eye, who was nodding in agreement, 'No need to say a word, but please behave yourself!'

Norma and her mother never mentioned that incident again, but from that day on she forbade David to ring her, at home, at the station, or on her mobile. David Subirana wasn't a parallel relationship, he wouldn't be her friend or confidant, and they wouldn't spend the day talking on the phone or exchanging teenage messages saying how much they missed or longed for each other. At most, they would meet up now and then and make love in secret, with no romantic declarations, promises or backbiting. Norma had sworn to herself she'd never confess her little affair to Octavi, convinced that, although she was occasionally unfaithful, she retained an idiosyncratic loyalty.

'God, you're up and about early!' said Inspector Permanyer, as he looked up from his computer keyboard to see a radiant Norma in the doorway.

'Well, you've been here for a while yourself...' she retorted, smiling broadly.

'Someone has to do some work in this place,' the inspector said ill-temperedly.

'In fact, I wanted a word with you,' Norma said, as she looked on the sly at the report the inspector was writing.

Before she interviewed the professor's widow, she wanted to know what her forensic colleagues had found out about the Porta case and have a look at the file.

'Well...?' said Norma, raising her eyebrows.

'Hell, Norma, can't you wait till I've finished?' the inspector grunted sourly.

That morning the inspector's expression was on the gloomy side and Norma imagined he and his wife must have quarrelled again. Recently she spent the weekends reproaching him because of the little time they spent together, but as Norma knew the inspector didn't like to talk about his private life at the station, she opted not to ask anything.

'Come on, give me a clue...' she begged, making it obvious she was trying to read his notes from the other side of the table. 'I'll be a good girl and bring you a coffee.'

'Milk and sugar, please.'

'First, the report of the Porta case. What do we have?'

The inspector looked at her over his spectacles and sighed.

'Very little. According to forensics, the weapon used was a standard kitchen knife, with a serrated edge, but the man must have taken it with him because the lads didn't find it. There were lots of prints and traces in the flat: his daughter's, his son-in-law's, the cleaning lady who went once a week...'

'According to Carrasco's report, he's already cleared the family and the cleaning lady,' Norma interrupted him. 'They all had good alibis.' And she added, seeing how sceptical the inspector seemed, 'Carrasco is what he is, but he knows how to do his job.'

'Don't get too excited,' the inspector smiled maliciously, savouring the reaction he anticipated he'd provoke in Norma, 'but we also have some hairs we've yet to identify and that were very close to the body.'

'I knew as much!' whooped Norma.

'I imagined you'd like that piece of news.' The inspector smiled, feeling pleased with himself.

'Now all you need to do is check whether these hairs match any you found in the professor's office,' Norma said, thinking aloud.

'Are you trying to tell me how to do my job, Deputy Inspector?' the inspector asked sarcastically. 'Don't you worry, we've sent everything to Sabadell. Martí's seeing to it.'

'I'm sorry,' Norma apologized, smiling. 'I'm rather in a rush this morning.'

'That's blindingly obvious.'

'With a bit of luck, we can establish a link between the two cases. I'm sure they're related. Now I'll get you your coffee. You've earned it.'

'With milk and sugar,' the inspector reiterated in a would-be military tone.

'Goes without saying, senyor.'

After taking him his coffee and drinking her own, Norma went in search of an empty office, shut herself inside and rang David. The Egyptologist was on his way to the Autònoma, where he was going to give a lecture that morning, and they both agreed to meet the next day in the attic flat David had on Carrer Ganduxer. When she hung up, she sat still for a few seconds, remembering the last time they'd seen each other, barely nine months ago. On that occasion, David had stayed a week in Barcelona, participating in a series of lectures for postgraduates. He and Norma spent three afternoons together during which they made love and whispered sweet nothings. David had tried to persuade her to have dinner in a restaurant, but Norma had refused and he'd responded rather angrily because he felt she was overdoing the discretion.

She immediately decided she must forget David and her ethical dilemmas, if only for a few hours. Before questioning the professor's widow, she wanted to familiarise herself with the context of the Porta case. With a sigh, she picked up the file and read it from beginning to end, took notes, and added some question marks in red. The time went quickly, and it was almost ten-thirty when she jumped up and rushed out of the office.

'Do you know where Inspector Roca is?' she asked Officer Mata on her way to the lift.

'I think he's in a meeting with the chief,' the woman whispered. After hesitating for a few seconds, weighing up whether it was the right moment to bring the subject up, because the deputy inspector seemed to be in a hurry, the corporal plucked up courage and said, 'Deputy Inspector, I'd like to ask you for a favour...'

'Go on then. I've not got much time,' said Norma, looking at her watch impatiently.

'I was wondering whether you could ask Inspector Roca to let me work with you. If you agree, naturally...' And she added, looking down, 'I've been assigned to Deputy Inspector Carrasco's team...'

'You're with Carrasco now?' Norma exclaimed, her eyes

flashing. And she shook her head and added, 'That's bad luck.'

'Working with the inspector isn't easy,' the corporal explained, smiling shyly.

'I guess it isn't.'

Norma tried to imagine the shrinking violet Officer Mata acting as skivvy for that coarse, foul-mouthed animal, and clicked her tongue. The corporal was twenty-four, and for a female officer she was quite petite and her fragile appearance aroused pity rather than fear among criminals. Obviously, she didn't dare stand up to the deputy inspector, but at the same time, she was resourceful and always got her own way.

'I'll see what I can do...' said Norma, feeling sorry for the corporal. 'But don't get your hopes up. I know he's a relic from the past, but somebody has to work with Agustí. And he can teach you a lot. He is what he is, but he's a good cop and knows the streets better than anyone.' But when she saw the young woman's hangdog expression, she said, 'Alright, I'll speak to Roca and see what we can do.' As she entered the lift, she added, with a smile that made it very clear who was in charge, 'By the way, you must call me Norma. It's about time you left the formalities for when the top brass are around!'

18

The combination of it being Monday and an economic crisis meant half of Barcelona was under roadworks, and Norma took longer than she'd calculated to reach the Plaça de la Universitat. Professor Parellada's widow lived very close by, near Carrer Aribau, in an elegant building, a flat in which time had stood still in the era of crocheted table covers, antimacassars, lurid flowery wallpaper and hand-sewn velvet curtains. A maid with a Galician accent, dressed in black, who must have been almost seventy, answered the door and led Norma at a snail's pace to a sitting room where a tearful Mercè Parellada was waiting, silently surrounded by her nearest and dearest. A grave Jordi Parellada warmly welcomed her and shook her hand, and almost apologised for the contingent of relatives who'd insisted on being present at the interview. He and his mother did the introductions, and Norma, surprised to be confronting such an array of family, told herself that at least it gave her an opportunity to meet them all, and she greeted them one by one, ritually offering them her condolences.

Senyora Mercè, as she was referred to in that household, was a slight woman, looking shy and fragile, and her face was furrowed by a thousand wrinkles. She sat silently on the two-seater sofa she was sharing with her daughter Eulàlia, who had one arm around her back and gripped her hand with the other. Eulàlia was four or five years younger than her brother, Norma reckoned, while her husband, by the name of Artur, who was sitting in the winged armchair by the window slightly apart from the others, was at least ten years older despite the youthful appearance given by his casual dress and long, curly hair. The other sofa was occupied by a po-faced Gerard Muntaner and his wife Anja, who were holding hands.

'I imagine this won't take long, Deputy Inspector?' murmured Eulàlia Parellada, genuinely anxious. 'My mother's not very well, as you can see...'

'Don't worry, I won't keep you long. We'll be done in no time.'

Norma walked over to Mercè Parellada, who, head bowed, was nervously holding a white lace handkerchief she was using to wipe away her tears.

'Senyora Mercè,' she said, touching her hand. 'Do you mind if I sit next to you?'

Mercè Parellada looked up and stared at Norma as if she didn't understand who that woman was or what she was asking, while her daughter Eulàlia stood up to make way for her.

'Offer the young lady a coffee,' she said quietly, looking bewildered.

'No need. I'll soon be finished. Just a few questions I'd like to ask... Do you know who I am?' Norma wasn't in uniform and was aware she didn't look like a cop.

'I don't remember...'

'I'm Norma Forester and I am a detective,' Norma felt 'detective' sounded less alarming than 'female officer'. 'I'm trying to find out what happened to your husband.'

Mercè Parellada glanced around the room and nodded. Her yawns, absent look and lack of focus, as if she wasn't completely there, betrayed the fact she was under the influence of tranquillisers.

'I need to ask a few questions...' Norma said tactfully.

'My husband is dead,' she whispered.

TERESA SOLANA

'I know. That's why I am here,' replied Norma softly. 'Senyora Mercè, I understand that on that night'—Norma decided to cut to the chase avoiding 'the night of the murder' or 'the night he was killed'—'your husband stayed on late to see a student. Did he by any chance say who he was or what his name was?'

'He only said he was a young man from the Autònoma who wanted to talk to him...' she said, sobbing. And then added, as if it still pained her, 'I was quite annoyed, because Dolors and Miquel were coming to dinner...'

'Is that all he told you?' Norma persisted. 'What his name was, who he was, or why he wanted to see him...'

Mercè Parellada looked down and switched the handkerchief to her other hand. Then shook her head.

'Are you sure, Senyora Mercè?'

She wiped away a tear that had started to roll down her cheek and nodded, still not looking up.

'I'd also like to speak to you about something else,' Norma said, changing the subject. 'I know that recently you attended the funeral of a friend of your husband.'

'Víctor.'

'Precisely, Víctor Porta. He and your husband had just had a meeting, right?'

'He came to dinner from time to time. As he was a widower and lived by himself...'

'Do you recall if he came to your home the last time they saw each other?'

'I don't know. I don't remember...'

From the other side of the room, Eulàlia chipped in to try to help her mother remember, 'Mother, I think you told me he and Father had agreed to meet mid-morning in a bar. It was a day when we were going to have paella for lunch and you were afraid the rice would stick, don't you remember? You didn't know whether to tell Herminia to serve the paella or wait until Father arrived...'

'Perhaps...'

140

'That was three weeks ago, perhaps a month,' clarified Eulàlia, addressing Norma.

'Now you mention that... I think they met in that bar on Carrer Girona, I don't recall its name...' said Mercè Parellada.

'You mean the Cafè Central,' commented Jordi Parellada.

'That's it,' she agreed. 'Francesc liked the place. And it's near where Víctor's daughter lives...'

'Did he tell you what they talked about? Perhaps he told his friend he was worried about something...'

'I don't remember.'

'It's important,' Norma emphasised.

'I don't know...' whispered Mercè Parellada.

'And did you think he was worried or anxious after talking to Víctor?'

Suddenly Gerard Muntaner jumped up, looking tense, and confronted Norma. *He's very tall*, thought Norma, and his wife, who was German, seemed surprised by her husband's reaction.

'I thought,' he said politely but firmly, 'you'd come here to investigate Professor Parellada's death, Deputy Inspector.'

'Yes, senyor, that's what I'm doing,' Norma replied, trying to sound respectful.

'I don't understand why you are so interested in this Víctor...' Gerard insisted curtly. 'Senyora Mercè has enough on her plate...'

Gerard Muntaner was the only man of the three in the room wearing a tie. He displayed the confident air of an individual accustomed to giving orders and moving vast amounts of money, and unlike his sister, who was more discreetly dressed, everything about Gerard Muntaner was ostentatious, from his haircut to his shoes. The eau de cologne he used reminded Norma of the one worn by Judge Gallardo, even though she was sure it wasn't the same.

'We are following several leads,' Norma said, to justify herself, though she didn't want to go into detail.

'What leads?' asked Gerard Muntaner, trying to intimidate her by looking her in the eye.

Without flinching, Norma stared back but didn't reply, and a tense silence filled the room. Jordi Parellada stood up and started walking around the room.

'I think we should let the deputy inspector do her job. I am sure she has a good reason to ask us these questions.'

'I'm sorry, I only wanted to...' said Gerard Muntaner less aggressively. But he didn't finish his sentence.

'I know it's all very trying,' said Jordi Parellada, running his hand through his hair and looking at his wife out of the corner of his eye, 'but we must let the police pursue their investigation.'

Norma felt rather uneasy but, following the chief superintendent's orders, she was obliged to bite her lip and took a notebook out of her pocket, making it obvious she was consulting her notes while deciding what to do next.

'Now you mention it,' Mercè Parellada said suddenly, looking up, 'Francesc told me Víctor had written a kind of book of memoirs. Things to do with the war, from their youth...'

'Víctor's is one dramatic story,' Jordi Parellada whispered quietly so his mother couldn't hear. 'His father died in the prison in Burgos, just after the end of the war, and his mother committed suicide. He was brought up by an uncle and aunt.' And he added, surprised by that revelation, 'But I didn't know he'd written a book.'

'Are you sure you can't remember anything else?' Norma insisted, directing her question at Mercè Parellada and trying to soften her tone even more.

'That happened so many days ago...' came her barely audible reply.

'Maybe Víctor's daughter can tell you more, if you think it's important. Isn't she a nurse at the Hospital de Sant Pau?' asked Mònica Muntaner, appealing to her husband.

'In obstetrics, I think,' he answered. 'She's a midwife.'

'I'll speak to her, thanks,' said Norma, remembering that Carrasco had mentioned her though his report made no reference to any memoirs. And getting up from the sofa, she said, 'I think we can leave it there. In any case, if any of you remember something you think might help our investigation, don't hesitate to contact me or one of my colleagues.'

'To tell the truth, I can't see what connection there could be between what happened to Víctor and my father's death,' murmured Eulàlia Parellada, who'd got up from the winged armchair her husband had vacated for her and sat back next to her mother. 'Víctor was killed by thieves who broke into his flat, while my father...' Her voice petered out.

Although she was wearing light makeup and was trying to keep herself together, Norma could see she was very out of sorts.

'There may be no connection,' Norma admitted cautiously, 'but we must investigate it, we can't dismiss it out of hand.'

'Deputy Inspector, if you have no more questions...' Jordi Parellada got up from his chair and walked towards the door, a subtle hint to Norma that it was time for her to leave. 'I think my mother should rest.'

'Of course. Sorry for intruding. I know these are difficult times.'

Norma reiterated her thanks and politely said goodbye to everyone, ready to play to the very last the role of the discreet, obsequious female officer the chief superintendent had told her to perform on this case. Once she was back in the street, she lit up a cigarette and rang Gabriel, who was still at the School of History.

'Wait for me. I'll be there in a jiffy,' said Norma.

'I've got good news!' Gabriel exclaimed euphorically. 'You won't believe it, I've found a student who claims she and her girlfriend saw a suspicious guy leaving the department just after nine pm. Isn't that amazing?'

'A suspicious guy?'

'They'll drop by the station this afternoon and you can question them,' said Gabriel, unable to hide how pleased he was with himself.

'Chapeau, Sergeant! But no need to make them go to Les Corts. I'm on my way to you right now...'

'They had to leave. What's more, they like the idea. I've promised to introduce them to Permanyer.'

'To Permanyer?' Norma explained, surprised. 'What the hell has Permanyer got to do with it?'

'Well, now that CSI is so trendy... Didn't you know? Besides, they're real pretty.'

And with a sly smile Norma couldn't see but could imagine, Gabriel added, 'Don't worry, boss. They're both over eighteen.'

Before heading to the School of History, Norma decided she could do with a coffee or beer, she couldn't decide which, and while she was walking along the Gran Via towards the parking lot, she looked for a bar that would fit the bill. She saw a bar on the other side of the street, and had just decided to cross when her mobile rang.

'You must come to the station immediately, Norma,' said Inspector Roca, sounding anxious.

'What's wrong?'

'Violeta is in jail. She's been arrested.'

'What do you mean she's been arrested?'

'There was a shit-show on Via Laietana this morning. A squatter demo that ended in a battle royal,' the inspector explained. 'But don't worry, she's fine.'

'You sure she wasn't hurt?' asked Norma anxiously.

'I'm sure. I personally saw her and spoke to her. The problem...' Norma heard the inspector sigh, 'is that she won't leave.'

'She won't leave? But didn't you say they'd arrested her?'

'Nebot was prepared to turn a blind eye and make sure she didn't end up in front of a judge, but you know your daughter... I think it's out of my hands now.'

'What an idiot!'

'Would you like me to ring Octavi?' asked the inspector.

'No, I'll give him a call.' Crossing Gran Via when the light was red, she gave a driver a fright and forced him to do an emergency stop to avoid hitting her. 'Keep an eye on her. I'm on my way.'

TERESA SOLANA

19

Violeta was in a cell at Les Corts station that she was sharing with a dozen youngsters who look terrified despite their bolshie attitude. The mix of Palestinian scarves, piercings, dreads and army boots unequivocally identified them as members of the squatter collective, and Norma contemplated them one by one without comment. From behind bars some complained about being beaten up when arrested, while the most daring chorused slogans, insulted the Mossos and gestured obscenely. Norma immediately identified Violeta, who, unlike her companions, was sitting meekly in a corner and acting as if she'd not noticed her mother. Norma suspected her daughter hadn't told her friends that her mother was a cop, so she decided not to compromise her and said nothing. Once she'd seen with her own eyes that her daughter was all right, she turned tail and headed towards her office.

On the way to the station, Norma had rung Octavi and her friend Rita. Octavi left the clinic in a flash and was in Les Corts in twenty minutes, but Rita took a little longer.

'Where is she?' Octavi asked anxiously.

'Where do you think she is?' Norma shouted, in a rage. 'She's in the slammer with a load of losers!'

'Is she OK? Have you seen her? Has she been hurt?'

'Calm down, she's fine. They didn't wallop her.' And she added, looking impatiently at her watch, 'When Rita gets here, they'll take her to one of the interview rooms and we can speak to her.'

'Can't we do that now?' Octavi insisted, worried by what might happen to his daughter.

'What do you want to do? Embarrass her in front of all her friends? She'd never forgive us! If you'd seen the look on her face when she saw me...! And I'm not even in uniform!'

'I suppose you're right,' sighed Octavi. 'We'd better wait for Rita. Did she say she'd be long?'

Rita Soler was a lawyer who specialised in defending abused women, unfairly sacked workers and illegal immigrants, and right at that moment she was in court trying to persuade a judge to withdraw joint custody from a father who was acting irresponsibly towards his son in order to take revenge on his wife. The lawyer arrived a couple of hours later, breathlessly dragging her ninety-six kilos along the station's corridors, and, after kissing and hugging Norma and Octavi, and greeting Inspector Roca, she slumped on a chair and apologised for being so late.

'I'm sorry, you two. I was defending a case and it went badly. What's happened?'

'They arrested Violeta during a squatter demo on Via Laietana,' Norma explained rather despondently. 'They threw stones, broke windows and burned containers.'

'More of the same...' sighed Rita.

'I heard a couple of anti-riot guys were hit.'

'Were any of the demonstrators hurt?'

'Some got hit with truncheons, but Violeta is fine.'

'Do we know what's she being charged with?'

'Not yet.'

The lawyer scratched her neck, raised her eyebrows, and said nothing. Then suddenly she looked at the time, sighed again and got up.

'We'd better talk to her, and see what can be done,' she said, walking towards the door. And, shaking her head, she muttered, 'Young people...'

Rita Soler knew what it was like to confront the anti-riot

brigade and the damage they could do with rubber bullets and truncheons because in her youth she'd confronted Franco's police and been hit more than once. She was four years older than Octavi, and, when they first met they'd had a fling. Rita was a member of the PSUC at the time and Octavi was studying for the exams to become a forensic scientist. Their affair barely lasted a few months, but a good friendship had flowed from that relationship, and over the years it had firmed up to the point that both had almost forgotten how once they'd been an item. Of her own volition, Rita hadn't had children, but she'd been married and divorced three times, and Norma and Octavi had seen how with each divorce Rita put on a few more kilos she never managed to shed and then became resigned to them. Over time, she and Norma had become good friends, and in fact, apart from Norma's psychoanalyst, Rita was the only person who knew about the existence of David.

Violeta appeared handcuffed in the interview room, solemnly escorted by a Mosso only a few months older than her, but fifteen centimetres taller. She looked frightened, and Norma and Octavi stood up and rushed to give her a hug.

'Are you alright?' asked Norma anxiously.

'What do you think? Your mates whacked me with their truncheons!' said Violeta sullenly.

'I was told you'd not been touched...'

'Let me have a look,' said Octavi, alarmed. 'Where did they hit you?'

'On my legs. But they don't hurt anymore.'

'Let me have a look,' insisted Octavi. 'Slip your trousers down.'

'Maybe it was only once...' muttered Violeta, trying to change the subject. 'I dodged them as best I could... It's nothing really.'

Norma sighed and swayed her head, and a relieved

Octavi glanced at her sternly, but didn't pursue it. It wasn't the first time a detainee had complained about bruises and beatings that disappeared during the first examination as if by magic or were far less shocking than the detainee claimed.

'You know Rita.'

'I don't want a lawyer.'

'Don't be silly!' shouted Octavi, who'd been simmering ever since he'd arrived at the station. 'You need a lawyer. You're under arrest. Or haven't you noticed?'

Violeta stared at the floor and pushed her chair back, as if wanting to distance herself from her parents.

'I don't want any favours because I'm a cop's daughter,' she said, avoiding their gaze.

'Favours?' repeated Rita, leaning forward, as if she'd not heard Violeta clearly.

'The chief was prepared to turn a blind eye, but she refused to leave,' explained Norma. And, turning to her daughter, she added, 'Don't worry, even if you changed your mind, he wouldn't be able to help you now. It's too late.'

'That's so very intelligent of you...!' Octavi reproached her, raising his voice. 'Frankly, Violeta, I don't know what goes on inside that head of yours.'

Violeta, who knew her father usually kept his cool even in the tensest of situations, looked down nervously.

'Fine. You don't want any favours. I get that, but you must have a lawyer,' Rita suggested gently, 'that's not a privilege, it's a constitutional right. It's how the system works.'

'A system that's rotten...' retorted Violeta. 'Besides, my companions don't have money to pay for a lawyer and they'll get the duty lawyer. That's who I want too.' And she looked up and added loftily, 'I don't want to be different.'

'Well, if that's the problem, no need to pay me,' said Rita, with half a smile. 'I'll represent you for free. Happy with that?'

'That's not playing it straight.'

'Come on, darling. I expect you're going to be accused of taking part in an illegal demo, destroying municipal property and resisting the authorities. Frankly, it's not looking good,' said Rita, trying to put the wind up her.

'Fuck if I care. If I have to go to prison, I'll go. That's my decision,' retorted Violeta defiantly.

Norma banged the palm of her hand on the table and jumped up in a rage, shoving her aside with her arm and almost knocking her to the ground. She felt like giving her daughter a good hiding, grabbing her by the ear and taking her home like a little girl. Octavi, who sensed Norma was about to lose it, gently gripped her arm and got her to sit down again. The possibility the judge might accuse Violeta of aggressive behaviour and decide to send her down for a stretch in Can Brians was real enough, and the prospect of Violeta ending up in a cell with drug dealers, thieves and murderers who'd sooner or later find out she was a cop's daughter didn't help to calm her nerves.

'Are you in your right mind?' she snapped. 'Or have some aliens got to you?! The charges you face are extremely serious!' Then, lowering her voice and trying to calm down, she added, 'This isn't a game, Violeta. They can lock you up in jail. And that's not a very pleasant experience, believe me...'

'And if you go to prison, that won't make the system any less rotten,' argued Octavi, appealing to his daughter's common sense.

'I won't be complicit,' Violeta fired back.

'Complicit in what? What the hell are you talking about?! I've seen the video, you went on the rampage, you broke shop windows, burnt containers and threw bricks at the anti-riot squad! You organised a right shit-show!'

'We were showing solidarity with our comrades in Sants whom the Mossos evicted violently yesterday,' muttered Violeta bitterly, 'If they attack us, we've the right to defend ourselves, haven't we?'

'Breaking windows and throwing stones at the police doesn't solve anything, my love, it makes things worse,' said Octavi. 'You should know that by now.'

'Whatever, but I still don't want a lawyer.'

A silence descended on the small interview room for a few minutes. Sighs and deep breaths were all that could be heard. Finally, Rita half got up from her chair, leaned back and stared at Violeta in a phlegmatic pose Norma and Octavi knew well.

'Violeta, my dear... Who're you trying to fool?' the lawyer asked in a condescending tone. 'Do you really think I'm swallowing all this?'

Violeta looked up from the floor and stared at her in dismay.

'Do you know why you don't want a lawyer and prefer to go to prison?' continued Rita softly. 'Do you think I don't know?'

'I don't want any favours,' Violeta insisted.

'No, my dear,' said Rita, shaking her head. 'Don't give me that fairy tale. You want to be locked up because you think that's the way to become a heroine in the eyes of all your mates. I can hear them now, right? A cop's daughter inside! That Violeta is the real deal!'

'You're out of order,' said Violeta, red-faced.

'And, yes, you *will* end up in jail,' continued Rita, ignoring the hatred flashing in Violeta's eyes. 'Obviously, while you're still in the jug acting the martyr, you won't be able to continue fighting against the speculators and corruption. Though naturally,' she continued after a short pause, 'you'll have a whale of a time acting big in front of your friends and you can brag about how courageous you are while you drink a few beers and smoke spliffs...' Rita paused again, measuring Violeta's reaction out of the corner of her eye. 'Yes,' she nodded, playing with her long necklace of garnet stones, 'it can be so very gratifying to play the martyr!'

Violeta looked her up and down, her eyes glowering.

'You speaking about me or yourself?' she snapped.

Rita burst out laughing and, still fidgeting with her necklace, sat back on the chair. She didn't seem at all insulted by Violeta's comment.

'You're so clever...! Listen,' she now adopted a more matey tone, 'I like you squatters. Indeed, I've defended a good number, and I dare say that if I was younger and weighed thirty kilos less...' she sighed.

'Wonderful, that's all we needed, for you agree with her!' interrupted Norma, who hadn't understood where Rita was going.

'But do you reckon I could do anything for the unhappy folk the system marginalises if I spent my time burning containers and throwing stones at judges whenever they give out a sentence I consider unfair?' Rita continued, ignoring what Norma had said. 'Come on, my love, let's be clear, do you really want to change things? Do you really want to fight for a fairer society? Because if you think this is all a game, I've enough work to get on with without wasting my time here. Right now, I've got to prepare a claim for a desperate woman whose idiot ex is making her life hell and endangering her son's life.' Rita paused. 'Obviously, if you really do want to fight the speculators and the corrupt, as you say you do, what you must do is use your brain, and not be led by your emotions. Going to prison won't help one bit.'

Violeta lowered her gaze rather sheepishly and didn't retaliate. A few seconds later, when she considered Violeta had had enough time to digest the little sermon she'd just delivered, the lawyer went on with a shrug, 'Fine, if what you want is to go through life acting the victim...'

Violeta blushed again and, head lowered, looked at Rita out of the corner of her eye.

'Very good,' the lawyer continued, moving her chair closer to the table and putting her shabby briefcase on it.

'Now we understand each other, tell me your version of what happened and what exactly you were doing when they arrested you.'

20

After a while Violeta returned to the cell smarting, but represented by a lawyer who was an institution in the court rooms of Barcelona. Octavi, who was late for a meeting he could not miss because they were finalising preparations to move the Forensic Pathology Service to the new installations in the City of Justice, had to get a move on, while Norma was in a hurry to meet up with Gabriel, who'd been waiting an hour with the two students who'd seen the suspicious man in the entrance of the School of History on the day of Professor Parellada's murder. All three were currently with Inspector Permanyer who was showing the girls the modern devices they used in the scientific laboratory at his usual leisurely pace.

'Roca isn't here. Best if we go to his office,' suggested Norma, who was slightly more relaxed now Violeta had agreed to be defended by Rita.

In Les Corts station the news that Deputy Inspector Norma Forester's daughter was in the clink was on everyone's lips, and Norma, who wasn't in any mood for jokes or sarcasm, wanted to avoid colleagues parading past her desk asking after Violeta. There weren't enough chairs in Inspector Roca's office and Norma sent Gabriel to look for a couple more.

Before questioning them, Norma silently looked the students up and down. One was dyed blonde, chubby and wore her hair long and the other was dark, small and had short hair. Both were caked in makeup and sported tight-fitting jeans, high-heeled boots and hoop earrings, and for a second Norma tried to imagine her daughter dressed like that. She wasn't enchanted by the image that came to mind and decided she preferred Violeta with piercings and baggy trousers to a Violeta larded with face paint and tarted up to go clubbing.

'Sergeant Alonso informed me you saw a suspicious individual leave the department on the 31st at about nine pm. Is that correct?' Norma asked drily.

The two young women looked at each other, unnerved by the unfriendly tone they detected in the deputy inspector's voice, and nodded rather despondently.

'I suppose you know that making a false statement is a crime that can carry a prison sentence,' Norma warned them, looking serious, while she acted as if she was consulting her notes and tried to intimidate them with her deliberately hostile attitude. The truth was Norma was afraid Gabriel's charms might have caused both students' imaginations to run riot.

'But it's true!' shouted the long-haired girl. 'We *did* see someone odd! We didn't invent him!'

'Odd? Barcelona is full of *odd* people,' Norma objected in that same chilly tone. 'Why did you happen to pick on that particular student?'

Now it was the turn of the short-haired girl to reply with a question she hadn't anticipated.

'Was he a student? He didn't look like one...'

Norma looked up from the pile of papers and stared at her.

'Why do you say he didn't look like a student?'

'I don't know... He just didn't,' the girl insisted.

Her friend nodded.

'It's true,' she said. 'He looked odd and was old-ish. That is...' She quickly corrected herself, calculating the age the unfriendly cop might be, afraid she might have offended her, 'I mean he was older than us.'

'I've an idea,' suggested Gabriel, smiling seductively, seeing that the students felt uncomfortable. He couldn't understand why his colleague had decided to question them as if they were two hostile witnesses. 'Why don't you tell the deputy inspector what you told me?'

The two students looked at each other hesitantly, and finally the blonde sighed and took the initiative.

'Laia and I had just left our lecture and we were chatting in the entrance,' she exclaimed, uncrossing her legs and sitting more demurely in her chair. 'We didn't have a lighter, and were looking for a smoker to give us a light. Then we saw him leave the department and light up,' she said, looking to her friend to back her up. 'We went over and asked him for a light, but the guy shoved Laia out of the way and ran off.'

'He started running?' asked Norma.

'He didn't exactly break into a sprint,' said Laia, lowering her head, closing her eyes and making an effort to remember the scene. 'But he did walk away very quickly, as if he wanted to get away from us.'

'That was when I shouted 'bastard'. Because of the way he shoved Laia,' the blonde explained.

'So what was he like? Tall? Short? Thin? Fat?' asked Norma.

'He was a bit shorter than Neus,' said the dark-haired girl. Neus got up from her chair so Norma could calculate his height.

'He came up to about here,' she said, putting her hand level with her eyebrows. Norma reckoned the girl must be one metre seventy, so the stranger must be around one metre sixty-five. 'And he wasn't what you'd call thin,' she added.

'Or particularly fat...' her friend added. 'Though he wasn't skinny...'

'He was a bit like the policeman Gabriel introduced us to,' said the blonde, referring to Inspector Permanyer. The inspector certainly wasn't fat, but he was starting to get a bit of a belly.

'Very good. You say he didn't look like a student. Might he have been a lecturer? I suppose there are lots in the department and you don't know them all...' Norma suggested.

'No way!' They both shook their heads. 'Lecturers don't dress like that.'

'Do you remember how he was dressed? Can you describe him?'

The students glanced at each other and stayed quiet for a few moments as they tried to remember.

'He was wearing one of those leftie shirts, without a collar... I think it was grey, with thin stripes,' the dark-haired girl said after a while.

'It was blue, grey-blue,' replied her friend, who'd crossed her legs again.

'OK, but it *was* striped,' the dark-haired girl insisted.

'Yes, you're right.'

'And he wore black jeans.'

'And was carrying one of those bags that eco-freaks and lefties carry.'

'What was it like exactly? Do you remember?' asked Gabriel.

'It was purple, wasn't it?' asked Laia, addressing her friend.

'Yes, corduroy, I reckon,' said her friend. 'He was carrying it like this,' and she made a diagonal gesture to explain he wore it across his back.'

'The sign for peace was painted on the front,' said the other girl. And added contemptuously, 'Very flowery-powery.'

'Do you remember anything else?' Norma concluded the girls were telling the truth and sweetened her tone.

'He was also wearing shades,' said Laia.

'Ray-Bans. But I think they were fake...'

'And a military cap. You couldn't see his hair.'

'A military cap?' repeated Norma, raising her eyebrows.

'Well, perhaps not exactly military... It was khaki,' the dark-haired girl corrected herself.

'Oh...! And white trainers, like tennis pumps. I remember them because they didn't go with his outfit.'

'He was quite scruffy,' said her friend, adding very self-confidently, 'And not very friendly.'

Norma sighed, as she tried to imagine the man they'd just described.

'Do you think you could identify him, if you saw him again?'

The two girls looked at each other again and hesitated for a few seconds.

'What with the cap and the shades, you couldn't see his face,' said Laia. Her friend nodded.

'In any case, we'll try to do an identikit likeness we can show to students and lecturers,' Norma decided, addressing Gabriel. 'Who knows, we might strike it lucky?'

Suddenly the blonde girl threw her body back, opened her eyes wide and exclaimed, 'I know why he didn't look like a student! He was more like one of those conmen on La Rambla!'

Norma, Gabriel and her friend looked up and stared at her.

'A conman?' asked Norma.

'I mean one of those guys who stand around the one dealing the cards or shaking the dice. You know,' she said, acting the expert, 'those that act as if they're laying bets and winning lots of money to attract people. They usually disguise themselves as tourists, businessmen or students... But you can see from a mile off they belong to the gang!'

'It's true...' her friend whispered. 'Now you say that, he did look like a conman.'

'You mean he looked as if he'd disguised himself to look like a student?' asked Norma, making sure she'd understood what the girl was trying to explain.

'Yes, I'm sure with those looks he was no student. Besides, as we said, he was old-ish.'

Norma thought those young women seemed too observant for her to doubt their judgement, and nodded. Before she let them leave, she asked if they knew Dr Parellada.

'We're in the second year. I think he only teaches post-grads,' replied the dark-haired girl.

'You must think we've invented all this, right?' asked the dyed blonde, chubby girl, who still seemed rather offended by the way Norma had initially treated them. 'I swear it's the truth.'

Norma smiled and stood up. The two students did likewise.

'I believe you. But I had to make sure, I think you can understand that.' And she added, with a sigh, 'There are people who love to invent things when they're talking to the police. I'm sorry if I was rather abrupt at the start.'

'What do you reckon? Should I take them to see Marc?' asked Gabriel.

'Yes, go with them and get an identikit pic done. It can't do any harm.'

'When we've done that, if you don't mind, I'll go out for a bit. I promised these girls a Coke and I said I'd tell them a few amusing stories,' said Gabriel.

'A Coke? You cops drink Coke?' asked the long-haired girl, looking disappointed.

'Well, when I'm on duty...' Gabriel smiled sweetly and winked.

Norma raised an eyebrow, looked at the time and saw it was almost six-thirty.

'That's all good, no need to come back.' And, addressing the two students, she added, 'But don't get him too excited, right? And don't be duped by the sergeant's butter-wouldn't-melt smile...'

The two girls lowered their heads, exchanged knowing glances and smiled as they argued the toss over which of them would land Gabriel and carry him off to their bed that night.

21

On Tuesday morning a Violeta intimidated by judicial trappings was appearing before the judge while Norma and Gabriel were heading to the Hospital de Sant Pau to question Víctor Porta's daughter. Violeta had begged her mother not to come to the hearing so she wouldn't have to give explanations to her friends. Norma had reluctantly agreed, deciding that her presence might be counterproductive if the judge misinterpreted it and considered she was trying to exert pressure. Fortunately, thanks to Rita's good offices, the judge released Violeta without the prosecution presenting charges after it had been noted that she didn't appear in the videos taken by the police, while the anti-riot squad who drew up statements were aware she was a colleague's daughter, and didn't identify her among the demonstrators who'd thrown stones and burned containers. As soon as she left the court building, Violeta called her mother and gave her the good news.

'You should come home for a few days to get over the shock...' she suggested in the faint hope that Violeta would accept. She tried – and failed – to not make it sound like a reprimand: 'Your father and I were very worried... And so was Guillem. He's rung several times from Madrid to ask how you are.'

Violeta's arrest had caught Guillem in Madrid, accompanying Robert to exhibitions, artists' workshops and trendy bars. When they heard the news, Guillem and Robert quickly brought forward their departure and now had return tickets on the AVE that same afternoon. Norma suggested to Violeta they should all have dinner together.

'What do you think? You know how Guillem tends to be so melodramatic, and he won't stop until he's sure you are well and aren't traipsing the world with a ball and chain tied to your ankle...' she said, trying to add a touch of humour to overcome any reticence her daughter might have.

'Oh, I'm not sure...'

'Come on, we all really want to see you...' she said positively.

Violeta, who deep down felt guilty for the upset she'd caused her family and the cock-up she'd created, readily agreed and accepted her mother's invitation. As fortunately neither Mimí nor Octavi's parents had been informed about her arrest, they all decided not to tell them anything. At most, they'd say that Violeta had some exams and was coming home for a few days in order to concentrate on her revision.

The news of Violeta's release radically improved Norma's state of mind and Gabriel was pleased his superior was finally her usual cheerful self and had lost the anxious expression she'd had ever since Violeta's arrest. Violeta's call had caught her on the way to the Hospital de Sant Pau, and, as she was driving this time, the moment they reached the vicinity of the hospital, Norma stopped the car and asked him to find a parking space. She had to make a few calls, she said. Gabriel sat behind the steering wheel, and, since it was still early, they agreed to meet up in one of the bars on the Avinguda Gaudí for a coffee before going into the hospital.

Norma entered the bar and quickly rang Octavi to give him the good news, but her husband already knew because a contact of his at the court had just rung to tell him how the hearing had gone. Violeta had no record and the judge had decided to be charitable, but she'd also warned her very solemnly that the next time they caught her playing the fool she wouldn't get off so lightly. Head down, Violeta had silently left the courtroom under the judge's severe gaze.

Norma then rang Guillem, told him his daughter was back out on the street and invited Robert and him to supper. Guillem sighed theatrically and passed on the news to Robert, who was sitting next to him. If there were no delays, said Guillem, they'd be in Barcelona at seven. Norma rang David, with whom in principle she had a date that afternoon, and told him what had happened.

'We won't be able to meet today, but we could tomorrow,' she suggested.

'Out of the question, I've got to catch a plane early,' said David, sounding disappointed. 'I've a meeting at my college at five and I must be there.'

From her bar stool, Norma could see Gabriel through the window walking towards her and she told David she must ring off. Luckily, Gabriel's arrival meant Norma didn't have time to mope about that missed encounter and torture herself because she wanted to see a man who wasn't her husband. Gabriel, who hadn't noticed any changes in Norma's state of mind in the ten minutes he'd taken to park the car, sat down and ordered a tuna roll and a Coke. Norma was feeling drowsy and ordered another tallat.

'Just as well it all came to nothing...!' said Gabriel, as he took a big bite of his roll.

Norma still had David on her mind and she eyed Gabriel with dismay, but then realised he was referring to Violeta's arrest.

'The anti-riot squad were a help, because they told me Violeta threw quite a number...' she sighed. 'Although it seems, her aim is poor...' she added with a smile.

'She's very pretty,' said Gabriel, pretending to focus on his roll.

'At the present time, I don't think getting involved with a member of the forces of repression forms part of her plans.' Norma glanced at him sardonically. 'Come on, hurry up, it's almost a quarter to one.'

Gabriel polished off his roll and drink and they both left the bar. They'd agreed to meet Montserrat Porta at one in the cafeteria in the Hospital de Sant Pau, during one of the nurse's breaks, and Norma didn't want to arrive late. Even though Carrasco had already questioned her, she wanted to talk to her and ask about her father's life in Mexico and his relationship with Professor Francesc Parellada.

'Do you know it's my first time here?' asked Gabriel, surveying the building that was the entrance to the site. 'It's beautiful.'

'Yes, too beautiful to be a hospital for the poor...!' Norma said with a sigh. 'That's why they've built a new one further up.' And added, shaking her head, 'It's a pity...'

'Come on, the new hospital will be more up to date. This one's a bit on the shabby side.'

'If you say so...' replied Norma, in a tone that expressed her total disagreement with Gabriel.

The modernist buildings of the Hospital de La Santa Creu i Sant Pau dated from the beginning of the twentieth century, but the origins of the institution conceived as a hospital for the poor and pilgrims went back to 1401. The Hospital de Sant Pau, as it is popularly known, was the most important Catalan modernist building in Barcelona and too much of a temptation for politicians and speculators who'd finally decided to deprive doctors, nurses and patients of that privileged area of gardens and colourful buildings, and transfer the hospital infrastructure to a new, anodyne building that was far from inviting. They were restoring the wings and wards and transforming them into headquarters of various political institutions; from now on they'd only be enjoyed by politicians. In the new hospital, meanwhile, doctors complained their offices had neither windows nor natural light.

With its pathways and avenues and poor lighting, Sant Pau had become a labyrinth for those who weren't used to it, and Norma and Gabriel struggled to find their way between the different wings, most of which were being modernised. When they finally found the cafeteria, they took one glance and saw it was packed. They had to wait outside for a good while, because the nurse was twenty minutes late.

'I'm Montserrat Porta,' she said, holding her hand out and catching her breath. 'You're waiting for me, right?' Norman and Gabriel nodded and introduced themselves. 'I'm very sorry. We had a twin birth that took quite some time.'

'Don't worry,' Norma smiled. 'We know you don't have much time. Shall we go in and get a bite to eat while we talk?'

'I don't feel hungry. And at this time of the day there's a lot of bustle and noise in the cafeteria. Why don't we sit on that bench?' she suggested, pointing to the only bench that was free.

There was a chilly breeze, and Montserrat Porta, who was wearing the nurse's uniform under a thin cardigan, sat down at the end of the bench that caught the sun. Norma and Gabriel, who wore thicker clothes, sat next to her in the shade.

'Any news? Have you arrested them?' the nurse asked optimistically.

'Not yet. But we're still investigating and we have a few new leads. That's why we wanted to ask you some more questions.'

'I'm all yours.'

Montserrat Porta spoke Catalan with a gentle Mexican lilt that got stronger when she switched to Spanish, and her long black hair, the almond shape of her eyes and brown colour of her skin revealed Indian antecedents that couldn't have gone back many generations.

Norma reckoned she must be into her forties and looked well on it, and Gabriel, who marked women out of ten, rated her a seven and a half.

'Don't get me wrong,' Norma began tactfully, 'but I must ask you if your father had any enemies in Mexico.'

'Enemies? No, not that I know,' replied Montserrat Porta, surprised by the question, wrinkling her eyebrows as if she didn't understand where the deputy inspector was going with that.

'Perhaps he had left some unfinished business...'

'Unfinished business?' repeated Montserrat Porta.

'Your father owned a restaurant, right?'

Monserrat Porta first looked rather disconcertedly at Norma and then Gabriel, hesitated for a few seconds and finally, realising the track they were on, straightened her body and answered defensively, raising her voice, 'My father was never involved in any criminal activity, if that's what you are thinking!'

'I'm sorry, I wasn't trying to...'

'Yes, he lived in Mexico City, my mother was Mexican, as I am too! But we're not criminals!' she declared aggressively.

'I assure you I wasn't insinuating...'

'My father wasn't a drug dealer, an arms dealer, or anything of the sort. He didn't gamble or drink and didn't have debts or accounts to settle with anybody!'

'I realise this is all very painful and unpleasant...' whispered Norma. 'I was thinking rather of the restaurant your father owned in Mexico. Did he ever have any problems with anyone, before or after he sold it on?'

'It was a small tourist restaurant, not far from the house of Diego Rivera the painter, in Coyoacán,' she explained, calming down. 'He and my mother ran it between them, she did the cooking. In seasons when there was more demand, Arturo helped them, but when she was diagnosed with cancer, my father sold the restaurant so he could care for her. As far as I know, there were never any problems. That was all five years ago.' And she added, getting emotional as she remembered, 'The cancer was very advanced and the poor dear only lasted six months... Father stayed on in Mexico for another year, but my husband and I finally persuaded him to come to live in Barcelona.'

'I heard your father had written a book...' asked Norma, changing the subject.

'You mean his memoirs? Yes, he'd been working on them for three years. He focused on it when he returned to Barcelona.'

'Do you happen to have the manuscript or his notes?'

'No.' Monserrat Porta was again very surprised by the question. 'Now you mention it, it is very strange, because when we emptied out the flat, we didn't find the manuscript or his notebooks. It never occurred to me.'

'The thieves took his computer. Maybe your father didn't have a hard copy,' Gabriel suggested.

'No, that's not true, he did have one. He had it bound with one of those black spirals and a transparent plastic cover. I remember because it was on the top of his desk the last time I went to his place. Its title was *Black Storms*, the first words of the *Varsoviana*.' She added, with a smile, 'My grandparents belonged to the CNT.'

'It was the anarchists' hymn,' explained Norma, who was sure Gabriel wouldn't know what kind of song the *Varsoviana* was. 'Do you know how long the manuscript was?'

'I don't know. It was about that thick.' Monserrat used her thumb and forefinger to indicate a thickness of some three centimetres.

'Around two hundred pages,' Norma calculated. 'Did you get to read it?'

Monserrat rubbed her arms to warm herself up and sighed.

'He said he didn't want anyone to read the book until he'd finished writing it. The fact is I didn't nag him, because what with work, the house and the kid, I barely have time to read...' she justified herself. 'But why are you asking me about my father's memoirs? They were only a kind of hobby, a way to kill time, I imagine.'

'I've reviewed the list of objects they took, the one you helped us to put together, and I do think it's rather peculiar,' Norma said, knitting her brows, 'The so-called thief or thieves stole the gold watch that, according to you, your father kept in his bedside table drawer, but they didn't take his wedding ring, which was gold too. On the other hand, they did steal his briefcase and laptop, though they left the printer, television and sound system, that were all brand new.'

'You're right, it is rather peculiar,' she agreed, looking at her watch. 'But I imagine my father caught them in the act and they took fright. That's why they killed him, I assume? That's what that policeman told us...' She was referring to Deputy Inspector Carrasco.

'That's what we thought initially, but we want to discount other possible motives.' Norma didn't want to go into detail about the new line she and Gabriel were pursuing.

'If you think the book is important, maybe you should talk to Berta,' suggested Montserrat Porta, looking at her watch again. 'But I think the other policeman did talk to her.'

Norma nodded, remembering she'd seen the name of Berta Macià, a close friend of the victim, in the file Carrasco had given her. You couldn't say the old cop hadn't explored all the leads.

'Berta and my father used to meet up a lot,' Monserrat Porta added. 'In fact, I think they were an item, or something of the sort. She too was widowed and retired, but she works as a volunteer librarian in the old people's centre in Poble Sec, where my father used to go,' she said, moist-eyed. 'Indeed, I was pleased my father was going out with her, though I think he found it hard to talk about, because of my mother.'

'In these situations, one never knows how the children will react...'

'I suppose not. Do you know? My father grew up in that neighbourhood. It would have been easier all round if he'd found somewhere near my house, but I imagine those streets brought back happy memories. The poor man hadn't been back in the area since he was twenty-two...!'

'If you remember anything you think might be useful, please do give me a call,' said Norma, getting up from the bench and giving her the card with her number.

'Do you think there's any chance you might catch them?' asked Monserrat Porta, shivering from the cold as she put the card in her top pocket.

'I can assure you we are doing our level best.'

22

'So what do you want us to do now, boss?' asked Gabriel as they walked back to the exit.

'We should give that Berta a ring first and see what she has to say.'

'The girl said Carrasco already talked to her…'

'That was when everything pointed to a robbery, and Agustí, reasonably enough, only asked her the usual routine questions. Nobody thought of telling him the dead man had written some memoirs.'

'I suppose they didn't think it was relevant. Do you really think it might be?' asked Gabriel sceptically.

'If the two murders are connected, it's possible the book Víctor Porta wrote might provide a clue or two. In any case, I want to know what Berta Macià knows about it. He may have given her a copy of the manuscript.'

'I think it's a bit too recherché,' said Gabriel. 'Are you sure you're not making up some kind of drama? Some people in the department think you read too many novels…'

'Two men of the same age have been murdered only two weeks apart, and they were friends,' retorted Norma, who didn't feel offended by Gabriel's comment. 'One was a historian specialising in the Civil War and the other had written a book about his childhood in Barcelona in the post-war period. Don't you think that's too many coincidences?'

'Yes, but maybe that's all it is, a coincidence,' said

Gabriel. 'Remember both were old men who couldn't defend themselves. If the motive was theft...'

'Thieves aren't that stupid. There must be something else...' whispered Norma, sticking to that hypothesis.

Gabriel had parked on Carrer Cartagena, and, as they'd just exited through the hospital's main entrance, they had to walk up Sant Antoni Maria Claret and around the whole complex. Norma took her mobile from her bag and dialled Berta Macià's number, reckoning that at lunchtime she'd find her at home. She was indeed in her kitchen and picked up the phone almost immediately. When she heard it was a female officer at the other end of the line, she panicked, but Norma quickly calmed her down and said they only wanted to talk to her because they were pursuing a new lead.

'If you like, we can drop by your place. This afternoon would be fine if it suits you,' Norma suggested. 'You don't need to come to the station.'

'I've an appointment at the medical centre at seven...' replied Berta, recovering from the shock.

'Don't worry. We won't keep you long. We'll be with you at five.'

Norma saw it was already two and hurried even more. She and Gabriel had to be at Les Corts at three, so she'd have little time to see her daughter.

'Drop me at home and go and get some lunch,' she said.

'Are you sure you want me to go home? Remember Roca's expecting us at three and he'll be angry if we're late.'

'I want to see how Violeta is. I'll have a quick bite while I'm at it.'

'If you want, I can pick you up...'

'No, you have lunch in peace and try to arrive punctually. I'll catch a taxi.'

At lunchtime timetables were usually quite chaotic, as Norma and Octavi never knew when they'd get home or how long they'd have for lunch, so Mimí wasn't at all surprised when her daughter turned up unannounced, saying she was in a rush. Violeta had been there some time and had shut herself in her bedroom, reading or pretending to, but when she heard her mother's voice she immediately left her bedroom and went to the hallway. Norma hugged Violeta as if she were still her little girl and she let herself be cuddled without too much of a protest, showing minimal resistance. She had showered and changed, and Norma thought she looked well despite the bags under her eyes; as she said, she'd not slept at all well. Mimí, who was pleased to have her only granddaughter at home, ran to the kitchen to defrost a steak and put another plate on the table.

'Guillem and Robert will come for supper,' Norma announced, trying to sound as natural as possible.

'But weren't they coming back from Madrid tomorrow?' Mimí asked.

'Robert has some urgent business, so they decided to bring forward their return,' Norma lied. 'But I can't cook today, I've got too much work on. We'll have to order some food in.'

'Bah, don't worry. There are eggs and potatoes in the pantry. We'll rustle up some omelettes and some ham and pa amb tomàquet. Everybody likes ham,' Mimí said, looking at her granddaughter out of the corner of her eye.

'When I leave work, I'll pop into the grocer's and buy bread and ham. And tomatoes too, mustn't forget them. And we can have a big salad,' Norma added, smiling at her daughter.

'I do eat eggs...' muttered Violeta, then added, for the benefit of her grandmother, 'I can do the omelettes.'

'In that case, we'll have a grand supper!' Mimí kissed her loudly. 'Violeta makes the best omelettes!'

Norma left Violeta, Mimí and Senta eating dessert and hurried off to Les Corts. The conversation pending with

Violeta would have to wait, because Inspector Roca had summoned them to get the latest on the investigation before his meeting with Chief Superintendent Nebot and he was waiting impatiently. That afternoon Nebot had called the inspector to his office to find out what progress they were making on the Parellada case, a meeting that in turn had been set up after he received a call from the director general of police who was being harried by Minister Roig to make that case an absolute priority.

Norma apologised for being ten minutes late and sat down. Inspector Roca was always on edge when he was about to see the chief superintendent, but contrary to expectations, Norma found the inspector to be in a good mood. He'd had a haircut and was clean-shaven, and for the first time in a long time was wearing a clean, ironed shirt that looked as if it was brand new.

'Meeting the chief does something for you...' Norma commented sarcastically after she'd given him the once-over.

'I'm having dinner with a colleague tonight,' he confessed with a smile. 'But I don't intend to tell you who she is.'

'We'll find out sooner or later, as you well know...'

'Could we focus on the case? I've got my meeting upstairs at four,' he said, looking at his watch. 'So, what's new?'

'I think we have two murders and one assassin,' Norma said. 'We're waiting on results from the laboratory, to see whether there are any links between the two crime scenes to back up my hunches.'

Norma summed up what she and Gabriel had discovered over recent days, and told him they had an identikit image of the man whose face hadn't been visible, and statements by the two student eyewitnesses. The widow had confirmed that the Poble Sec pensioner and professor had met just before the former's murder, and also that the pensioner had written some memoirs that had disappeared.

'We have an appointment to question his woman friend who lives in

Poble Sec,' Gabriel explained. 'Norma thinks it could be an important lead.'

'And what do *you* think?' The inspector looked up from the notes he

was taking and peered at him over his glasses.

'Well, you know the deputy inspector... She usually gets :t right,'

Gabriel said with a grin.

The inspector wrinkled one brow, picked up the phone and dialled

Inspector Permanyer's number.

'Francesc, Roca here. I'm with Norma and Gabriel. How's it going? Have you found anything?'

'I'm writing my report at this very minute,' said the inspector, who had in fact been woken up from his afternoon nap by the call. 'But I do have some good news. The hair we found in the Poble Sec flat and the professor's office belong to the same individual. And it's a man. Norma was right.'

Get a move on and send me this report as soon as possible. Before four, if possible...' begged the inspector before hanging up. And he then turned to Norma and Gabriel. 'You heard him. That means we can concentrate on finding a single suspect. I'll inform the judge in charge of the case immediately and see what he wants to do.'

'A: least you've got something solid for the chief. He won't haul you over the coals for something that's our fault,' Norma said with a smile.

'Talking of the chief, I should tell you he will inform the family unofficially tomorrow of the state of play,' said the inspector.

'The family? But didn't Gallardo decree that the case

should be kept secret?' Norma protested. 'He decided that to avoid any leaks to the press!'

'That's precisely why he will inform them unofficially,' the inspector justified himself. 'The judge is on board.' Then he lowered his voice, even though his office door was shut, and added, 'Everybody wants to be in the Muntaners' good books, starting with Gallardo, you know him. Indeed, it was his idea to organise an informal meeting with the family.'

'All the same, better not let the news get out that we are working on the assumption that the two cases are linked,' Norma said, mentally weighing up the consequences of a leak.

'Sooner or later the press will find out and start speculating,' said the inspector, shrugging his shoulders. 'You might as well get used to the idea.'

23

Berta Macià lived close to the Plaça Bella Dorita and what was left of the El Molino cabaret, that had been closed for years. The square and the cabaret were being refurbished (only the cabaret's emblematic façade with the windmill sails had been preserved), and the noise of the diggers resounded down neighbouring streets, working at a frantic pace, because elections were nigh and someone wanted to grandstand at the launch ceremony. Berta Macià lived on the fourth floor of a modest building that had neither concierge nor lift, and Norma and Gabriel had no choice but to walk up the dark, dingy stairs that, apart from stinking of urine, at that time of day also smelled of fried garlic.

Berta Macià was thin and petite, and her stunning blue eyes took a good look at them before she decided to invite them in. Despite her modern hairstyle and casual way of dressing, she looked her age, sixty-seven, maybe older. She welcomed them in, wearing black trousers and a lilac, knee-length smock, and her style of dress and long necklace reminded Norma of the New Age style preferred by Mimí. As she ushered them into the dining room, Norma calculated the flat was barely sixty square metres, but even so the room looked out on the world, there was a lot of light and it seemed attractive enough. It was freshly painted and everything seemed brand new. Indeed, that spruced-up, tidy interior wasn't at all like the gloomy, drab stairway they'd just climbed up.

'When my husband died,' Berta Macià explained, aware that Norma was scrutinising the room on the sly, 'I decided to redecorate the whole place in order to cheer myself up. I also modernised the bathroom and kitchen.'

'It's very pretty and very bright,' Norma said sincerely.

'If you'd have seen it before! We still had the same furniture we bought when we married...'

'Sometimes in life, you need to ring the changes...'

'All this makes me feel younger. Crazy, isn't it?'

The walls of the lobby, passage and dining room were painted a pale yellow and the furniture, some of which was white, was all modern in style, surely from IKEA, deduced Norma, after inspecting it. A couple of brightly coloured kilims lay on the dining room's new parquet floor, and there were colourful boxes, scented candles and sticks of incense everywhere. Exhibition posters, in wooden frames, adorned the walls, and Norma was struck by how not a single item in the flat revealed that Berta Macià had lived there almost forty years with her husband. There were no old photos, no ceramic figurines, no souvenirs of times past. From the sofa where they'd sat down, Norma couldn't help looking at the titles of the books on the shelves, most of them novels written by women and self-help books. Various CDs of Vangelis, Kitaro and Enya, among others, were oddly lined up on one shelf. Right then, with the volume very low, Norma identified a theme by Enya.

'My husband and I never had children,' she said with a sigh, 'and meditation and yoga have helped me come to terms with his death. I mean,' she quickly corrected herself, 'with the help of a few antidepressants, I wouldn't want to mislead you.'

'Everything helps,' said Norma with a smile that was intended to express her sympathy. 'Did your husband die a long time ago?'

'It'll soon be five years. And now poor Víctor!' she said with another sigh, lowering her head.

'It must have been hard for you.'

'We'd known each other just over a year. It's not the same as losing someone you've lived your whole life with, obviously... But to die like that... I still have nightmares at night.'

'That's normal enough. But you seem like a courageous woman...'

Berta Macià shook her head sadly, got up from her chair and went to look for a tissue to wipe away the tears.

'Forgive me, I've still not got over it.'

They'd met at the old people's centre where she volunteered as a librarian, and they'd been in a romantic relationship for about a year. Víctor Porta was a fine, good-natured man, she said, and as far as she knew, he'd never quarrelled with anyone.

'He was considerate and well-mannered, and his only vices were smoking cigarettes and drinking the occasional glass of tequila. Though he wasn't a big drinker, you know?' she added, to make sure the two police didn't get the wrong idea. 'He only drank now and then after lunch or dinner. And he didn't smoke a lot either.'

From what they gathered from her explanations, Víctor Porta led the life of a retired man with few health problems and a tidy sum in the bank that enabled him to live not lavishly, but without having to skimp. He was on good terms with his daughter and son-in-law, and proof of that was that he lunched with them on Sundays and the odd national holiday, which, she said, had led to a number of arguments because on the days he ate at his daughter's, she was left on her own. Víctor Porta adored his grandson and got on well with his son-in-law, and when he was with her, he was too much of a gentleman to hide that he still missed his wife.

'I couldn't begrudge him that,' she added, nodding her head.

Berta Macià assured them she had little idea of the

contents of the book that Víctor Porta had written because he'd never allowed her to read it. She knew that on his return to Barcelona he'd spent his time researching the circumstances around the tragic deaths of his parents, and that finally, after talking to different sets of people, he'd discovered why his father had ended up in the prison in Burgos at the end of the war and why his mother had committed suicide.

'Above all, he was obsessed with his mother's suicide. He said he couldn't understand why she'd taken her own life, and orphaned her three-year-old son,' she said sadly.

'Did he tell you what he uncovered?'

'There was a man who was stalking his mother,' said Berta Macià, leaning forward and lowering her voice, 'someone who'd been a lifelong friend of Víctor. Evidently, he never forgave her for rejecting him.'

'So what happened?'

'Shortly after the end of the war, this individual betrayed Víctor's father to the Falangists and they took him to Burgos. The poor man died in prison soon after. From tuberculosis, it was said. In fact, according to Víctor, the truth was never known.'

'What about his mother? What happened to her?'

'Víctor discovered that man was making her life so impossible, she could stand it no longer, and one day she threw herself off their balcony, but I don't know any of the details. In the end, Víctor was brought up by an uncle and aunt, I imagine you know that.' And she added, 'They both died years ago.'

'Do you know who that man was? What his name was?' asked Norma.

'Not a clue. Víctor always refused to tell me his name. He said it was a very delicate subject because it involved other people.'

'Other people?'

'The children of the man who had betrayed his father.

When the war was over, this man became a Falangista and married. Things went very well for him...' And making an effort to hold back her tears, she added, 'Víctor explained it all in his book, but he wasn't too sure about taking it to a publishing house. When I asked why he didn't, he said that he must first ask a friend for advice. He wanted the truth to be known, but he didn't want to hurt any innocent people.'

'Do you know this friend's name?' asked Norma.

'It was that history professor who was killed not long ago at the university, I can't remember his name...'

'Professor Francesc Parellada,' said Norma.

'That's him. He and his wife came to the funeral.' And she added, looking down. 'He seemed very affected. They'd been friends from childhood...'

'Do you know if he gave him a copy of the manuscript?'

'He sent it by registered post. I accompanied him to the post office.'

'Do you remember what day that was?'

Berta Macià sighed and closed her eyes, trying to remember.

'It was a day when I went to the hair salon, so it must have been a Monday. Víctor came to pick me up and had to wait a long time, because they were very busy.'

Norma took her diary from her bag and looked at the calendar.

'Senyor Porta was murdered on October 15, that was a Monday,' said Norma, wrinkling her eyebrows.

'So it must have been the previous Monday... yes, it was the week of the 12th of October,' said Berta Macià, looking at the calendar. "I remember because Friday was a holiday and it was a long weekend. That day Víctor went to his daughter's for lunch and I was quite annoyed.'

'Do you know where he sent the packet to? To his home? To the university?'

'To the university. He asked me to look up the address.'

And a few seconds later, as if she'd just realised it might be important, she added, 'Víctor also sent the manuscript to someone else.'

Norma and Gabriel exchanged glances on the sly. If Berta Macià was right, there must be a third manuscript in circulation they might still be able to track down.

'Who did he send it to? Do you remember the name?' asked Norma.

'Oh, I'm so sorry!' Berta Macià said suddenly. 'I am so discourteous. I've not even asked you if you'd like something to drink... A coffee perhaps?' and she half got up as if to go to the kitchen.

'No, please don't bother,' Norma gently took her arm so she couldn't stand up. 'So who did he send the second packet to? Was it a publisher?'

'I don't think so. In fact, Víctor refused to tell me, but I'm sure it was someone connected in one way or another to the tragedy of his parents.'

'Connected how?'

'I don't know. But he did say something like: if you were going to do something, you should do it properly. I thought maybe he'd decided to send the book to the family of the man who'd been responsible for the deaths of his parents, but I can't say for sure. I didn't ask.' And she added, as if she were making a confession, 'Actually, I was quite hurt that Víctor wouldn't confide in me. I often asked him to let me read the book, but he always refused. He said he didn't want anyone to read it until he'd made up his mind.'

'About what?'

'About whether to take it to a publisher or throw it in the bin. He sometimes thought he might be wrong and that it wasn't worth stirring up the past, and at other times he said the dead have a right to see justice done. He couldn't ever decide.'

'And when he was murdered, didn't it occur to you that there might be a link between his death and his research?'

Norma asked, trying not to make her question sound like a criticism.

'Frankly, it never did,' said Berta Macià, rather perplexed she hadn't even contemplated that possibility until then. 'The truth is everyone in the neighbourhood thought it was a robbery that went wrong. That it was a drug addict or one of those gangs from Eastern Europe who kill at the drop of a hat... They've burgled loads of flats recently, I'm sure you must know? And that policeman said that as well...' She was referring to Carrasco.

She added in disbelief, 'Do you really think they killed him because he'd written a book? All that happened years ago and nobody remembers any of it...!'

'I really couldn't say,' Norma acknowledged genuinely. 'That's what we're trying to find out.'

24

The moment they left Berta Macià's flat, Norma asked Gabriel to go back to the School of History and try to locate Víctor Porta's manuscript among the professor's papers. She'd call Jordi Parellada and ask for permission to look around his father's study in the flat on Gran Via.

'He may have taken it home,' she said half-heartedly.

Norma called his mobile. She was in luck, because Jordi Parellada was with his mother and was happy for her to carry out a search without a legal search warrant.

'My father was quite organised,' he said, opening the office door. 'If it's here, I think it will be easy to find.'

The professor was a painstaking academic, and in his study nineteenth-century methods of working based on yellowing handwritten cards coexisted with a modern computer. Norma spent a good hour opening drawers, until she decided to give it up as a lost cause and ring Gabriel.

'Well, it's not here either,' said Gabriel drowsily. 'Either it got lost in the post or someone took it.'

Norma still had to pop to the grocery store, and, when she realised it was almost eight, she decided to catch a taxi so she'd get there before it closed. She left the store laden with bags, and when she finally arrived home, she discovered Octavi had been there a while and that he and Violeta were closeted in Octavi's study. They were talking about the precarious state of the world without touching on the delicate subject of Violeta's arrest and her possible participation in acts of hooliganism. Norma said hello from the doorway and told them she was going to shower and change. It was true she needed a shower, because the smell of fried garlic from Berta Macià's staircase had impregnated her clothes and hair, but she also didn't want to interrupt them. She knew Octavi was more deft at dealing with Violeta, so she quietly pulled the door to and headed towards the bathroom.

Octavi had decided to hold off and not scold Violeta. He was aware that, however he went about it, at that point in time no common-sense statements from him could ever compete with the fraternal atmosphere of political camaraderie, sex and fun he imagined surrounded the girl's life in Gràcia. A life of shared emotions and empty shelves, of litre bottles of beer, joints, dry tuna rolls, fleas and lice, where Octavi also suspected there must be a prince in blue with piercings and dreads who stirred her endorphins and was responsible for the happiness that gleamed in her eyes. Octavi was sensible enough to realise that open confrontation would be futile, so, rather than arguing with his daughter and telling her off because of her behaviour, he'd opted to proceed philosophically and have recourse to what had best worked with Violeta ever since she was a child: patience and intellectual complicity.

Ever since Violeta joined the squatters' movement, Norma and Octavi had been following the activities of the alternative groups in Gràcia on the Internet. Deep down, neither could avoid feeling some sympathy for those youngsters who were disillusioned with politics and called themselves anarchists. They devoted their energy to denouncing property speculators and occupying houses rather than spending their days in gyms and clubs, trying to ape the tinsel glamour of the apolitical youths in American TV series. Even the flea-infested dogs that accompanied them everywhere lent a sympathetic touch that contrasted with the aggressive aesthetic of Mohawks, buckles and military boots displayed by the most extreme of them, thought Octavi. Despite their noisy parties and often rude, bolshie attitudes, he had to recognise there was a genuine enough spirit of romantic rebellion in those youngsters who'd adopted the style of less gilded, more combative bohemians and were striving to live according to their ideals. Norma and Octavi felt a great deal of ineffable pride in their daughter and her rebellious, philanthropic ideals, though they were well aware that such romantic escapades and alternative projects often ended badly, and they hoped Violeta would see sense and her flirtation with alternative lifestyles would be short-lived.

The relationship Violeta had with her biological father was a good one but quite different. In fact, seen from the outside, it was more like one between an uncle and a spoilt niece rather than father and daughter. Violeta loved Guillem and was delighted to be able to boast she had a gay father to her alternative friends, but from early childhood she'd always thought of Octavi as her father. They'd never hidden from her the reality that Octavi was really her uncle and that Guillem was homosexual, and the natural way Norma's household reacted when Guillem returned from San Francisco and announced he'd like to be a part of their lives again contributed to the fact that Violeta never suffered any traumas from that family imbroglio. Violeta was eighteen months old when Norma and Octavi fell in love, three years old when they married and five when she met Guillem for the first time.

Norma and Octavi had met when she was sixteen and he was twenty-six. It was the first time Norma stepped inside Guillem's house, and Octavi, who was preparing for his exams to enter the forensic service, had spread all his medical books across the dining-room table, and didn't even look up when his kid brother introduced a friend from secondary school and told him they were going to the bedroom to study. Guillem's parents were out that afternoon and Norma only caught a brief glimpse of Octavi from the back and against the light before they headed to Guillem's bedroom. Absorbed in a sea of paper that flew off the table now and then, because it was hot and the window was open, Octavi didn't take a proper look at Norma either, who wore her hair waist-length back then and painted her nails a dark red. Later on, when Guillem declared his love and they started going out, Norma and Octavi occasionally met, but Octavi took no interest in his brother's young girlfriend and nor did Norma feel intrigued by that serious-looking doctor who spent his day surrounded by books and barely made the effort to say hello to her. Guillem always got into a state of panic when he talked about the macabre profession his brother had chosen, so he simply told Norma that Octavi was preparing for the competitive entrance exams to the hospital.

At the time Octavi was living with his parents but spent little time at home, and Guillem preferred to stay at Norma's place to spare himself his mother's interrogations and insinuations. Unlike Isabel, who was a drag, Mimí let them get on with it and didn't spend her time going in and out of Norma's bedroom to see what they were or weren't doing, and when Guillem slept over, there were no questions or reprimands the morning after. Norma's family's laid-back attitude, so different from his own parents', meant that Guillem felt at home in a place where everyone got on with their own business and treated him hospitably, with warmth and respect. Compared to the inquisitorial atmosphere in his own home, Guillem found the family scene at the Foresters liberating.

The flat rented by Guillem's parents was in Hospitalet and was tiny compared to Norma's place, but nevertheless it had three bedrooms so the brothers didn't have to share a bedroom. Maurici managed an ironmonger's, the same one in which he'd started working at fourteen, and Isabel, who gave up her secretarial job when she married, looked after the house. Indeed, when Norma met Guillem, neither he nor his brother knew how to make their beds or fry an egg, and one of the things that most surprised Guillem was to discover that Norma's stepfather helped with the domestic chores even though they had a maid. Most of Guillem's friends' families were like his, families who often found it hard to survive until the end of the month and were paying for their television or car on instalment plans, with brothers and sisters fated to inheriting their older siblings' faded hand-me-downs or broken toys. Families with parents who worked from dawn to dusk and mothers who were stay-at-home mothers or helped the family economy by working as part-time cleaners to boost their income, who often had to look after a sick grandparent, families who lived crammed into flats and staircases that at midday stank of lentil and chickpea stews and in the evening of potato omelettes and sardines. Those modest flats, furnished with stuff dating back to when the parents got married and that had never changed since, because to change the furniture or flowery wallpaper they'd have to wait until they won the lottery, weren't anything like the grand apartment Norma's family occupied in the Eixample. Norma lived on Carrer València, near the Rambla de Catalunya, and Guillem was impressed by the size of the flat with a view of the sea from both sides. The window of Guillem's bedroom looked over a dark inner courtyard and it couldn't be opened in the summer because mosquitoes swarmed in, while Norma's bedroom, like Roger's study, looked over an Eixample patio that was blessed with the rays of the sun in the early afternoon. Guillem had always liked the smell of wood and old books in Norma's stepfather's study, and often, when he wasn't there, he'd invent an excuse to slip in and breathe in that aroma.

25

Guillem and Robert arrived at Norma's just before nine, smiling, travel-weary, with a bottle of cava. Before they sat around the table, while an astonished Robert scrutinised the Ming vase in the lobby and realised it was genuine, Guillem went to look for Violeta and chatted with her for a few minutes in her bedroom, behind closed doors. As Mimí and Senta knew nothing about Violeta's stay in a cell at Les Corts station and they didn't want to alarm them, nobody mentioned it over supper. Robert, who knew any silence was uneasy given the secret hovering over the table, went out of his way to gossip, telling anecdotes about his profession under the attentive gaze of Mimí, who was beginning to smell a rat. Although good vibes reigned in the dining room, Mimí suspected her family was hiding something. But what was it? An illness? A money issue? Perhaps Violeta was pregnant, as had happened to Norma when she was the same age, and they couldn't think how to tell her. In fact, Mimí had noticed ever since Violeta's return home that her granddaughter looked sheepish and seemed to have given up on her rebellious stance. Something didn't fit. In the end, she could stand it no longer and erupted.

'Fine, now would someone like to tell me what we are celebrating?' she asked, dead set on getting to the truth. 'Or do you think I was born yesterday?'

Mimí's words caught everyone by surprise, and for a few

seconds they all swallowed, and exchanged worried glances, Guillem was the only one to react.

'Hell, Mimí, you don't miss a thing!' he said, smiling broadly. 'The truth is we wanted to wait until it was dessert time to give you the news, but since you insist...'

As everyone looked on in amazement, Guillem stood up and ceremoniously raised his glass of wine.

'Family, Robert and I have decided to tie the knot. We're getting married!' he said, gesturing theatrically.

Like the rest of the family, Robert sat and gawped, not knowing what expression to adopt. Before anyone had time to say anything, Great-grandmother Senta leaned forward and asked, 'Who do you say is getting married?' Since her hearing was poor, she'd not understood.

'Guillem and Robert, Mama,' said Mimí with a big smile and raising her voice. Visibly relieved, she added, 'So that was what it was all about...! Christ, you had me worried because I thought something bad... Congratulations, my boy! May it last for many a year!'

'Congrats!' murmured Norma and Octavi, still feeling uneasy.

'*Felicitats*, Dad,' Violeta chorused sarcastically.

In fact, Robert had several times suggested to Guillem they could have a town hall wedding, but Guillem had always changed the subject. Now, after that declaration, Robert didn't know what to think. On the one hand, he was pleased because he imagined that after such a public announcement in front of the whole family, Guillem would find it hard to backtrack, but on the other hand, he felt disappointed. Robert had always fantasised about a candlelit supper and a proper proposal, and Guillem had just shattered that dream.

'I bet you weren't expecting that, were you?' Guillem whispered in his ear.

From that moment on the question of the marriage, the how, when, who and where, became the focus of the conversation. Initially, Robert listened in silence, blank-faced, nodding from time to time, but finally, before that peculiar family not only organised their wedding but also their honeymoon, he decided to make a desperate attempt to change the subject, and again asked Norma about the investigation she was involved in. Norma realised Robert had resorted to a desperate manoeuvre and didn't dare clam up, so she decided to tell them what she suspected and the ins and outs of the manuscript that had vanished.

'However, if we don't catch the guilty party, I don't think we'll ever read it,' Norma said finally. 'That is, if he hasn't destroyed all the copies...'

'What a pity!' said Robert, who seemed genuinely interested.

'Bah, there must be a copy somewhere,' Guillem chipped in. 'You say they stole his computer? Maybe before they stole it, he emailed it to himself.'

'And why would he have done that?' asked Mimí, confused. 'I really don't understand...'

'Well, it's what I do with some documents I don't want to lose,' Guillem explained. 'It's to ensure a copy is safe and sound.'

'Uploading important documents online isn't at all safe, my love,' Robert scolded him. 'I hope you haven't uploaded anything really important.'

'In any case, we don't even know if he had an email address,' Norma said with a sigh. 'I suppose we could check it out, but...'

'And what about looking into his credit cards?' Violeta suggested. 'If he had an email account, maybe his cards will be associated with it.'

Norma and Octavi stared at their daughter as if they'd just seen a creature from outer space.

'Well, what? I watch crime series on telly too, you know?' Violeta defended herself.

'Indeed, we could talk to the lads in the computer

department,' said Norma, thinking aloud. 'But I think we'd have to be very patient. Because right now they're swamped by all the corruption cases.'

Mimí, who'd been pondering for a while, finally said, 'If it involves computers, you should talk to Aunt Margarida, my dear. I'm sure she'll solve it,' as all heads turned and stared at her, not understanding where she was going.

'To Aunty?' exclaimed Norma, laughing.

'I may have overstepped the mark.'

'What do you mean?'

'She does things,' said Mimí mysteriously. And closing her eyes, she added, 'Obviously they're not always legal...'

Norma mentally added up the glasses of wine her mother had downed that evening, looked at Octavi and shook her head. Robert, after all that had happened, felt like one of the family, so he grabbed the bottle of wine and filled his glass.

'What kind of things does Aunty do?' asked Violeta, intrigued.

'I can't tell you.'

'What's got into you all of a sudden?' Norma rasped. 'Come on, Mum, I think you've drunk too much.'

'I can't tell you, because *you* are a cop,' said Mimí, raising her chin. 'But if you wanted her to, Aunty could give you a helping hand.'

Norma didn't have a clue what her mother was talking about and glanced at Robert, asking him to pour her another glass. Aunt Margarida was certainly an eccentric character, and, just in case, she decided not to ask. However, Mimí had already reached a decision, and before Norma had time to reply, she jumped up and left the dining room with a wily expression on her face.

'Mum, where are you off to?'

Mimí just smiled at her daughter and came back a few moments later holding her mobile. She sat down again and dialled a number.

'Marga. Hello, love, it's Mimí. Is this a good time to talk?'

'But what...!' exclaimed Norma incredulously.

The nun must have said it was good, because Mimí continued talking.

'Hey, Norma has a problem with a computer. Can you help her out?'

'Mum!' shouted Norma, not understanding what her mother was suggesting. 'What the devil...?'

'Love, what did you say the name of the owner of the computer was?'

Mimí asked, without flinching.

'You must be joking! I don't know what you're plotting, but I'm not going to tell you!'

'I think she said he was Víctor Porta,' said Guillem impishly.

'Yes, Grandma,' corroborated Violeta. 'Tell Aunty the owner was Víctor Porta. That she needs his email address.'

'Mum, please ring off!'

'Listen, Marga, you should try to find out if this Víctor Porta has one of these email addresses you use... And the password, naturally. He is dead, and they stole his computer.' And she added, in the tone of a professional bloodhound, 'Norma wants to know if he sent himself something before he died.'

'A document,' Violeta specified.

'A document,' Mimí repeated.

'I don't want anything!' protested Norma. 'Please give me that phone!' she said, as she got up and tried to grab it.

'Shut up, I can't hear a word!' said Mimí, raising her voice. 'What do you say you need? Wait a mo, I'll hand you over to her. She's in a better position to tell you.'

Mimí handed the telephone to Norma, who grabbed it in a fury.

'Listen, Aunty, this makes no sense at all... No, you just listen to me, this isn't a game... And I forbid you to...'

But before Norma could finish her sentence, Sister Margarida had hung up.

26

Inspector Roca's unexpected call caught Deputy Inspector Agustí Carrasco in bed, coping with the hangover from his inevitable Friday night drunkenness when he wasn't on duty. It was barely eight am, and as he'd gone to bed at five that Saturday morning, and in theory today was a holiday, when he heard the phone he cursed, put a pillow over his head and turned over. A couple of minutes later the jingle on the phone woke him up again. After the third round of this, he couldn't stand the noise anymore and decided to get up and switch off his mobile so he could sleep some more. When he saw the name on the screen, he hesitated, and sat on the edge of his bed in his underpants for a few seconds holding the ringing phone. He finally decided to answer, reluctantly and with a thick voice, and immediately regretted it because the call obliged him to dress quickly with no time to pop into the bar on the corner for his usual coffee and cognac and a painkiller for his headache. There'd been a murder in Badalona that looked as if it was a narco issue, Inspector Roca told him. He wanted him to go at once and take a look with Officer Mata. The officer was there in less than ten minutes, made-up, in her uniform, her hair still damp, and, when he saw her walk through the door, Carrasco gave her a withering look and grunted a greeting.

'Don't you dare switch on the siren!' he growled.

As he had a hangover, the deputy inspector sat next to

the corporal and let her drive. It was cold but the officer had to open the window to avoid being sick, Carrasco hadn't showered and stank of putrefying liver. The deputy inspector noticed nothing and started to snore, and, when they reached Badalona, the officer had to shout to wake him up and remind him where they were and what they had to do.

The body was half-hidden between the demolished walls of one of the abandoned factories that still lingered by the railway track. It was a couple of hours since a group of youths who were all ready to see the night out on that wasteland had come across the corpse and informed the police, and when Deputy Inspector Carrasco arrived, Inspector Permanyer's men had already emptied the dead man's pockets and noticed he wasn't carrying his wallet. However, they hadn't taken his mobile, which was switched on and charged. The deputy inspector looked at the mobile sceptically and let out one of his usual curses.

The corpse was face up, but everything indicated the body had been moved before the police arrived, perhaps to turn it over. The victim was shortish, not the muscular, sporty kind, and had been shot twice in the chest. His face had been shot to pieces and his brain scattered around and about. As it was difficult to ascertain his age at a glance, the deputy inspector bent down to examine the backs of his hands and concluded the man was between forty and fifty years old. He hadn't started to smell yet, and, according to the forensic examiner, he'd been dead some twelve hours.

'I reckon he kicked the bucket around nine last night,' Carrasco muttered.

'More or less,' said the forensic examiner, taking his gloves off. 'I imagine they shot him when the train was trundling by to hide the sound of their shots.'

The dead man was wearing cream polyester trousers that didn't look new, a sky-blue shirt, also made of polyester, and a cloth jacket that had seen better days. His ridiculously small feet were funnelled into black, fake-leather moccasins and cream socks. Apart from the mobile, the police had found on him a couple of wraps of coke, of decent quality, they said, though not the best you could find on the market. The deputy inspector reluctantly crouched down again to take a closer look at the corpse, but he slipped and almost fell on top of him. Officer Mata yelled, and, putting a hand over her mouth, she ran towards some bushes and started vomiting.

After helping the deputy inspector to get up, and cracking a few jokes at the corporal's expense, one of the uniformed policemen showed Carrasco a transparent plastic bag that contained the pistol they'd found near the body. It was a Glock 17, a gun commonly used by petty criminals, that fetched between a thousand and fifteen hundred euros on the black market.

'Shit...' was the deputy inspector's only reaction.

'Come on, don't complain, they've made it easy for you this time, Carrasco?' one of the forensic team smiled sarcastically as he collected up samples of soil.

'You just fill up those bags, Sherlock, you've not got a fucking clue.'

'I bet it was a dealer who wanted to swindle his supplier,' the policeman insisted. 'Or a customer who owed him too much dough.'

'I told you, you've not got a fucking clue.' Shaking his head contemptuously, he said, 'Lads, reading makes you lose the plot. Too much university, too many devices,' the deputy inspector was referring to the sophisticated devices and computer programmes the forensic team used, 'But when push comes to shove, I'll be the one to save your bacon.' And in the same bad-tempered tone, he added, 'And you dragged me from my bed for that...!'

Still growling, the deputy inspector took out his mobile and started dialling Inspector Roca.

'Boss?' he said, as the paramedics put the body inside the ambulance. 'I don't know what this is all about, but you got it wrong. This isn't a drugs issue. And no way was a professional killer involved...! This is a really shoddy job.'

'Are you sure, Agustí? They told me they'd found coke on him...' In a conciliatory tone, remembering it was Saturday and Carrasco must have a hangover, he said, 'I know it's your day off today, but you're the drugs expert and forensics say he might be a dealer.'

'Those forensics don't have a fucking clue.'

'Agustí, don't get started.'

'Come and take a look for yourself, if you don't believe me,' Carrasco replied, scratching the inside of his ear with his little finger. 'I'm off. Someone else can take charge.'

'Sentís and Teixidor are on duty today. And if in the end it does turn out to be drugs...' The inspector didn't finish his sentence: 'You know those two are a bit wet behind the ears.'

'For fuck's sake, I told you it's got nothing to do with drugs!' roared the deputy inspector, about to devour the phone. 'Look, boss, the guy or guys who did this took his wallet and smashed his face in, so it would make identification more difficult, I imagine, but the idiots forgot to take his mobile, that's switched on, charged and working perfectly. What's more, they left a couple of wraps of coke on him. Do you think dealers are that stupid? This was done by an amateur!'

'Yes, but...'

'Bernat, get off my back, it's Saturday and I'm going back to bed. You got my opinion, which is what you wanted. Get it? I mean, call Sentís and Teixidor and let them deal with it. And if they're green, time they ripened! I'm off to bed!'

And in a rage, he switched off his telephone, went over to his car and soon started snoring.

27

The five bullets Octavi extracted from the corpse belonged to the Glock 17 Inspector Permanyer's men had found next to the body. The only prints on the pistol were the victim's, but their tests showed he hadn't fired a weapon because there was no powder on his hands. As Carrasco had anticipated, the mobile they found in his pocket made identification easy, and, by the evening Deputy Inspectors Senís and Teixidor already knew the dead man was Antoni Falgueres, from the Sant Antoni district, a lawyer by profession.

Early the following morning, the forensic team searched his flat on Carrer Joaquim Costa while Deputy Inspector Sentís questioned Mary at the station. They found little more in the flat except dirt and poverty, but during the search Inspector Permanyer's attention was caught by travel brochures with destinations to tropical countries and a parcel untidily wrapped in shiny paper containing a corduroy bag with a trendy design that seemed quite new.

'And what's that? Who was he going to give that to?' asked the inspector, examining the bag and finding it empty.

'It's hardly his woman's style, is it, boss?' laughed one of his men, as he selected samples and put them in a plastic bag. 'Did you see the collection of filthy tangas on the clothesline?'

'You know, this bag seems familiar,' said the inspector,

looking at it again, and trying to remember from where he knew it. 'Show it around the station and see if anyone recognises it.'

The man who did the identikit image of the suspect in the Parellada case recognised it immediately, and Norma asked Gabriel to summon the two students to the station to confirm. The girls examined the bag and were dead sure it was the one that stranger was carrying, the one who'd not given them a light but a shove in the faculty entrance before running off.

'You see, we didn't make it up!' crowed the girl with long blonde hair at Norma with a grin as she was about to leave.

The bag established a link that couldn't be a chance coincidence between Antoni Falgueres and the murdered professor, and Norma asked Inspector Permanyer to compare the lawyer's hair with those they'd found at the scenes of the murders of Porta and Parellada. In the meantime, Deputy Inspector Carrasco had offered to help out finding where the Glock had come from, delighted to be useful in a case that allowed him to visit low dives and meet old acquaintances. They'd erased the gun's serial number, but a couple of days later Carrasco made a triumphal entry into Inspector Roca's office and informed him that Antoni Falgueres had bought the pistol from a thug in the Barceloneta who charged him two thousand euros.

'This Falgueres was well-known to the hoodlums in the area,' the deputy inspector explained, taking a packet of black tobacco from his pocket, and putting a cigarette between his lips.

'Agustí, you can't smoke here.'

'They told me,' the deputy inspector went on, lighting up, 'it was the first time he'd bought a pistol. He told the seller he had no idea about guns and was doing a favour for a friend.'

'Who knows if that's true.' Deputy Inspector Teixidor,

who'd joined the meeting because he was now officially in charge of the case, shook his head sceptically.

'You can say what you like,' thundered Deputy Inspector Carrasco, offended by a comment that questioned his proverbial savoir faire in the underworld. 'You know those petty thieves never try to trick me. They know which side their bread is buttered.'

'There's always going to be a first time, Agustí,' Inspector Roca retorted in a conciliatory tone.

Deputy Inspector Carrasco smiled contemptuously at both men.

'The guy was a cokehead and often had problems paying his dealers, but he wasn't the type to beat people up or a paid killer,' he said. 'In the neighbourhood they think he was working for a bigger fish.'

'Did he deal?'

'Sometimes, but only as a favour, when he owed people. The whore he lived with was also hooked on coke.' And he added, unable to repress a lecherous smile, 'An ugly slut, with great tits...'

'So the guy was a little angel!' said Inspector Roca with a sigh.

'If they did him in, he must have been in deep water. But whoever did him,' Carrasco declared, throwing his fag end out of the window, 'is an amateur. I'm sure of that.'

The DNA analyses confirmed that the hair found at the Porta and Parellada crime scenes belonged to Antoni Falgueres, and Inspector Roca hurriedly called Norma and Gabriel into his office. Everything pointed to Antoni Falgueres as the man responsible for the murders, but the evidence was circumstantial and the investigation had yet to establish a motive.

'Tomorrow morning, Gabriel and I will go back to Antoni Falgueres' flat and do a new search,' Norma announced. And looking at her watch, she added wearily.

'If you like, I'll get the file and we can review our notes...'

'It's almost eight,' replied the inspector, with a grimace that was meant to indicate he was exhausted. 'Why don't we get out of here and chat about everything over a gin and tonic? I've been cooped up here for over twelve hours. I need a breath of fresh air,'

'I could do with a G&T,' agreed Norma. 'Why don't we go to Casa Fuster?'

'Casa Fuster? Hell, Norma, you do like the high life...' growled the inspector, as he got up.

'Well, at least it's quiet.'

'But you can't smoke there,' replied the inspector.

'And from what I recall, drinks cost an arm and a leg...' added Gabriel, who knew all about Norma's expensive tastes.

'Don't worry, they're on me.' Norma sighed, standing up. 'I don't want to arrive home with my clothes stinking of cheap fry-ups, right?'

Ever since Casa Fuster had been converted into a luxury hotel, its designer lounge had become a fashionable bar, an ideal place to do business or have a quiet conversation without being deafened by background music. You'd find bevies of women in their Sunday best gossiping about their love-lives over a pot of tea, stressed-out executives celebrating their successes or drowning their failures with single malts, publishers who didn't read and who contracted books as they bargained with literary agents on just mineral water. At that time of night the bar was packed, and Norma suggested a small table by the window, slightly away from the others. She and Inspector Roca ordered Bombay Sapphire G&Ts while Gabriel, who wasn't keen on spirits, opted for a beer.

'We know what the professor and the retired guy from Poble Sec had in common,' said Norma, after savouring her first gulp. 'They'd been friends from childhood, had been brought up in the same neighbourhood and both were interested in the Civil War. What I can't figure out, is how a flat-broke cokehead lawyer, who lived with a whore, is involved.'

'Well, he is the murderer,' said Gabriel, as if that was self-evident. 'He killed them.'

'Sure, but why? To steal that manuscript? And, by the way, the memoirs Víctor Porta wrote still haven't surfaced.'

'It's still not clear what the motive behind the murders was,' Gabriel reminded him.

'The evidence we have doesn't hold up,' interjected the inspector, taking a big swig of gin and tonic and lolling back in his chair. 'The fact that we've some of his hair at both crime scenes doesn't prove he killed them. And, right now, that hair is all we have to put before the judge.'

'But it's as clear as daylight he did them in!' protested Gabriel, not understanding where the inspector was heading.

'What Bernat means—' Norma crossed her legs and angled her body slightly towards Gabriel '—is that no judge will ever convict Antoni Falgueres because of a handful of hair. Even so I think, as far as our investigation goes, we can work with the hypothesis that he did kill them both.'

'He must have killed them for money,' hazarded Gabriel, shrugging his shoulders. 'If not, where was he going to get the money for a holiday in the Caribbean? Remember his bedside table was full of brochures...'

'Gabriel's right,' said the inspector. 'We've found no connection between him and his victims, which means either he was a psychopath or else someone contracted him to kill them.'

'According to Carrasco, Antoni Falgueres wasn't a hired killer, and I don't think he was a psychopath. I'm sure he must have had a motive.'

'Perhaps he was contracted to be an intermediary and

decided to do the job himself,' suggested the inspector, knocking back the last drops of his gin and tonic. 'Perhaps he was fed up with getting the crumbs and thought he could hit the jackpot for once.'

'That's possible. We need to find out who he was working for.'

'It won't be easy,' said the inspector, gesturing to the waiter to come over. 'Permanyer said they found nothing at his place or in his office.'

'But he was getting money from somewhere. Somebody must know something,' replied Norma.

'You'd better question the woman he lived with again,' the inspector suggested. 'I'll have her brought to the station tomorrow.'

Norma and the inspector ordered another round of G&Ts and Gabriel continued on the beer. While they waited for their drinks to arrive, they told him they were going into the street for a moment.

'Next time we must go to a bar where you can smoke,' grumbled the inspector, lighting up.

'Smoking in bars will soon be a thing of the past,' retorted Norma. 'We might as well get used to that.'

'But I thought you'd given up?' said the inspector, surprised to see Norma take a packet from her bag.

'Officially, I'm an ex-smoker. I mean, not a word to Octavi, right?' And she added, in self-justification, 'I smoke very rarely.'

'Don't you worry,' said the inspector with a shrug of the shoulders and a complicit smile. 'I'll keep your secret.'

There were others in front of the hotel entrance who'd come out to smoke, mostly women. Some were on their mobiles or simply smoking with an absentminded air. The ashtray by the side of the door was full of butts and Norma went over to stub hers out.

'To change the subject,' she said, 'I want you to assign Officer Mata to me.'

'You want to work with Laura?' The inspector shook his head and sighed. 'Carrasco will be livid.'

'Carrasco can get lost,' said Norma, unflinching. 'Right now, I've three corpses on the table, and I'd like to remind you it won't be me or him that will get a lambasting if we don't solve this case soon.'

'It's true the chief is starting to get a bit edgy,' agreed the inspector, hesitating over whether to light up another cigarette.

'Find some excuse, but transfer Laura over to me,' Norma asked. 'I'm sure you'll find someone delighted to work with such an experienced cop as Carrasco.'

'You must be joking. I suppose, as things stand, I can't refuse you anything...' said the inspector with a resigned shrug, taking out his lighter.

Before he had time to light the cigarette he was holding, Norma grabbed his arm affectionately, and guided him towards the hotel entrance.

'Come on, Bernat,' she said, 'tepid G&Ts are a waste of effort.'

28

Antoni Falgueres lived on Carrer Joaquim Costa close to the Teatre Goya, and on Wednesday morning, while a couple of Mossos were tracking Mary down to a tatty boarding-house where she'd moved with her scant belongings, and taking her to the station, Norma and Gabriel returned to the deceased's flat to carry out a fresh search. This time they knew what they were after, and soon found black jeans and trainers that fitted the description given by the two students. Inspector Permanyer's team the previous day hadn't found a computer or manuscript, but Norma insisted on turning it all upside down again in the hope of finding a lead they'd missed.

'There's fuck all here,' said Gabriel after a while, admitting defeat.

'You're right,' sighed Norma, taking off her latex gloves. 'Permanyer did a good job. It would make more sense to take a look in his office.'

'We won't find anything there either.'

'I know, but I just want to give it a go. It's nearby, so it won't be such a waste of time.'

The Mossos had discovered that Antoni Falgueres rented a small office on the Ronda de Sant Antoni, a five-minute walk from his flat. The office comprised a minute room opening onto scabby stairs and a tiny, unventilated lavatory. There was a desk that looked as if it had been rescued from a rubbish tip, a couple of rusty-legged chairs, a bookcase with dusty law books and an empty filing cabinet. The computer on the desk was an ancient model that didn't work, and the office had neither fax machine nor telephone.

'Sentís was right, this doesn't look like a lawyer's office,' Gabriel observed, wrinkling his nose.

'But he did put his diploma and the course photo on the wall,' said Norma, looking at the certificate and the yellowing photo.

'I don't reckon he had any clients,' commented Gabriel, opening the desk drawers and seeing they were empty. 'Petty criminals, at most.'

'The office must have been a cover. An address to receive mail and to use for shell companies. I bet Antoni Falgueres was a frontman.'

'It won't be easy to find out who he worked for. No address book, no files...' remarked Gabriel, leafing through a pile of old newspapers. 'And he'll have been paid cash, because there's no sign of any income in his bank account...'

Norma smiled, picked up her bag and took out her mobile.

'I've just had an idea.'

It had just occurred to her to ring Rita Soler and ask her if she knew a lawyer by the name of Antoni Falgueres, or if she'd heard his name mentioned in the corridors of the law courts. Rita said it rang no bells but she'd send out a few feelers to her colleagues and have a look online.

'If there's one thing lawyers like it's gossip,' she said. 'I'm sure someone will know him. But I must leave you because I've a hearing and I don't want the magistrate losing it because I'm late.'

When they left the building, Norma saw it was drizzling and suggested to Gabriel they should have a bite to eat before returning to the station. It was almost two, and Maria del Carmen Expósito, alias Mary, had been waiting almost four hours shut in the small interview room, and she was desperate because the Mosso on duty had warned her you couldn't smoke inside. She wasn't arrested, they'd told her, but they wouldn't let her leave.

From the moment she'd been told her man had been murdered, Mary assumed it was bad news and was scared of being implicated. The proof was that they'd taken her to the station. The police knew of her connection to the dead man, her coke habit and line of work, and she was sure they'd not accept she knew nothing about her lover's business deals. Nonetheless, it was true she knew almost nothing, and when Norma and Gabriel finally arrived in the interview room, Mary had decided to come clean and tell them the little she did know in the hope they'd let her go.

'I know he was working for lawyers. And I reckon the things he did weren't always very legal...' she confessed wearily. 'They made him sign documents, on behalf of companies...'

'What companies?'

'I don't know. He never told me a thing.' Looking down, she added rather shamefacedly, 'In any case, if he had, I don't expect I'd have understood a word.'

'Antoni Falgueres is a suspect in two murder cases...' said Norma, not managing to finish her sentence.

'Antoni was no saint, but he was no murderer either,' she said, adding, as if it constituted proof, 'He never ever laid a hand on me...!'

'You mean, you'd put your hand in the fire and swear Antoni Falgueres was incapable of murder...' Norma replied sarcastically.

'Hey, dear, I wouldn't go that far, I mean...' retorted Mary, crossing her legs and adjusting her fake-leather miniskirt. 'At this stage in life, I put my hand in the fire for nobody.'

Norma smiled and acted as if she was consulting some papers.

'Maybe he had an accomplice. Male or female...' she blurted, trying to scare her.

'You mean me?' Mary leaned back and laughed nervously. 'Now that's plain stupid!'

'You swear he never spoke to you about a history professor or a pensioner who lived in Poble Sec...' Norma persisted.

'No. Yes. I mean he never mentioned them.'

'Maybe he let something slip...'

Mary shook her head and looked down. She was starting to panic.

'All I know is that like two weeks ago he walked in with a new laptop and left it in the wardrobe. A few days later, he told me he'd sold it on.' And she added, 'I don't know where he got it, but I didn't ask him either...'

'Who did he sell the computer to?'

'I haven't a clue,' she declared, shaking her head. And she implored Norma, 'Hey, can't I smoke in here? Just one cigarette... I've been here ages!'

Norma glanced quickly at her watch, with a gesture that indicated she'd all the time in the world for an extended interrogation, and finally, after a lengthy pause, she said, 'It's up to you when you leave here. If you decide to collaborate and tell us all you know. For example, about that computer...'

'I swear I don't know where he got it or what he did with it.'

'And what can you tell me about the lawyers he worked for?'

'I told you I don't know who they are. I never saw them. All I know is they paid him some kind of wage and got him to sign papers,' she repeated wearily.

Norma went quiet, thinking it was past four o'clock and the poor woman had eaten nothing for hours. Although Mary was acting calmly enough, she seemed scared, and Norma was beginning to regret using her authority to shut

TERESA SOLANA

her up in that small room without formally accusing her of anything or allowing her a lawyer. She had good alibis, and it was most likely she'd not been involved in her lover's murders or murky business ventures.

'Would you like a roll?' Norma asked.

'I told you what I want is a ciggy.'

Norma nodded and took out a packet of Marlboros from her bag and Mary started smoking with gusto. She was dark-skinned, but her hair, long and dried out like an old mop, was dyed a yellowy pink which set off her pallor. Her swooping neckline showed off firm, large breasts that were definitely not fake, and her skirt was so short that, when she was sitting down, she couldn't hide her red lace knickers. She wasn't pretty, and although her ID card said she was thirty-eight, she looked ten years older.

'How did you meet Antoni Falgueres?' asked Norma, adopting a warmer tone of voice.

'I met him as a customer at the club. He came a lot and one night he suggested I should go and live with him.' She gave a disillusioned sigh. 'He told me one day he'd earn loads of money and take me off the game.'

'And you believed him?'

Mary shrugged her shoulders, adjusted her miniskirt and sighed again, lighting up a second cigarette.

'Know what?' she whispered. 'It's not true that us girls like working the street. Who the hell would like opening their legs and giving blow jobs all fucking night? I'm no youngster, and if a guy offers to let me live in his flat for free in exchange for a few frolics and says he wants to get me out of that...'

'His death doesn't seem to have affected you very much.'

Mary looked Norma up and down and gave her a smile that reflected years of disappointments and battering.

'You know, I don't want to have to eat his shit,' she eventually said. 'Mine's bad enough.'

'If we find out you're hiding something, the prosecutor

208

can accuse you of being an accomplice to murder,' Norma warned her.

'I'm a flat-broke whore who's growing old,' she replied. 'I know perfectly well you can do whatever you want. Are you going to accuse me of killing somebody or other?' Mary shrugged her shoulders and acted defiantly. 'That's up to you. But I've done nothing and know nothing.'

'I can suggest rehab programmes that could help you. I can give you a number...'

'Course you can. People leaving university can't find work, so they're bound to take me on as a secretary...!' Mary retorted sardonically. 'Come on, don't make me laugh!'

'In any case,' Norma said, taking a card from her bag and putting it on the table, 'there's my number. If you remember anything or change your mind...'

In the morning, while they were eating breakfast in the kitchen, Norma told Octavi she fancied going out for dinner. Violeta had decided to go back to her alternative friends in the Gràcia squat, and Norma was worrying about her daughter again and realised she was beginning to take out her bad temper on her family. Tonight she wanted to have a good time, drink a good Rioja and spend a few hours alone with her husband without having to pretend to her mother that everything was fine. She was tired of putting on a cheerful front when she arrived home so Mimí wouldn't interrogate her, and, additionally, she was annoyed that they seemed to have reached a dead end in the investigation.

'I'm sure Antoni Falgueres did in the pensioner and the professor,' Norma said, as she smeared mango chutney on a poppadom while waiting for the first course to arrive.

'So all you have to do is find out who gave him his orders and you're there.'

They both liked exotic cuisine and that evening they'd

chosen an Indian they'd recently discovered in the Eixample.

'It's not that simple,' Norma sighed, 'The evidence we've got amounts to very little. His hair was found at both crime scenes, but there's no DNA to link the victims with the murderer or the murderer with the victims. We don't even have any indication that they knew each other.'

'Perhaps they didn't,' Octavi suggested.

'Bernat thinks Falgueres was contracted to kill them. But his account was in the red, and we haven't found any cash.'

'They must have killed him to avoid paying up,' declared Octavi, straightening his glasses.

'You know, nobody contracts a killer to do what he doesn't want to do and then kills him to save a wad of money,' Norma replied sarcastically. 'Besides Carrasco says he wasn't a professional, so maybe Falgueres thought he could extract more cash by blackmailing the individual who contracted him.'

'A typical beginner's mistake,' replied Octavi, pouring himself some water and gulping it down. 'Careful with that sauce. It's on the hot side.'

They spent the rest of the meal talking about Violeta and her hasty decision to go back to Gràcia after receiving a call from a certain Micky. This time Norma hadn't criticised her daughter or insisted she stay at home, because she'd already asked Officer Mata to find out who Micky was and what he did.

'Trias didn't find any traces of drugs in her hair,' said Octavi, scouring the last grains of rice from the bowl. 'He called me today with the results of the analysis. Good news, don't you think?' he added, trying to cheer her up.

'Of course. But I won't feel better until I hear something back about this Micky,' replied Norma.

'Norma, there'll always be a Micky... You can't police your own daughter.'

'Can't I?'

'Can't you see you're acting worse than my mother?' Octavi scolded her, sighing.

'Yes, I'm appalling.'

Octavi looked at her tenderly and smiled. The waitress began to take the plates and brought the dessert menu, but they were both full and decided to go straight to the tallats.

'What about the suspect's clothes? Where've you got with them?' Octavi asked suddenly.

'We found black jeans and trainers, that, according to those students, are just like what the man they bumped into was wearing on the day the professor died,' Norma replied.

'If he killed the Poble Sec pensioner, his clothes must have been splattered with blood, I bet. However much he washed them...'

'We've analysed everything in his wardrobe and found no traces of blood. He must have got rid of them. And there was no blood on the jeans and trainers because the professor was strangled.'

Octavi raised his eyebrows, looked around and grinned.

'Perhaps Permanyer's lads should have been looking for something else. Hey, I've just had an idea.'

He quickly took his mobile from his pocket and called Inspector Permanyer. It was eleven, but the inspector was up and answered at once.

'You should look for traces of urine on the black jeans the students identified and compare the DNA with the professor's,' Octavi said, after apologising for the late call.

'I really can't imagine what you're hoping for,' said Norma after Octavi hung up.

'The professor pissed himself as he was being strangled. With a bit of luck, if the murderer was wearing those trousers and didn't wash them, there still might be traces. As he strangled him from behind, the victim must have fallen back against his body, that is, there must have been contact.' And he added angrily, 'I should have thought of that before.'

'Hey, Antoni Falgueres's flat was no pristine palace, but I don't think he'd have put jeans that had been pissed on in his wardrobe,' replied Norma, lowering her voice when she saw the young couple on the adjacent table giving them disapproving looks.

'I don't mean he pissed on him. Just a little contact would have been enough to leave a few cells on the trousers,' said Octavi. 'I bet the murderer didn't even notice. I'll show you at home. Don't make me perform here.'

'In any case, Antoni Falgueres was working for somebody else, that's obvious,' added Norma. 'Perhaps in the end we will prove he killed them, but I've got to find the individual who contracted him. I'm sure he didn't do it on his own initiative.'

'Ah...!' Octavi leaned back, shrugged his shoulders and straightened his glasses again. 'I can't help you with that. You know my speciality is blood and guts.' He picked up the bottle of Rioja with a glint in his eye, and, seeing it was empty, asked, 'How about a drop more?'

29

The following morning, while reviewing the witness statements in the station and trying to tie up loose ends, Norma received a call from Rita. She'd wasted no time finding the lawyers Antoni Falgueres was working for; it was an important practice on the Plaça Francesc Macià.

'I've emailed you their coordinates,' said Rita. 'Naturally, they'll deny it, but my contact assured me Antoni Falgueres had been working for them for some time.'

'You mean they employed him as a front man?'

'Yes, they used him to front dicey operations and tax avoidance schemes.' And she added, with a click of the tongue, 'He was a pathetic guy. They paid him a pittance.'

'I owe you one.'

'Only one?' Rita replied in a jokey tone. It changed as she asked, 'How's Violeta? Is she back home?'

'No, she's back in Gràcia, with someone called Micky. How are you?'

'Under the cosh as ever. I'm going out with a notary.'

'Someone I know?'

'I don't think so. I'll introduce you one of these days.'

'Be good!'

'You must be joking!'

After hanging up, Norma switched on her computer to read the email Rita had just sent. She was about to open it when her mobile rang a second time.

'Norma?' she heard a very quiet voice say, 'Listen. I've not got much time, because it's time to pray. Write down what I'm about to tell you.'

'Aunty?' asked Norma, surprised to hear Margarida's piping voice. 'Is that really you?'

'Who else!' the nun whispered. 'Come on, hurry up, I've not got much time, take note!'

Norma sighed but said nothing. She grabbed pencil and paper and wrote down what the nun was dictating.

'But what...?' she reacted when she saw what she'd just written.

'It is what you were after, isn't it?' said the nun.

'Yes, but... Listen, Aunty, how the hell...?'

'I'll tell you one day,' she muttered mysteriously. 'Now I must leave, because the Mother Superior is on her way and I don't want her catching me.'

'Aunty, wait, don't hang up...'

'Goodbye.'

Norma sat stock-still, the silent mobile by her ear, and looked in bewilderment at what the nun had dictated: an email address and a password. She didn't think twice, entered Hotmail and keyed them in. When she saw she was opening Víctor Porta's inbox, she gave a start in her chair and smiled in admiration. In less than a week her aunt had been able to find Víctor Porta's email info by connecting to the Thyssen Museum network from a clandestine computer in a convent cell.

'Aunty, I owe you one too,' she whispered, as she looked around and saw that everyone was busy and nobody was paying her any attention.

Not stopping to wonder whether she ought to eavesdrop on Víctor Porta's messages without a warrant from the judge, she examined the inbox and saw that Guillem was right. The pensioner had sent himself a document with the title of *Black Storms* that she now rushed to open. She gave it a quick glance to check it was legible, downloaded it to her desktop and made a safe copy. Then she read Rita's email and went to tell Gabriel what her friend had discovered.

'The practice is the Carreras i Ribot partnership,' Norma said, reading the message aloud as she printed it out. 'Here's the address.'

'Do you want me to go right away?'

'Yes, and take Laura with you. And put the screws on them.'

'You're not coming?' Gabriel asked, perturbed.

'If you want promotion, you'll have to start taking the initiative. Besides,' she added, avoiding looking Gabriel in the eye so he didn't guess what she had in mind, 'I've got a job to do.'

'You give the orders.'

'Get a move on. And don't be fooled by their bespoke suits and silk ties. This lot of lawyers are a gang of crooks, and don't you forget that.'

'Don't worry. I'll try to do my best for you.'

Gabriel left with a smile on his lips and Norma quickly printed out the document. The manuscript was under two hundred pages, and, since she didn't want to be disturbed, she shut herself in an empty office and unhooked the phone. If her hunch was right, those memoirs would provide the key to solving the three murders Inspector Roca had placed on the table, but equally she might have got it wrong. Maybe Víctor Porta's memoirs had nothing to do with the assassinations, she told herself, trying to hold her euphoria in check. Maybe it was only a coincidence she had misinterpreted.

The first pages of the manuscript were enough to show that Víctor Porta wasn't gifted as a writer. He'd have struggled to find a publisher. The guy had done his best, but his text was full of fancy words, clichés and clumsy syntax and, from the point of view of comprehensibility, some paragraphs were completely opaque. Third-person memories of an orphan brought up in the post-war period by a childless aunt and uncle were mixed up without rhyme or reason with the research he'd carried out on his return to Barcelona forty years later, which he tried to explain minutely in the first person. Víctor Porta had decided to scour the streets of his parents' neighbourhood with the patience of a retriever until he came across people who still remembered his parents and the tragedy they experienced, and, thanks to them, he'd been able to contact Conxita Planes, a friend of his mother who was still alive and who, despite being ninety-one, had a lucid mind. Her memories had allowed him to fill the gaps in the patchy tales told by other contemporaries of his parents, and she wasn't the only one who remembered the name of the man who'd betrayed Ramon Porta to the Falange. Most of the individuals interviewed by Víctor knew he was a friend of his father by the name of Pau Muntaner.

Ramon Porta and Pau Muntaner were the same age, had been born in the same neighbourhood and had grown up playing together in the street. As children they'd gone to the same school, and, according to Conxita Planes, they were friends, though not close. Ramon's best friend was Andreu. Conxita didn't remember his surname, but he was a well-built lad who'd acted as a witness at his friend's marriage. Later on, when the war broke out, Andreu and Ramon had joined the Durruti Column and gone to the front in Aragon, but whilst Ramon managed to survive, Andreu died in the Battle of the Ebro. By the time Ramon and Mònica married, he and Pau Muntaner had distanced themselves from one another, and the friendship ended for good the day Ramon discovered his friend had taken advantage of his absence at the front to harass his wife with all kinds of promises and threats. According to Conxita Planes, Pau Muntaner was a resentful, evil-natured lad who'd developed a morbid passion for Mònica that was a mixture of desire, jealousy and envy, and, when the war was over, he joined the Falange and engineered a tribunal that sentenced Ramon to twenty years forced labour in the Burgos prison by accusing him of something that was true: of being a clandestine anarchist and soldier. Ramon didn't last two years in prison, and, terrified by Pau's constant threats, his wife finally threw herself out of a window, hoping her death would protect her family. Pau Muntaner left the district, the neighbours lost track of him, and as far as Víctor could make out, nobody ever thought of establishing a connection between him and the powerful Muntaner family or the laboratories that bore their name.

Before reaching the end of the manuscript, Norma knew she'd found the piece that would enable her to solve that puzzle: the Muntaner family, that had no doubt the most interest in silencing an episode that, if it became public knowledge, would sully their name and put a question mark over the source of its wealth. Pau Muntaner's descendants, pondered Norma, couldn't be at all amused by the possibility their name might be splashed across the dailies with a story of sexual harassment that, on the rebound, would spotlight the family patriarch's links to the Falange. Of course, Pau Muntaner wasn't the only Catalan entrepreneur who'd built his economic empire in the shadow of Franco's regime, but his involvement with Ramon Porta's incarceration and his role in Ramon's wife's suicide was a story that was too juicy for journalists not to sink their teeth into it. Unlike other entrepreneurs and industrialists, Pau Muntaner hadn't just got filthy rich benefitting from the advantages of life under a corrupt fascist regime, but he'd also donned the blue shirt and red beret of the Falange in order to betray a friend and terrify his wife to the extent that she took her own life. Everything pointed to the fact that someone had decided to intervene by contracting Antoni Falgueres to kill Víctor Porta and ensure that the manuscript and results of his research disappeared.

Norma reviewed Gabriel's notes and saw that the Muntaner family wasn't that large. Pau Muntaner married a young woman from a high-born but impoverished family, and they'd had only one child, Gerard, father of Gerard and Mònica, who'd died in a car accident almost fifteen years ago. Mònica and Gerard's mother had Alzheimer's and had been living in a luxurious residence for years; of the two children, Mònica was the only one with offspring. Gerard had no children, there were no aunts, uncles or cousins, so that reduced the Muntaner family to Mònica and Gerard, a mother with Alzheimer's and two adolescents. However, by chance the son of Víctor Porta's best friend had married Pau Muntaner's granddaughter, and even though Norma knew the professor hadn't got around to reading the manuscript Víctor had sent him, she wondered whether he or his son had been in the know. Did they know who Pau Muntaner really was and what he'd done? Norma put question marks after the names of Francesc Parellada and Jordi Parellada which she'd written on a sheet of paper and rang Gabriel, who at that very moment was threatening one of the partners in the Carreras i Ribot practice for the nth time with the accusation of being an accomplice to murder.

'Ask them if they have any connections to a member of the Muntaner or Parellada family, and if they know whether Antoni Falgueres knew them,' Norma asked him.

Gabriel hardly had to put any pressure on a lawyer who was shitting himself, to get him to confess he knew Antoni Falgueres. The lawyer also admitted Gerard Muntaner was a client of the practice and that he thought Antoni Falgueres and Gerard Muntaner had met once or twice. Indeed, Antoni Falgueres administered one of the many companies Gerard Muntaner had set up through that practice to defraud the tax authorities. Although he denied Falgueres was a front man, the lawyer covered his back by saying that, if he was, he knew nothing about it.

Gabriel quickly informed Norma, and she immediately tied up the loose ends. When Gabriel returned to the station, they both met Inspector Roca and told him what they'd found out and he at once phoned Chief Superintendent Nebot, who summoned them all to his office.

'So according to you, Gerard Muntaner, alone or with his sister as accomplice, contracted Antoni Falgueres to kill Víctor Porta and Francesc Parellada and steal the manuscript,' the chief recapitulated.

'That's right.'

'And a few days later Gerard Muntaner summoned Antoni Falgueres to a piece of wasteland and killed him with the pistol he himself had contracted him to buy.'

'That seems more than likely.'

'But you don't have any evidence, right?'

'That's why we need a search warrant,' said Inspector Roca, looking at Norma out of the corner of his eye.

'In fact, we need more than one,' Norma corrected him. 'We should search the homes and offices of both brother and sister.'

'If you fuck this up, you can shake the dust off your uniforms, because I'll be sending you to patrol La Mina,' said the irked Chief Superintendent Nebot, as he picked up the telephone.

The chief called Judge Gallardo, explained the situation and asked him for a warrant to search the homes and offices of Mònica and Gerard Muntaner. The judge listened silently to the chief's explanations, and after a few seconds' silent reflection, refused, saying they had no evidence linking the Muntaner family with that case and therefore, under the circumstances, it would be excessive to treat them as suspects. He said Norma had accessed Víctor Porta's emails illegally, and as a result the manuscript couldn't be accepted as evidence, and, in any case the prosecutor's office already had the official version of what had happened: Antoni Falgueres was a drug addict, thief and murderer, and the fact that Francesc Parellada and Víctor Porta knew each other and were friends was pure coincidence. Conversely, despite what the police reports might suggest, the public prosecutor was sure Antoni Falgueres had been the victim of a drug-gang settling of accounts. The case was practically closed. Before hanging up, and, without giving the chief an opportunity to reply, the judge reminded him the three cases were subject to secrecy while the investigation was still ongoing and warned that stirring up the past by making those memoirs available in the public sphere would only help to hurt innocent individuals and imperil his career and that of Deputy Inspector Forester.

'I'm sorry, Norma,' the chief apologised. 'You heard the judge. My hands are tied.'

Norma left the chief's office in a rage and, without saying anything to anyone, she went straight to see Jordi Parellada. He was in his office, and betting everything on a single card, Norma gave him a copy of the manuscript and told him what conclusions it drew.

'Are you sure about this?' asked Jordi Parellada. His face had turned pale as he went from feeling incredulous to indignant.

'Yes, I am.'

'I know my wife. She's not involved.'

'And your brother-in-law?'

'All I know is that he has political ambitions,' he acknowledged. 'I suppose if his grandfather's past hit the headlines, it would make all that more difficult.' And almost reluctantly he added, 'He's not like Mònica. He's ambitious but doesn't like hard work. Obviously, to do what you are insinuating...'

'If I've come to see you and tell you all this, it's because you're a powerful man and there are strings you can pull,' said Norma. 'People who are way above Judge Gallardo.'

'I'll see what I can do,' said Jordi Parellada,

accompanying her to the door and looking aghast. 'For the moment, I'd ask you to keep this quiet.'

A couple of days later, Jordi Parellada phoned Norma and suggested they meet in a low-profile cafeteria. He told her he wanted an informal chat, and they agreed to meet an hour later in a very central café where their presence would go unnoticed. Jordi Parellada started by thanking her and her team for their hard work, and then apologised and said exactly what Judge Gallardo had told the chief: that the case was closed, and that stirring all that up would only bring grief and headaches and that he too had a family to protect.'

'My brother-in-law has gone to live in the United States,' he said. 'He and his wife have separated. He'll be there a good long while.'

'Is that all you have to say?' retorted Norma angrily. 'I'd like to remind you that your brother-in-law had your father and Víctor Porta killed and that possibly he himself killed Antoni Falgueres.'

'It's also possible things didn't happen like that,' he replied, looking down.

'How? What did your brother-in-law tell you?'

'Is this conversation on the record?'

'I suppose it isn't. No, it isn't.'

'Well, let's imagine,' said Jordi Parellada, lowering his voice even more, 'that one day Víctor contacted a certain person to tell him what he'd discovered about the deaths of his parents.'

'You mean Víctor Porta was intending to blackmail your brother-in-law?'

'No. Víctor only wanted this person to know what he'd found out before he published the book.'

'Go on.'

'This person,' he sighed, 'took fright, and, thinking through the consequences, decided to contract Antoni

Falgueres to dispose of the manuscript.'

'The manuscript and its author,' Norma corrected him.

'This person didn't tell him what he had to do or how he should do it. He only asked him to sort out the problem. Antoni Falgueres decided to go to Víctor's house and steal his computer and the manuscript. The person who contracted Antoni Falgueres doesn't know if he'd decided to kill him from the outset or if Víctor surprised him and he panicked.'

Jordi Parellada paused, took a handkerchief from his pocket, and wiped the beads of cold sweat forming on his forehead.

'It turns out that, while Antoni Falgueres was turning the house upside down, he found a post office receipt and discovered that Víctor had sent a copy of the manuscript to a university professor. Then he decided to steal the copy and murder my father. Of course, he didn't know that Francesc Parellada was my father or that I was married to a Muntaner.'

'So then, according to you, the only one guilty of your father's death is Antoni Falgueres.'

'When the man who'd contracted him discovered that Antoni Falgueres had killed my father by mistake, he lost his temper and killed him.'

'And you swallow that?'

'It seems a reasonable enough explanation,' Jordi Parellada protested.

Norma gave him an icy stare.

'You know as well as I do that your brother-in-law ordered the killings of Víctor and your father,' she said, 'or maybe it was your wife?' she added, trying to rattle him.

'Mònica knew nothing about any of this,' he said, shaking his head. 'I swear to you. I wouldn't be telling you all this, if my wife was involved, would I?'

'And what do you reckon happened to Víctor's parents and the book he wanted to publish?'

'That all happened so long ago. What would be the point of dragging all that up now?' muttered Jordi Parellada.

'I suppose you'd think I was being ridiculous if I said it is about seeing justice done?' Norma retorted indignantly.

'No, I don't,' Jordi Parellada said with half a smile. 'My father spent his life trying to make sure justice was done, and don't you ever forget that.' Then he added in a faint voice, 'But I also have a wife I love and children I must protect.'

'Protect from the truth...'

'Please, I beg you not to make things any more difficult. It's already painful enough.' And he added, as if to justify himself, 'Horrible things were done on both sides in that war... Those were different times. It's better if we forget all that now.'

'Congratulations,' Norma said abruptly. 'I couldn't sleep knowing that I'd let the murderer of my father go free.'

'Who told you I can sleep?' he replied sadly. Although he hadn't taken a sip of the coffee he'd ordered, he gestured to the waiter that he wanted to pay the bill, while adding, 'I'm grateful for all the efforts you made. I know you did everything with the best of intentions. But I must ask you to drop this matter.'

'You know I can't do that.'

'You are a great professional, but Mònica is very powerful. Don't endanger your career, Deputy Inspector. It's not worth it, believe me.' He said that reluctantly, without his voice sounding at all threatening.

'My career is my business. And I like to sleep at night with a clear conscience,' Norma replied defiantly.

'Unfortunately, there are wars that not even someone like myself can win.' And getting up, keeping his head low, he said, 'Have a good day, Deputy Inspector.'

It had been a couple of years since the socialist government had passed the Historical Memory Law that pleased no one. The victims' associations found it fell short, and conservative politicians opposed it because many of them were the children or grandchildren of famous Francoists and still retained an admiration for the Franco regime to which they couldn't confess publicly but which they boasted of in private. They argued the victims of the Civil War were of no interest to anyone now, that too many years had gone by; the pact underpinning the transition endorsed forgetting and silence, and devoting time to disinterring bones from ditches only helped resurrect the old spectre of war. There were good and bad deeds on both sides, they said, and it had even become the fashion among some intellectuals claiming to be on the left to emphasise the excesses committed by the Republican side and forget the size and scale. Stalin and the failure of communism allowed them to advance the theory that in Spain in 1936 communists and fascists were alike, the same fanatical dross, and that, if it hadn't been for Franco, communism would have installed its own dictatorship and turned the country into a satellite of the Soviet Union. Victims, they said, were equally worthy on both sides; war, by definition, was a cruel activity, and numbers weren't relevant. That the leaders of the insurrection had systematically organised the massacres of Republicans in order to sow terror in a disorganised opponent with few resources didn't count either.

Norma loathed that cynical attempt at rewriting history and denying the massive crimes of Francoism, or rather at silencing it completely, in the name of a reconciliation that never happened. She considered it to be a joke in the worst possible taste. She hadn't anticipated that the son of Francesc Parellada, a man who had devoted a life of research to ensuring the Republican dead weren't forgotten, would react in that way. She sat in her chair for a good while thinking over the conversation they'd just had, and the only conclusion she could draw, yet again, was that another murder would go unpunished in a fog of reactionary arguments. Norma was very clear that silence wasn't an option.

She'd been turning over an idea for days and, all of a sudden, she picked up the telephone and called Aunt Margarida.

'Aunty? Have you got a moment? I need you to do me a favour.'

Perhaps it was no coincidence that it was the twentieth of November. That's what Norma was thinking after she'd spoken to the nun. While a few were nostalgically lamenting the death of the dictator with shouts of ¡Viva Franco! and ¡Arriba España! Aunt Margarida shut herself in her cell and began sending Víctor Porta's manuscript anonymously to the newspapers, a number of judges and all the associations dedicated to the recovery of historical memory she'd been able to find on the Internet. At that very moment, dressed much more elegantly than usual, Norma and Octavi were toasting Aunty with a glass of cava in the Liceu's Hall of Mirrors in an interval during the opera Norma.

'Violeta's right,' said Octavi in disbelief, 'There's too much that is rotten... It's incredible the judge has closed the case and that Gerard Muntaner hasn't been put on trial.'

'Gallardo's father also had a glorious past in the Falange,' Norma said with a smile. 'But don't you worry, this is only the start. In the end, Gerard Muntaner won't get off scot-free. And Gallardo will get his comeuppance, you just wait.'

'What you've done might cost you your career...'

'Don't worry, I'll be fine.'

'You're an optimist. And always have been.'

'It's funny. Every day we curse journalists and, in the end, we had to have recourse to them so they can do what we can't. I only hope Aunt Margarida doesn't get into deep water,' added Norma, shaking her head.

'Where the hell did she learn so much about computers, and at her age? Living, as she does, in a convent...'

'I've no idea. But, between you and me, she's been brilliant.'

'Do you know what?' Octavi laughed, putting his arm around Norma's waist. 'You and your family are a special case!'

'No, more like a lost cause!' she added, with a sigh.

Epilogue

Jack Forester arrived in Barcelona's Estació de França on 23 October 1936, carrying a small cardboard case under his arm and struggling to control the waves of emotion surging through him at the prospect of setting foot in the city about which he'd heard so much. It was the first time he and his friend Bob had left Manchester. As the train slowed down to enter the city, dazzled by the blinding blue of the sky and the fierce, dusty heat of the Mediterranean coast, his eyes feasted on everything. Barcelona was preparing to start the revolution within a war that had erupted a few months earlier and already claimed its first victims, and Jack and his friend were ready to fight fascism, convinced they would be on the winning side.

On the long, long journey from Manchester to Southampton and Le Havre first, and Paris to Portbou and Barcelona second, Jack had watched how the autumnal landscape gradually changed and, as they moved southwards, how the sun became hotter and the sky bluer. They'd left behind the rain, the grey clouds and the damp, monotonous green fields and asphyxiating stench from the canals that eviscerated Manchester, not to mention the peasouper and black smoke from factory chimneys, a mixture of soot and sulphur, permanently enwrapping the city like a dirty, stinking shroud. In the Estació de França they could smell the briny aroma of fish and sea, of algae and decomposing shellfish that the waves washed up on reefs and sand. An aroma, Jack would later discover, that impregnated everything, the walls of houses, the clothes hanging from balconies, especially in an easterly wind, an aroma that could often be unpleasant, because there were days when the sea rebelled and sent back to the city the piles of detritus its sewers had spewed into the sea in the form of poisonous waste. That stench was the source of constant complaints voiced by the inhabitants of the Barceloneta and the dark, narrow streets of medieval Barcelona, packed into tiny flats where they cherished hopes of prosperity and bucolic memories of childhood, as they eked out a life on lousy wages or handouts from neighbours. Pungent oil fumes from merchant ships also issued from the port, and were so penetrating they stuck to the inside of your mouth and made those unused to it feel nauseous, but Jack reckoned that mix of saltpetre, fish and oil was infinitely more tolerable than the stink from the murky waters of the River Irk, constantly churned up by barges that were always stirring the rubbish rotting in its depths. Jack had grown up near the river in Old Town, in one of the city's oldest working-class districts, and he had never seen the sea.

To reach Barcelona, he and Bob crossed England in goods trains to Southampton where they boarded the French ship that took them to Le Havre. In the course of traversing the rough sea of the English Channel, Jack felt seasick and vomited the little there was in his stomach, and, for the first time in his life, was afraid he might die. When they arrived in Portbou, they were greeted by the blue, transparent waters of the far kinder, more welcoming Mediterranean, and Jack and his friend felt the south made everything different and possible. Even winning a war against a professional army of fascist insurgents and creating a revolution.

When they jumped off the train, both were bright-eyed, and felt lumps in their throats that prevented them from speaking, but they had no need. As they tried to find their way through the station, inaugurated seven years earlier on the occasion of the Universal Exhibition, both were overwhelmed by the same euphoria, the same vertiginous feeling that their lives were about to change. For the first time a future of hope extended before them writ large, a future that moved forward in step with slogans and heroic anthems that spoke of revolution and freedom with resonant words and martial rhythms. They had reached the city of black flags, the city where, they believed, that whole web of dreams of libertarian fraternity on which they'd so often fed for lack of a decent meal would be fulfilled. And they were both going be part of it.

War had broken out three months ago, and, in the street, most passers-by stared at them curiously. Too fair, too pale and too tall not to stand out. Bob was a couple of years older than Jack, much taller and brawnier, and, when they were together, Bob's one metre ninety made Jack look titchy, especially when they were with the lasses, Jack would think rather enviously. On the street where Bob had grown up, nobody could understand how that lad had grown so tall, with the hunger he'd suffered as a child, and the neighbours imagined Bob had inherited the robust build of a father he'd never known. His mother had been impregnated by a Scottish sailor she never saw again, and she died from TB when Bob was four, so the young boy had been raised by a prematurely aged grandmother who worked in textile factories and wasn't always in work. Grandchild and grandmother often had to rely on the charity of neighbours to fool their stomachs with a slice of bread or bowl of tasteless soup, hounded every hour of the day by fleas, hunger, creditors and the cold. Bob's grandmother was a widow, and the tiny room where they lived in Long Millgate was near Jack's aunt and uncle. This coincidence, as well as the fact that Bob and Jack had no siblings, meant the two lads immediately struck up a friendship.

Jack's aunt and uncle didn't have children. At most the pregnancies of Rose, Jack's aunt, lasted for two or three months, and the homespun remedies of neighbourhood midwives, more skilled in provoking abortions than avoiding them, were futile. She always lost her babies, who, perhaps foreseeing that entering this world to suffer wasn't worth the candle, never managed to cleave to her belly. When Jack's mother died, Rose had already lost seven or eight, and she and her husband, resigned to not having their own offspring, were quick to give a roof to Jack and his father, thinking that shy, undernourished nephew would fill the void left by her own frustrated attempts to give birth. Jack's mother, Mary, was twenty-five when they buried her next to her daughter in the paupers' cemetery that was by one of the banks of the Irk. Jack had just made it to three.

His maternal grandmother was a widow and lived at the other, northern end of the district, near the commercial centre, with a daughter who was also widowed and was in service with a family that lived in a well-off neighbourhood. Aunt Margaret, for that was her name, had lost her husband and two of her children to the same flu epidemic that had taken Jack's little sister and mother, and every day she was forced to travel to the other end of the city to work as a maid. However, it was a good job because her masters turned a blind eye to the leftover food she stole and hid under her skirts, and everyone said she was very lucky. Now and then, she would drop by Rose's with leftover roast beef, steak and kidney pie, sausages or biscuits. 'For your lad, who's still growing', she'd say, ruffling his hair. Jack always shared those unexpected banquets on the quiet with his friend Bob.

Jack's other relatives, on his father's side, were Irish, and Jack never did meet them. Some had died in France in the Great War, blown to bits in the trenches by German bombs, but the rest were still in Ireland where they barely survived as shepherds and agricultural labourers. They went hungry and their children died, and all that misery had led Jack's father to board a ship at the age of twelve, excited by stories he'd heard about prosperous Manchester factories and the opportunities they gave to workers. His only childhood memories, apart from hunger, were of being beaten by his father, his mother's tears and the ritual procession of white coffins on their way to the cemetery. 'Why the hell did I bother?' he used to say when he got drunk and discovered he'd no pennies left in his pocket. The loss of his wife and daughter had made him sad and taciturn, and the few times he came home and wasn't drinking himself silly in the pub, he refused to talk about his family and childhood in Ireland. Jack only knew that his grandfather was a shepherd, and a Fergus, and that he'd inherited the stormy-sea grey-green of his eyes.

After his mother died, Jack was often thrashed by his father when he was the worse for drink. Apart from losing his wife and daughter, Jack's father was frequently on the dole. The crisis in the textile industry forced factory owners to cut production and sack workers, and he wasn't helped by his fondness for the hard stuff. Whenever he could, he drank. But those thrashings stopped one day when Jack received a wallop that split his lip and caused his father and uncle to come to blows. From then on, his father didn't dare lay a finger on him. The scar was still visible, and, when he touched it, Jack remembered his father's forlorn, drunken gaze and Rose's tender caresses.

Jack was seven when his father disappeared. Everybody assumed he'd fallen into the Irk after squabbling with other drunks or simply because he was sozzled out of his mind, and that, swept away by the currents, his body ended up in the Irwell and then the Mersey, which must finally have spat him out into the Irish Sea. Nobody bothered to look for him, and, since alcohol had made him nasty, even his drinking companions forgot him. When he disappeared Jack's aunt and uncle, tired of his shouting and boozing, felt relieved, as did Jack, who'd always been terrified they'd be thrown out of that comfortable home because of his dad's antics.

In the 1920s, Old Town was still one of the most poverty-stricken districts of Manchester. The portrait Engels had drawn eighty years before to describe the inhuman living conditions of the working classes still held. In its streets, ravaged by constant epidemics of typhus and cholera, and by tuberculosis, venereal diseases and alcoholism, Jack and Bob shared their hunger and cold, their fleas and dreams, and learned how to survive by helping each other. From the first day they met, Bob's imposing physique led him to assume the role of big brother and protector, and his friendship was the reason why they went to work in the same factory and agitated in the same union. It was Bob who guided him through the local women on the game the day Jack made it to thirteen and who persuaded Maggie, the only prostitute whose teeth weren't rotten and who didn't spit blood when she coughed, to make a man of him in exchange for a handful of coins he'd saved for the occasion. It was Bob who took him to his first political meeting with men who spoke passionately, in foreign accents, about justice and revolution. In that clandestine meeting, Jack heard for the first time the name of Bakunin and the words of the *Varsovian* sung by a handful of Russian Jews drunk on hard liquor and nostalgia, and understood that a different world was possible and that he could be part of it.

Bob was present that first day when Jack and Senta met and fell in love in the bomb shelter in the Plaça de Catalunya metro station. He was also there the day they got married. Together they said goodbye to her in the train station on their way to fight on the Aragon front, and it was there, as bullets whistled by, that Jack received Senta's letter telling him they were expecting a child. Jack read the letter to his friend, hugged him and asked him to be his child's godfather, and Bob was so moved that tears welled up. That night they laughed, cried, sang and drank until the early morning caught them by surprise plastered and ecstatic: they didn't yet know the war was definitively lost. Nor did they imagine a few months later, as they retreated, that a bullet would hit Bob's head and shatter their dreams. Jack buried him with his own hands under a storm of fire and tears, then returned to Barcelona defeated and alone.

The fascists' entrance into the city was imminent, but Senta still hadn't given birth. Stubborn as he was, Jack refused to leave for France alone. When Barcelona fell, the fascists were quick to arrest and lock him in the Model. He wasn't there long. Three or four days, nobody knew for sure. One morning they ordered him to climb into a lorry, drove him to the Camp de la Bota and Jack knew it was all over. In front of the firing squad, shivering with cold and fear, hatred and anger, he made his final review of the few worthwhile things in his life in an attempt to keep sane. As he heard the soldiers load their guns in the early light of morning that would be his last, he closed his eyes and thought of the wife he loved and the friend he had lost, of his dead mother and the uncle and aunt who had brought him up. He thought of the burden of sadness in his father's eyes and Aunt Margaret's cheerful generosity, of the banter he'd shared with his comrades at the front and Mary's caresses, the first time he kissed Senta, and the rainy afternoon he buried Bob.

Jack thought of all these things, and many others, but when the bullet entered his chest, he was only thinking of Senta and the daughter he'd never know, to whom he would bequeath the stormy-sea grey-green of his eyes.